FLIGHT
of the
KINGFISHER

J Merrill Forrest

Published by
The Moon Tiger
United Kingdom

Revised Edition: February 2015

Cover design by J Merrill Forrest
www.jmforrest.com

ISBN: 978-0-9567954-3-4

ACKNOWLEDGEMENTS

My heartfelt love and thanks to my husband for his endless support and encouragement.

My thanks to the readers of the early drafts for their praise, criticisms and proof reading: George Panos, Deborah Harrowell, Sonia Davies, Sue Davies and Sue Threlfall

in loving memory of

my brother
Stephen Thomas Forrest
1954-1984

&

my father
Thomas Miller Forrest
1931-2006

1951

Chapter 1

"Come on, sweetheart, up you come."

Though she weighs next to nothing, and he is as gentle as can be as he gathers her into his arms, she gasps in pain as he eases her up from the pillows. Gently, oh so gently, he persists, moving her little by little until she is sitting on the edge of the bed.

"I'm sorry, love, so sorry." He brushes away the beads of perspiration on her forehead and upper lip with his fingertips. "I'm trying not to hurt you, but you know I have to get you dressed and downstairs."

Her clothes are already laid out: underwear, petticoat, tights, her smartest, warmest dress, cardigan, her favourite low-heeled shoes that she's always worn for going out somewhere a bit special. Tenderly he places each garment on her tiny frame, hiding his distress at how nothing fits her any more. Even the shoes are too big. He brushes her hair, so fine now her scalp shows through the strands of white in narrow lines of shiny pink.

"I think we can do without make up, eh, love? I don't think I'd do a good job. Smear your lipstick and get more powder over me than on you, most likely. Anyway, you're beautiful as you are."

He steps back so she can see him. "And look at me, in my best suit and tie. I've even pinned on my medal and my shoes are so shiny you can see your face in them." He lifts up his right foot, but her gaze doesn't leave his face. She starts to slip sideways and he has to dash forward to catch her.

"OK, my darling girl, we're ready as we'll ever be. Let's do this."

Carefully, slowly, acutely aware of the sharpness of her bones and the sweet-sour scent of her skin, he raises her to her feet and wraps the thick quilt from the bed around her. She manages a few shuffling steps and it's obvious she cannot make it on her own.

Can he carry her? He has to, despite being old and weak, with probably less than half the strength of his youth.

"Well, my love, we're going to have to do this the hard way. Remember how I carried you over the threshold on our wedding night? I nearly took a tumble and you grabbed hold so tight you almost wrenched my neck. Remember that? I'm sure you do."

He can't risk the extra weight of the quilt or the possibility of tripping over a trailing piece of it, so he removes it from her body and tosses it on the bed, still talking all the while to distract her.

"It's like yesterday to me, our wedding day. You looked like an angel in your white dress, you know. Fair took my breath away. And that little suit you wore afterwards, showing off your tiny waist. A hat, too, I remember,

2

perched on your shining hair, which was all pinned up at the back so fancy. I thought I was a lucky, lucky man that day, and I've thought it every day since. Can you put your arms round my neck, love?"

He pauses, making sure the weight of her, slight as it is, is securely balanced against his body. Her head rests on his shoulder, and her feet dangle so that both her shoes slip off and land on the floor with a dull thud, thud.

"I'll come back up for your shoes, don't you worry. And the quilt. We must keep you warm, now, mustn't we."

He's at the top of the stairs now, already nervous about how he's going to make the descent safely.

After each downward step, shaking with effort, he has to pause and steady himself before taking the next one. He almost smiles at the bitter irony of not wanting to trip; what if she were to survive the fall and he didn't? It didn't bear thinking about. He had a huge responsibility here, and he couldn't afford to mess up.

"I have to be very careful, my love. I know this is uncomfortable for you, but you need to hold tight. Now, then, let's take it really slow and steady."

The narrow stairway means he has to turn slightly sideways to get them both down. He can't hold onto her as well as the banister rail, so must take it one step at a time.

Right foot down.

Shift her weight a little to keep his centre of balance.

Left foot down onto the same tread.

Steady.

Steady.

Pause and breathe.

Down and down, step by step, until he is at last standing on the hall floor. His breathing is laboured and his arms tremble with the effort he's made, but he has to carry her just a few more steps to the kitchen.

Once there, he lays her down on the thin mattress he'd placed on the floor earlier. Her skin gleams with sweat and has a ghastly yellow hue. He knows bruises are already forming on her arms and thighs where his hands have so firmly held her.

"I'm going back up for the quilt and your shoes, love. I'll be very quick."

When he returns, she is shivering and weeping, mewling like a newborn kitten. Quickly he covers her with the quilt and with a clean handkerchief wipes the tears from her sunken cheeks and kisses her forehead. His own face is wet, his throat tight, but he must not waver now. This is something he must do, a promise he must keep.

A promise he *wants* to keep, with all his heart.

His voice just above a whisper, he tries to reassure her as he once more puts on her shoes and covers her with the thick pink and white quilt. "It's alright, sweetheart, it's alright, my love. Very soon now you won't be suffering, I promise, and everything will be wonderful again. For both of us. Just wonderful."

Her huge, once-beautiful eyes fasten on his face and his throat catches to see the tears well up again and tremble on her sparse lashes. She has no voice now, hasn't been able to speak for quite a time, but everything she is thinking shines from those eyes.

"Now, now, don't you be worrying about me. My mind's made up, and there's no changing it. Since the day we met, you've meant the whole world to me, and I couldn't go on without you. You know that, love, I've told you often enough. And this way I won't have to."

Satisfied that she is warm and as comfortable as he can make her, he bustles round the tiny kitchen, checking for the hundredth time that the sash window is securely taped

4

up. It is so cold, ferny fronds of frost pattern the glass on the inside.

"Just got to do the door now." His words plume in the freezing air.

From the wooden draining board, he grabs the roll of duct tape and the large knife he's had since his army days.

In minutes, the door is sealed to his satisfaction, and he puts the tape and knife away in a drawer, wanting the kitchen to be tidy. He has spent the past few days cleaning every nook and cranny of this house to be sure that it is immaculate.

There's a warning note taped to the outside of the front door and the letter to his sister-in-law, their only living relative, is propped against the clock on the mantelpiece. There's hardly any money for her, but Mavis can have any of their possessions she wants, including a pearl brooch that he knows she admires. He's sorry, though, that she will have to deal with the fallout on her own, and that plays on his mind constantly.

She's been so good, helping out, has Mavis. Many times he's wanted to confide in her as they sat drinking cups of milky tea after she'd changed the bed linen and done some baking so he'd have something wholesome to eat. But feeling sure she wouldn't understand, would certainly try and talk him out of it, he's kept silent and, he is sure, has put on a good act so she has no suspicions.

Besides, what possible alternative is there to the plan he is determined to carry out this day? He would be nothing without his wife. Nothing. Only war has ever separated them, and on either side of those terrible times they haven't spent a single night apart. He has no intention now or ever of sleeping without her by his side.

So this is the way it has to be.

He kneels beside her, croons softly, "Just one more job, my darling, and I'll be right beside you. It'll be just like we talked about; we'll simply drift off to sleep. Yes, we'll go to sleep and then we'll wake up on the other side, and everything will be wonderful."

Grabbing two corners of the mattress and trying not jolt her fragile body any more than he has already, he positions her so that her head is a little closer to the open oven door.

He turns all the gas jets full on and quickly burrows under the thick quilt, stretching himself out beside her, his beloved, his dearest friend, his soul mate.

Wraps his arms around her and tries to still her shivering body, even though his own hands are numb with cold.

Plants a gentle kiss on her dry lips.

Puts his lips close to her ear, and whispers. "Breathe deep, my love, and if you get there first, wait for me."

PRESENT DAY

Chapter 2

"Doors are open, Alex. Ten minutes."

Alex jumped up from his seat and started to pace the length of the dressing room. Even in here, sequestered from the people who had come to see him, he could sense their expectations permeating the walls.

To calm his nerves he curled and stretched his fingers and concentrated on his breathing: deep inhalations through the nose and slow, controlled exhalations through the mouth.

Natalie listened to some chatter in her earpiece and announced, "Everyone's seated. Cameras are ready. Five minutes."

Alex faced his wife, Beth, and his brother-in-law, Paul, now also his agent. "Right, then. How do I look?"

It was Paul who answered. "Smart. I'm glad you listened to me and wore a suit and tie rather than your usual casual gear." He put his hand on Alex's shoulder and said, "This is the first of many, Alex, my friend. Make it a good one."

A middle-aged woman, with a mass of wiry hair and glasses perched on the end of her nose, marched briskly in and said, "Right, Alex, it looks like we're up. I'm looking forward to seeing you in action. I'll be watching on the monitors, so if you identify anyone in trouble just give the signal so I can get to them after the show."

"Okay, Fran. Thanks."

Beth adjusted his tie and the deep purple silk handkerchief tucked into the top pocket of his jacket, and reached up to muss his almost-black hair just the way she liked it. "Paul's right about the suit. You look amazing. They won't be able to take their eyes off you." She kissed his cheek and said, "Go get 'em, handsome."

Paul gave him the thumbs up, then unwrapped and furiously started to chew the first of the many pieces of gum he'd get through while the show was underway. He'd given up smoking years ago, but it amused Alex how this replacement habit persisted.

Alex followed Natalie as she led the way along the dimly-lit corridor to the studio.

"What's it like, Mr. Kelburn, seeing ghosts?"

"Oh, they're not ghosts, Natalie. They are people who have passed over into the afterlife and I can communicate with them. I suppose it's a little bit like how you hear voices in your earpiece, two, sometimes three people giving information and instructions. In my case, I hear maybe twenty or more. Sometimes many more. I rely on my dad to keep them in order, and when I make a connection, I can see them too. As clearly as I see you."

Natalie stopped in her tracks, her heavily lined and mascaraed eyes like saucers. "Your dad?"

Alex laughed at her expression. "It's a bit of story. I'll tell you some time."

As they reached the wings of the studio, the announcer was addressing the audience. "Good evening, ladies and gentlemen, and on behalf of Eselmont Productions, welcome. In just a few moments the man you've all come to see will be with you, but I'd just like to run through a few things to remind you how this event works."

Alex hardly heard what followed. His mind was already full of voices and faces, until his father quieted them and asked them to please wait their turn.

We're all ready here, Alex.

Thanks, dad.

The announcer raised his voice and said, "Would you please all put your hands together and give a very warm hello to... Alex Kelburn!"

There was a burst of music and Natalie gave Alex a gentle nudge. "That's your cue. Good luck."

He strode forward with a warm, confident smile he didn't yet feel and his hands held out in acknowledgement of the enthusiastic applause that greeted him. As the clapping gradually slowed and stopped, there was the usual clearing of throats and shuffling sounds as people got more comfortable in their seats, and then the auditorium fell silent. Even the voices in his head quieted for a few precious moments and he felt again the heavy weight of expectation pressing down on his shoulders.

Okay, Alex. Let's begin.

Alex saw his father motion to someone behind him. Another man came forward into view, looking a little bewildered but also very excited.

"I have a gentleman here... his name is... Ed... Edward?"

Edwin. I'm looking for my wife, Jessica.

"No, I'm sorry, it's Edwin. He's looking for Jessica. Is Jessica here? Can she speak to me please?"

9

There was a rustling that increased in volume as people shifted, looking around, murmuring low to each other, seeking out the lucky person who was about to receive the very first message. There was a commotion to his left, in the second row, as a very elderly lady sitting at the end of it was assisted to her feet by the younger woman next to her. She leaned heavily on two walking sticks, her thin and frail body trembling with the effort of standing, but her voice was surprisingly strong: "I am Jessica, and I recognise the name Edwin."

Hearing her voice, Alex felt a gentle tugging sensation in his solar plexus, and knew he had the right person.

"There's no need to stand; please, sit and get comfortable. May I call you Jessica?"

The rows of seats were well lit and steeply banked, with microphones arranged high above them to allow Alex to see and hear everyone clearly. He took a moment to study Jessica, his eyes taking in the deeply lined face and iron-grey hair pulled back in a bun, but his mind visualising her as she had been in her youth. He saw light brown hair swept back from a pretty, freckle-dusted face, large hazel eyes framed by long black lashes, neat and even white teeth except for a tiny chip on one of the front ones, adding to the charm of her easy smile. She had been a lovely, vibrant woman, and this was how Edwin still saw her.

"Are you comfortable, Jessica? Edwin tells me he is your husband."

"Yes, that's right."

"He is very agitated, and he's telling me that you urgently need to do something about the family finances. Does this make sense to you? Please just tell me yes or no."

The old lady licked her lips and replied with a firm "Yes".

Alex listened to Edwin. The contact was excellent.

She sits in front of my photograph, the one in a walnut frame that sits on the piano. She talks to me about this problem.

He relayed this information, and Jessica's hand flew to her mouth as she answered it was true. Alex noticed that her fingers, fluttering against her lips, were swollen and misshapen with arthritis.

Yes, it's a long time since she's been able to play the piano. She played so beautifully, too.

"Well, Jessica, Edwin is standing right beside you now."

Alex smiled to himself, as anyone still looking at him instead of Jessica at that point now turned with a collective intake of breath, and stared at her, half expecting to see her husband standing beside her. Jessica looked there too, her trembling hand still at her mouth.

Twenty-five years I've been gone and still she misses me every minute of every day, but I'm always with her. Please tell her that. And tell her that I was so proud of her when she went all the way to Durham for our granddaughter's graduation last summer. Tell her I loved her big hat with the feathers.

Alex repeated the message and waited as Jessica fumbled in the pocket of her lavender-coloured cardigan for a handkerchief.

"Edwin tells me that you have been making yourself ill worrying about these financial issues and he's come through now to give you some advice. He says there is a solution and you must consult a solicitor immediately for your son's sake. Don't fret about what it will cost, it will be worth it in the long run. The solicitor will know what to do, and will put your mind at rest. "

Our son's name is Michael.

"Your son's name is Michael, Edwin is telling me."

Jessica dabbed at her tears, although she had a wobbly smile on her lips now.

Alex paused again, listening to the message carefully so he could pass it on with accuracy, in exactly the way Edwin wanted. "He wants you and Michael to know that he's delighted with the way the three grandchildren have grown up, and happy that they all choose to live nearby so they can take care of you."

He paused, then gestured to the woman sitting next to Jessica. "You are the daughter-in-law? Susan?"

Round-eyed, Susan could only nod.

"He says he's relieved that you got away with just a broken arm and a very small scar on your eyebrow after the car accident. It could have been much worse."

Susan's fingers involuntarily went to a spot on her forehead, and she gave a little shake of her head in wonder. Alex could tell that she had come here a sceptic; maybe she'd be going home thinking differently.

"He is giving me these details so you know that it really is Edwin speaking to me now, and that he is always watching over you."

Jessica, weeping and laughing at the same time, waved the lace-edged handkerchief as a sign that she believed it.

"However, he is here particularly because the house and the money - your son's and grandchildren's inheritance, Jessica - are at risk and you must not be afraid to take action now because it can easily be resolved by law. I hope this makes sense to you? Do you understand Edwin's message?"

The old lady had by now lost almost all the colour from her face, except for two rosy circles on her cheeks. Susan gripped her hand tightly.

The tacit compassion of everyone in the audience helped, but Alex could tell that Jessica was too overwhelmed to speak. Edwin was still close to her, his hand on her shoulder, and the love on his face as he looked at his wife was wonderful to see.

He ended the communication by saying, "Jessica, I'm delighted to have brought Edwin through for you."

I love her so much.

"He loves you very much and begs you to remember he is always close to you."

I'm longing for the day she joins me here.

Ah, yes, but I hope you understand that it's better I don't say such a thing under these circumstances, Edwin.

Edwin chuckled. *Of course. Silly of me. Thank you for what you've done for us. It's been wonderful.*

Throughout this short mental exchange people had been applauding, giving Alex time to take a sip from a glass of water set on a small table. Then they started to shuffle and fidget and talk in whispers, and Alex waited patiently for them to settle down again so he could continue.

Ready, Alex? Here's a little girl to speak to you.

My name's Julie. I'm five.

He couldn't help but tense up for a moment, as receiving messages from a child was always a deeply emotional experience for the parents. An elderly man and a middle-aged woman, who introduced themselves as her paternal grandfather and aunt, flanked Julie, and said they would speak for her, as she was so young.

"I'm looking for the parents of a little girl called Julie. Over to my left again…near the back row."

A couple tentatively raised their hands. But it wasn't necessary for them to identify themselves as Julie had already skipped over to her mum and dad and was jumping from foot to foot in excitement.

Alex delivered the messages, short and sweet, and was pleased to see how the couple drew together, both tearful but beaming happily.

After that came some welcome humour from a grandmother who had many tales to tell of her time on this side of life, and a few cheeky stories about her family. Alex loved communications like this, because they brought laughter and some light relief to what could otherwise be an exhausting and emotion-charged couple of hours.

He was in his stride now, and had the 90-strong audience enthralled. The atmosphere in the studio was supercharged, almost crackling with energy.

I have a young man here, Alex. His name is Josh.

Alex stiffened, because the gravity of his father's voice alerted him that this communication was sure to be a tough one emotionally.

Hello, Josh.

Silence.

I know you're nervous. Why don't you start by telling me who you want to talk to?

My mum and dad. They're in the front.

"I have a young man called Josh with me now, and he's looking for his parents." Alex motioned to the front row. "Here, somewhere."

Josh's mother, already sobbing, had her head bowed and her hands tightly clasped in her lap. His father, sitting ramrod straight next to her, stared hard all around Alex, as if looking for his son.

Alex focused his senses on Josh's father, who was as tense as could be, and immediately discovered the reason for his dad's subtle tone of warning.

Okay, Josh. Be brave, now. Tell me what you need me to say to them.

He could see the boy clearly, short and skinny, about twelve years old with intense blue eyes and floppy, reddish-blond hair.

Dad wouldn't listen! I begged not to be sent back to the boarding school. I hated it there! I told him about the bullying and he just said I needed to toughen up. I...I wanted to give him a fright, that's all. I didn't mean it to go so far.

Alex could see the scene in his mind: the desperate young boy going to his room while his parents watched television, crying as he tied his dressing-gown cord round his neck... Just wanting his father to see how frightened he was about returning to school.

Alex tried to work out how to convey this information in the right way. The parents needed proof that he was in communication with their son, but he would have to be very, very careful how he chose his words.

Josh's mother was in a bad way, as was to be expected, but Alex was sure that the father was in an even worse state, even though outwardly he seemed calm. He reached out with his senses again and felt the guilt, the inability to forgive himself for not listening to his son.

It was clear to Alex that if he did not get this man the professional counselling he so badly needed, there was a very real danger that he might try and follow Josh.

In the prearranged gesture, Alex fingered the handkerchief in his top pocket, knowing Fran would see this and get herself ready to waylay and counsel this distraught couple at the end of the recording session.

Josh? Is there anything else you'd like to say to your mum and dad?

Tell them I'm sorry. I'm so very sorry. I didn't want to die! I just wanted them to take me out of that school. But I'm all right here. People are nice and I'm happy.

Alex gently talked to the bereaved parents, skimping a little on the details to preserve their privacy, but giving them just enough for evidence.

"The best thing you can do for Josh now is to live your lives to the full. And Josh is worried about his sister, as she misses him badly too. Remember that he will always be around you, and his family's happiness is all he wants to see. He tells me you've talked of moving house, and he thinks it's a very good idea."

He closed the communication by assuring them that their son was being taken care of, and he was well and happy.

For another hour, Alex worked hard, giving many messages, words of advice, encouragement and comfort from husbands and wives, grandparents, fathers and mothers, brothers and sisters, young children, friends.

So many people on the other side with so much to say.

Never enough time.

He could have gone on all night, but giving and receiving messages was mentally exhausting work. The last half-hour was a question and answer session, and he was relieved when he heard music over the speakers, starting quietly and slowly rising in volume as his cue to wrap up the session.

Well done, Alex. I think that was the best yet.

Thanks, dad.

Natalie met him as he came off stage and he followed her back to where Beth and Paul were waiting for him. They both bounced to their feet as soon as Alex entered, and Paul shook his hand hard.

"That was fantastic, Alex. You came across brilliantly from beginning to end. I've had word from front of house that people are absolutely buzzing about what they've just witnessed. They love you!"

"Of course they love him," cried Beth, throwing her arms round his neck. "How could they not love this gorgeous man with such a wonderful gift?"

16

Alex laughed and kissed her. "After a while I forgot about the cameras, and it felt just like any other evening of platform mediumship. The hardest part was the young suicide. I hope Fran can help that couple, because the father is right on the edge."

"You mean the parents of Josh? Poor kid. What an awful thing to happen."

"You handled that one well, mate," said Paul.

Natalie came in and offered them all a drink. The people who'd received messages were now being interviewed in private rooms to verify Alex's accuracy, but he was not involved in these. His job, for now, was done.

Eselmont would now spend weeks, or even months editing his two hours plus the Q&A and the interviews into a one-hour pilot programme. It would then be marketed to television companies, in the hope that one of them would commission a full series. Eselmont had told him they'd courier over a copy of the pilot when it was ready, but would he watch it? Probably not. He didn't much like the idea of seeing himself on screen.

"I'm bushed." He turned to Beth. "Do you mind if we go straight home?"

Beth squeezed his hand. "Of course not. I'll drive." She turned to her brother. "Dinner soon?"

"Yeah, that'd be great. I'll ring you tomorrow and set a date – and I'll bring a bottle of champagne to celebrate getting the first series into the can."

"A bit premature, Paul," said Alex.

"Well, yes, but having seen what I just saw I have no doubt whatsoever that you'll be back here very soon. You leave the negotiations to me. Trust me, Alex, this is just the beginning. I'm going to make you famous." He punched Alex playfully on the arm. "But you're psychic, so you know that already!"

When Alex threw him a ha-ha-not-at-all-funny look, he put up his hands and said, "I know, I know! Tired joke. Just couldn't resist it."

With Beth driving, Alex soon drifted off into a light doze, only waking fully as Beth turned the car into their drive.

Chapter 3

Lily grinned as Scott, wearing a red and white striped apron over his t-shirt and jeans, laid out their breakfast: toast, butter, jam, honey, a packet of cereal, jug of milk, plus a mug of tea for her and coffee for him. By the time she'd come down, he'd been out for a run, showered, and set the table with a clean cloth and polished cutlery. A card was propped against the salt and pepper pots.

She tore open the pale blue envelope and laughed out loud when she saw the picture and read the soppy, flowery rhyme inside.

"Hmm, not your usual style, but as it's one that I stock, I'm guessing you got Maisie to pick this for you? And you probably left it to the very last minute, right?"

"Guilty as charged on both counts. I hid round the corner and she slipped it out to me when you were busy out the back." He put his hand over his heart. "It may not be the one I would have chosen, and it may be gushy, but I do feel the sentiment. Now, then, does my lady require fruit juice with her breakfast?"

"Just tea, thank you."

"Tuck in, then. I'll be back in a sec."

Scott reappeared just as she bit into a piece of toast, a broad smile on his face and something held behind his back that was far too big to be completely concealed from view.

Lily dropped the remainder of the toast onto her plate and narrowed her eyes, pretending that she couldn't see the flowers. "Okay, what have you got there? A diamond bracelet? A Rolex? Keys to a sports car?"

Scott's expression changed to a mock grimace. "Well, no, I'm afraid not. Maybe next year, if we win the lottery and you continue to be a good and loving wife, you can have any or all of those things. But will these do for now, Birthday Girl?"

He gave a gallant bow and presented her with a basket arrangement of flowers, the centrepiece of which was a creamy pink stargazer lily, fully open to reveal its exotic speckled interior. A huge white bow was tied onto the handle, and tucked in amongst the blooms was a long black and silver box of handmade chocolates.

She took the basket and kissed him. "Oh, these are stunning! And they smell wonderful. You must have got this from Samantha?"

"Yep. I went in there and begged her – on my knees, mind you, as I only gave her a day's notice – to do something truly spectacular for my best beloved."

"On your knees, huh? I should think so! Oh, these really are truly wonderful." Lily placed the basket on the draining board and picked up the box. "And did Maisie sneak the chocs out to you, too?"

"Yep. She said you must like them, because you pinch one or two when you think she isn't looking."

"She's right, but I think the owner is entitled to snaffle her own stock." She took the lid off the honey and reached for a spoon. "So, are you taking the whole day off as you promised?"

"More than my life's worth not to, right? And have *you* taken the whole day off as *you* promised?"

She laughed. "Maisie insisted on it. She loves having the shop all to herself. So, what have you planned for my special day? Shopping at the designer outlet followed by dinner in a fancy restaurant? I'd love a new dress for Maisie and Jack's party; that's only three weeks away, you know."

"Maybe we, well, *you* could do that next weekend? You know I'm hopeless at shopping; you'd be much better off going on your own. But today, how about we go and look at a house?"

Her eyebrows shot up. "What on earth do you mean, look at a house? What house?"

Scott feigned innocence as he replied, "To answer your second question, the house is in Saxon Road. To answer your first question, we go there and we look at it! And no, I don't just mean we stand in the street and stare at the outside. The estate agent will be waiting to let us in at 10 o'clock. And to answer the question you haven't yet asked, we decide if we'd like to buy it and live in it."

Lily stared at him. "Scott, we haven't even discussed moving."

"We're discussing it now."

"But Saxon Road? Are you mad? We can't afford anything along there!"

"Ah, well, you don't know number 8, obviously." He pulled an estate agent's brochure from the apron pocket and placed it on the table. "Here're the details. You've got time for a quick look at this before we go, but please don't say anything until you've actually been inside."

The colour photograph on the front was of a Victorian red brick semi-detached house with a grey slate roof. Inside the brochure were pictures of the interior rooms, all unfurnished and, for the most part, unfinished. The patch of grass at the front and the long, narrow back garden were in need of attention too. The price was, indeed, a lot lower than she would have expected.

"This must be practically opposite Maisie's house. Scott, why didn't you tell me about this before?"

Scott rose from the table and kissed the tip of her nose before starting to gather up the breakfast things. "Because

21

I wanted to check out all the facts and figures first, and I wanted to surprise you on your birthday. I warn you, it needs a lot of work, which is what makes it just about affordable, but we can do most of it ourselves. Please, come and look at this with me, Lil."

"You've already seen inside it?"

"I spotted it on one of my runs, and I got curious, so…" He gave a disarming shrug.

"Scott, please tell me that you haven't already bought it!"

He laughed and hugged her. "Of course I haven't. I'd never do something like that. This is a decision for both of us."

"But you really like it?"

"Very much. It has good-sized rooms, lots of Victorian features, which I know you'll love. You can't hear the main road unless you're right at the bottom of the garden. And what a garden it could be! You've always wanted a garden."

He took the brochure from her and laid it out on the table so they could both see the picture on the front and the floor plan on the back. "We could make this place amazing, we really could. It'll be tight financially, but if we rent out this flat, dip into our savings, do most of the work ourselves, and use the money granny left me…"

"Scott, no! You and Duncan agreed that you'd both put your share of that money into expanding the garage."

He held his hands up. "I know, I know. But we've talked it over, and my brother's come up with a brilliant plan that suits both of us. I've thought hard about this, Lily, and it seems to me that a family home should be our priority."

She nodded slowly, a gleam of excitement beginning to shine in her eyes as she caught some of Scott's enthusiasm.

"You've certainly been busy behind my back."

"I know, but I wanted to be sure. Lily, believe me, this is a great opportunity that might not come round again for a long time. If ever. I say we go for it."

She put her arms round his neck and hugged him. "Okay. I absolutely love the idea. But are you sure about the garage? What are you going to do?"

"I'm going to concentrate on what I love best, service and repair, particularly of classic cars. Duncan is going to set up the sales side of the business on his own, and we'll come to some percentage arrangement on the income from both. Honestly, we're both excited about it."

"Well, then. Sounds like a plan." She opened the brochure to have another look at the interior shots.

Scott leaned over her shoulder. "It wouldn't be a problem, would it, living across the road from your part-time employee? We could always leave the front hedge as it is, it practically obscures the house."

Lily laughed and shook her head. "Of course I wouldn't mind. Maisie's a good friend."

"She saw me when I went to view it, and she promised not to tell." He grinned. "Which, clearly, she didn't, and I must admit that surprises me. Our Maisie is not known for her discretion."

"Oh, so *that's* why she's been looking at me in such a strange way lately! I felt that she had a secret she was bursting to tell me, but I would never have guessed it was anything like this. Look, you seem really positive about it, so I'm perfectly prepared to be convinced."

"Good. Finish your breakfast and get your coat on, woman. We've got a house to see."

Half an hour later they were standing on the kerb in front of the house, shaking hands with the estate agent.

He led the way up the path and unlocked the door. "Shall I let you show Mrs. Miller around, or would you prefer me to do the honours?"

"I'll show her, if that's okay."

"Sure it is. You have all the details. Take as long as you need and drop the key into my office later."

Lily could tell from his obvious hurry to get away that he didn't really believe he'd got a sale. It had been on the market for five months, not many had been to view, and Scott said it was likely that he was the only person to come back a second time.

They went slowly from room to room, Scott pointing out all the features, Lily saying very little. It was quite hard for her to gauge the size of the rooms with no furniture to act as guidelines, but she liked what she saw.

There was an unfinished two-storey extension at the back, and Scott explained that the plan was to create a big master bedroom with en-suite bathroom upstairs, and a lovely light-filled kitchen downstairs.

"You weren't wrong when you said this place needs work. The owners have obviously made this into a major project, but nothing's finished. Not a single room."

"They've not long started out property developing, apparently, and this is their third project. The estate agent told me that something unexpected has happened, he doesn't know the details, and they need to get shot of this place quickly. So that, plus the fact that there's so much to do, is why it's on at such a good price. But, Lily, don't you see the potential? Look at the ornamental plasterwork on this ceiling! And there are original fireplaces in just about every room."

Lily gazed around, her mind racing with colour schemes. It could be - it was - a lovely house.

Scott grabbed her hands. "We can do this, Lily, we really can! It's already been completely rewired and double-glazed. Dad can help with the plumbing, and he knows where to look for good-value bathroom and kitchen stuff."

Lily turned a slow circle, taking in the black and white tiles on the floor, the deep coving and the ornamental ceiling rose, the picture rail going round the walls, the narrow, steep staircase. "I'm a bit overwhelmed, to be honest."

"But in a good way, right? I was a bit worried about springing it on you on your birthday, but you can see how this house could be made into a wonderful family home, can't you? Let's go outside."

The back garden was long, with a gorgeous oak tree at the bottom and high hedges that blocked the sight and sound of the main road on the other side. Lily could see a ramshackle shed and a greenhouse with missing panes, half hidden behind a rotting trellis.

Scott said, "I'm sure you're already planning what could be done with this? Flower beds, meandering pathways, pond, veggie plot…"

His excitement gripped her again, as it had back at their flat. "Yes! Yes, I am. Oh, Scott, can we really do this?"

He stood behind her and pulled her into his arms, resting his chin on the top of her head. "Let's go talk to the estate agent."

***

Vincent was standing on the pavement across the road when the green car drew up to the kerb, right outside the house. A short, apple-shaped man in a loud pin-striped suit and a yellow tie got out and glanced at his watch and then up and down the road. In less than a minute, another car arrived and parked and a young couple joined him. They all looked at the house and Vincent knew they'd come to view it.

This was a scene he'd witnessed many times over the years. Normally he didn't pay all that much attention - no matter how proprietorial he felt about the place, he could not influence what happened to it - but there was something about the woman that caught his attention ...

He wanted to follow them inside and listen to their conversation as they walked around, but it was too risky. Instead, he stayed where he was on the other side of the road, his gaze fixed on the house, until the front door opened and they came back out.

The man was muscular and tall, considerably more so than Vincent, with a handsome face and dark brown hair fashionably spiked with gel. He seemed so confident, standing there in his black jeans and green t-shirt, looking at the front garden and then back at the house as if he already owned it. Vincent had seen him before on many occasions, usually in the early morning, but sometimes late in the evening, jogging along in shorts and chunky-looking running shoes.

The man opened the gate and waited for the woman to precede him onto the pavement. Vincent could see her face clearly now as she walked towards their car, and he almost staggered with shock. It was uncanny how like his wife she looked. Okay, the hairstyle was different, but it was that same light brown, like honey in the sunlight, and thick and straight. And, like his wife, she had large, light blue eyes and high cheekbones, the same lovely, dimpled smile that lit up her face. Her slim figure looked good in a pretty, becoming dress.

She was gazing up at the man - surely her husband - as he leaned down to kiss her, and Vincent heard the man say her name. How amazing: she'd even been named after a flower.

He sighed deeply at the memory of Rose. So sweet, so lovely. Rose had taken such care with her hair, her makeup and clothes. She'd kept the house immaculate, and she'd cooked good, wholesome meals every day, managing so well through the war-time deprivations of their *early years together. She'd budgeted the housekeeping money, too, so there was always a special treat on Sundays.*

Even when the much-wanted children had not come along, they'd been so happy together. So very happy.

Vincent mentally shook himself from his nostalgic thoughts and feasted his eyes on Lily as she and her husband got into their car. Once they were out of sight, he crossed the road and slipped quickly through the gate. Leading up to the house was a gravel path, the stepping-stones he'd set into the lawn long gone. The grass was overgrown now, and the box hedge that separated the garden from its neighbour was, like the one that obscured the front of the property, in dire need of clipping back. He flexed his fingers, wishing he could get his lawnmower and shears and make it all neat again.

Although he could not feel anything, he flattened his hand on the front door then ran his fingers over the dulled brass knocker. In his day, this same knocker, polished to a high shine every Saturday by Rose, had been positioned between two lovely stained glass panels that cast jewel colours on the hallway tiles. Now the door was a solid one, and had been painted many different colours over the years.

He entered the house and wandered through its empty rooms.

Under each new ownership, as changes had been made inside and outside, he'd watched them happen. The bathroom fittings had been replaced several times, in colours ranging from the original white to pale green, to brown, to pink, and back to white again. The beautiful parquet floor of the living room had been covered with rugs, then wall-to-wall carpeting. Now it was bare again, but in need of scrubbing and polishing to bring it back to its former shine. The walls had been wallpapered, stripped and painted, and wallpapered again.

But it was the kitchen that had changed the most, its appliances becoming more and more foreign to him. Now it was an empty shell, like the rest of the place.

Not a single room remained the same as when he'd lived there.

That was probably just as well, though.

He imagined the young couple here, Lily, and whatever her husband was called. He felt certain that they were going to buy it, and the idea of it pleased him, because the idea of Lily living in his house pleased him.

Chapter 4

Jack clicked the top of his pen and tucked it into his shirt pocket, at the same time pushing *The Telegraph*, folded on the crossword page, down the side of his chair. "How about a cup of tea, eh, before we go up and get ready?" He reached for his stick, but Maisie gestured for him to stay where he was.

"I'll make it, love, you need to rest. They're saying this is the hottest day of the year so far, and it'll be a long and tiring evening."

Standing in the kitchen spooning tealeaves into the rose-decorated china teapot, Maisie softly sang a medley of cheerful show tunes as she thought about the party. It was going to be a grand affair, organised by their children in celebration of her and Jack's golden wedding anniversary. Fifty years! She spread her left hand so she could admire the new diamond and ruby eternity ring on her wedding finger. It had been presented to her in a dark blue velvet box tied with a gold ribbon as soon as she'd woken up that morning, along with a single red rose, its thorns removed.

When she returned to the sitting room with the tea things laid out on a tray, Jack had the newspaper back on his lap, filling in some more of the cryptic crossword puzzle. She saw how he had to grip the pen hard and form each of the letters very slowly to keep them in the small boxes.

She poured a full cup for herself, and three-quarters filled the other one so he could manage to lift it to his mouth without spilling hot liquid over himself. She added milk and sugar to both and placed Jack's on the small table by his chair.

He absently smiled his thank you as he wrote in another answer.

Picking up her cup and saucer, Maisie sauntered to the window. It was 4 o'clock, and the sky was a clear blue with hardly a cloud in sight. She thought it likely that their party would spill out onto the lawns and terraces of the hotel, as it was obviously going to be a lovely evening.

She looked at the 'sold' notice nailed across the sale board opposite, delighted that Lily and Scott were going to be living there very soon. What a birthday present that had been for Lily a couple of weeks ago!

George Jameson was out with his dog, stopping every two feet while the huge, shaggy animal sniffed and cocked a leg at fences, hedges and lampposts. It must be so hot, having all that fur, she thought.

A silver estate car swept into the drive next door and Maisie wondered where they'd been all day. Probably visiting their newest grandchild? She'd find out later, at the party.

The rattle of Jack's cup in the saucer as he lifted it from the table brought her attention back to the room. She watched as he struggled to get the cup to his lips without spilling, trying hard not to read too much into the obvious fact that the weakness in his hands was getting worse. She wondered how much longer it would be before he couldn't even lift himself out of the chair. As if sensing her thoughts, he suddenly glanced up at her, and she covered her anxiety by saying, "I think I'll take my tea upstairs and have my bath now. Is there anything you need?"

"No, love, you go on up. I've nearly finished the crossword and then I'll come and get myself ready."

She heard the click of Jack's pen as she left the room. She had to force herself to stop thinking about his problems and to think happy thoughts instead. She had a tremendous party to look forward to. Her son and two daughters had hired the banqueting room in a hotel, and had arranged a fancy limousine to collect her and Jack and bring them home. The limousine even had a bar, she'd been told, and she couldn't help but laugh at the thought of such grandeur.

But she was so looking forward to celebrating this special event with her family and their old friends, most of whom were from Saxon Road and the previous streets she and Jack had lived in.

They had lived in the village for all of their married life. Their first home had been one of the tiny terraced cottages with long, narrow gardens backing onto the railway line. At night she'd loved to hear the soft rumble of the trains as she drifted off to sleep. As Jack had progressed in his career and their three children had come along in neat, two-year intervals, they'd moved into a semi near the primary school, then a larger semi and, finally, thirty years ago, into Saxon Road. And each time they'd moved, Maisie had insisted that the front door be painted her favourite colour, a deep ruby red, and furnished with polished brass numerals, lion head doorknocker and letterbox.

In their advancing years neither she nor Jack wanted to move to a bungalow, even though it was the sensible option. The Victorian house was far from ideal for Jack, but they'd had a few helpful gadgets installed to help him cope. But of course his ever-deteriorating condition, slow though it was, worried her dreadfully. For sure he'd have to give in soon and agree to a wheelchair, and at some point they'd have to convert the dining room into their bedroom once he could no longer manage the steep stairs.

The taps were turned on to full flow and her favourite bubble bath coloured the water and perfumed the steamy air. In the bedroom, Maisie removed the precious new

31

eternity ring, and put away her red and white skirt and white short-sleeved top. It was one of her favourites as it was decorated with an intricate Celtic pattern in silver sequins, and Maisie loved her sequins. Wrapping her cotton dressing gown around her and tying the belt, she returned to the bathroom, dipped her fingers into the water to test the temperature, and turned off the taps.

Before stepping into the fragrant water, she wiped the steam off the mirrored doors of the medicine cabinet to look again at her reflection. For the first time in decades, at the insistence of her daughters, her hair had been professionally cut and coloured. She loved the gleaming rich auburn and copper tones that had obliterated the harsh red of the home dye kits she usually used. Expensive, yes, but definitely worth it for this most special occasion.

Even more expensive was the outfit she would wear tonight, but as she immersed herself in the magnolia-scented water she allowed herself to consider how glamorous she was going to look in the new dress.

Having nagged her into submission about her hair, and insisted she also have a facial, manicure and pedicure, Caroline and Lorraine had frog-marched her into a clothes shop she would never have dared venture into on her own. The elegant and softly spoken owner had sat the girls down on a plush sofa, and they had sipped coffee as their mother's measurements were taken and several gowns selected for her to try on. When Maisie had emerged from the changing room – brightly lit with mirrors on the door and the three walls to give an all-round view – Caroline had had tears in her eyes, and Lorraine had acerbically commented that it was a far cry from her usual rag-bag hippy outfits in clashing shades of red.

Maisie had to admit that the dress they'd eventually chosen was flattering to her skin tone and figure, and once it had been altered for her height of five feet and half an inch, she'd known that Jack would love her in it.

Before getting into the bath, she just had to slip into the back room to admire the dress once more. Reverently, she fingered the soft, midnight-blue fabric and traced the delicate copper and gold beadwork at the cuffs and sweetheart-style neckline. It may prove to be a bit warm on a sultry night like this, she thought, but it was just perfect in every other way. Expertly cut, it would flatter her ample bust and still-small waist, and the way it flared on the hips would disguise her slightly protruding belly, the one part of her body she hated but couldn't get rid off no matter how she tried. Jack, who had long ago given up trying to get Maisie to wear more elegant clothes, was truly going to be astonished.

And the strappy high-heeled sandals that the girls had bought for her would also amaze him. Caroline had arrived yesterday morning and handed over a pale pink shoebox with a cheeky look on her face. Maisie had gingerly removed the lid and peeled back the pink tissue paper, exclaiming with dismay when she saw the height of the slender gold heels. But she'd been firmly told that she could manage them for just one evening.

Well, yes, Maisie had slowly replied as she held one of them up, she probably could. As long as she sat down for the entire evening and didn't dance even once.

She and Caroline had giggled at that, but their gaiety had been tinged with sadness, because it was ballroom dancing that had brought Jack and Maisie together more than fifty years ago. Jack loved to tell people how he had known the moment he'd taken Maisie's hand to lead her onto the dance floor that she was the girl he wanted to marry.

Maisie was sure that Jack missed being able to dance with her almost more than anything else.

But she didn't want to be sad about that, not tonight, and anyway it was time to help Jack get ready for the party.

Chapter 5

Lily skirted the packing boxes stacked by the door and nimbly skipped down the stairs. As she came out into the yard and rounded the corner to The Lilac Tree, she thought with excitement how there were just a few days left until they moved a quarter of a mile away to Number 8 Saxon Road.

She was so excited about the new house. So much more space, plenty to do to it to make it truly their own, a large garden just begging to be landscaped. Oh, they'd work so hard, every spare minute of every day, to make it ready for the family they both wanted to have!

When she thought about them becoming parents, she liked to imagine how their children would look. A boy first, that looked just like Scott. A little girl, a year or two later, that took after her. Then a third child. Here, she couldn't decide whether boy or girl, but it really wouldn't matter. They'd be the perfect family, with perfect children, all beautiful, bright, loving. Maybe they'd have a hutch and large run in the garden for pet rabbits or guinea pigs. Get a dog, either a red setter or a border collie. Or why not one of each breed?

She hugged this dream to herself as she rounded the building and walked the few paces to the shop, keys in hand ready to open up. She was surprised to find the door already unlocked, the interior lights on, and the sign on the door turned to 'OPEN'.

The Lilac Tree took up the ground floor, directly below their flat, of a late-Victorian building. It had for a long time been split into two shops, before being converted into one big floor space with just one door to accommodate a hardware store. When the hardware store had moved to bigger premises at the far end of the High Street, Lily had been able to buy and refit the shop with a small bank loan and a little extra help from her father.

The boarded-up doorway had been changed to a large bay window with small glass panes to give it an old-fashioned look, and she had been delighted to discover good quality parquet flooring beneath the tattered dull-brown linoleum.

Now the half-glazed door, painted a glossy black, led into the largest part of the shop. The merchandise was displayed on a range of shelves around the walls and in a central floor-to-ceiling column, which had revolving shelves within a glass casing. Customers wanting to look at cards, party balloons, wrapping paper, ribbons and bows turned left through a low archway just before the counter which housed the till and all the sales paraphernalia, and down two shallow steps.

At the back were a cloakroom, a kitchenette and a good-sized stockroom, which Lily planned some day to open up to provide more retail space. She didn't mind that 'some day' was now further away than she'd hoped when she had first thought of the idea, as they'd be putting all their cash into the house instead.

As she pushed open the door and went inside, she immediately felt her spirits lift even higher as the heavenly scents of lavender, sandalwood, lemon and vanilla filled her senses. "Maisie?" she called, "Where are you? I wasn't expecting to see you until later."

All she could see were Maisie's arms and legs as she came through from the back room struggling with a large box.

"Hey! Put that down, for heaven's sake. It's far too heavy."

36

"My daughter's taken Jack out for a couple of hours, and I wanted to be here to help you with the new stock," puffed Maisie, laying the box down on the floor and slitting the sealing tape with a scissor blade. "Especially as you have your hands full with the move." Her narrow gold-rimmed reading glasses swung on a thin cord around her neck; she hardly ever bothered to use them, preferring to squint and screw up her eyes rather than admit to poor eyesight.

"Well, thank you! You really are a treasure. It's going to be very hot again, so I'd better prop the door open." She pulled the heavy metal doorstop, in the shape of a Scottie dog, in front of the door, making sure its price tag was visible so customers would know it was for sale.

"That really was a terrific party on Saturday. And you looked absolutely stunning."

Maisie grinned. "Yes, I did, didn't I! The party was exhausting for Jack, of course, but he loved every minute. As did everybody else, I think."

"Oh, I've no doubt about that. Scott and I haven't danced so much in ... oh, I don't know how long. My feet still hurt. Well, if you're sure you're not too tired, I'm very glad you're here, because I don't think I'll be able to keep my mind on work. There's still so much to do before we move on Friday."

"Moving is a big thing, pet. All the packing, so many people to tell of your change of address, organising water, gas, electricity and telephone. Don't envy you all that." Maisie chattered on as she opened the flaps of the box and pressed them down the sides so she could reach in and lift things out. "When will your tenant be moving in upstairs?"

"In a week's time, I believe. We're leaving all that to the agent. Oh, the wind chimes!" She lifted out six packages wrapped thickly in bubble plastic and carefully cut them

37

open to reveal the wind chimes. Three, each beautifully decorated with coloured crystals and with metal chimes, were for indoors. The other three, made entirely from different kinds of wood, were suitable to hang outside. "They're even lovelier than I remember. Isn't that a gorgeous sound? We'll need to hang a couple up, Maisie."

A young man wearing a back-to-front baseball cap came in wanting a birthday card and was directed by Maisie to the racks. He took ages to decide, so Maisie asked him if he needed any help. The man's cheeks reddened as he said, "It's for my new girlfriend. I don't really know the best type of, um, you know, card?"

"Well then, dear, keep it simple, is what I would suggest. Have a look at these. And have you got your young lady a gift?"

Lily smiled to herself at Maisie's sales technique, and when the man asked for help in choosing a suitable gift to go with the suitable card, she winked at Maisie as the young man was guided to their selection of scented candles. She even talked him into buying a small box of the hand made chocolates.

As he left, a woman who was a regular customer came in, searching for a present for her daughter. Lily pointed out the new stock, and the woman was most taken with the crystal wind chimes and immediately selected one of them.

"Would you like me to gift-wrap it?"

"Oh, yes please. And, you know, I think I'd like one for myself. I've got just the right place for it. I'm always certain to find just the thing in this lovely shop."

Lily was delighted with the compliment. "I think I'll be keeping one of the wooden ones for myself. My husband and I are moving to a new house on Friday, and I'd like one for the garden."

At 11 o'clock the red mail van drew up outside and parked on the double yellow lines, hazard lights flashing. The driver, alarmingly spike-haired and tattooed, with numerous piercings in his ears, tongue, bottom lip and left eyebrow, was incongruously wearing fingerless leather gloves and orange knee-length shorts. The shorts and the chunky boots on his feet did nothing to enhance his skinny white legs. He strode in and thrust a handful of letters and a small package at Lily, mumbled something that sounded like 'gmornin', and strode out again. The van was gone with a roar of over-revved engine and a choking cloud of exhaust fumes before Lily had opened the first envelope.

"Have you noticed the huge holes in his earlobes? You can see right through them. And did he have his bottom lip pierced last time he was here, or is that new?" asked Maisie.

"I think it's new," said Lily. "I wonder if that's more painful than having one put in the eyebrow."

Maisie crossed her arms and leaned against the counter. "Mm, not something I'm ever likely to find out."

Lily laughed, remembering Maisie's hilarious tale of deciding to have her ears pierced just before her 50th birthday. She'd been so traumatised by the first piercing, she'd sworn like a trooper, shocking the poor girl doing the piercing, and almost walked out before having the other ear done. Now, though, she always wore ornate earrings that looked, to Lily, to be too heavy.

Maisie said, "I wonder if he has piercings in other parts of his body? You know, parts not usually on view?"

The thought made Lily shudder with disgust but she was curious too and said, "Perhaps we ought to ask him next time he comes in. Though I'm not sure he can actually speak."

She opened an envelope. "Invoice for those handmade cards from Jo Henley." She put it down and opened two more. "Statement from Mason's Toys, and another invoice - I'd better do some paperwork this afternoon. But now, I'm going to make us both some tea."

Leaving Maisie to price and set out the rest of the new stock, Lily went to the kitchenette.

Just as she came back through carrying two mugs of tea, the phone rang. Maisie was busy putting something in the window, so Lily put the mugs on the counter and picked up the handset. "Hello, The Lilac Tree Gift Shop."

"Hello, darling. How are you?"

Lily felt the usual mixed emotions rise at the sound of her mother's cut-glass vowels.

"Hi, mum. I'm fine, thank you. And you?"

"I'm very well, as always. Look, I'm sorry to call you at the shop, but I'm trying to organise who's coming to the villa and when. Your father and I are flying out next month. He'll be coming and going, of course, but I'll probably stay through September. Your Aunt Marion wants to come for a week with a friend. I wanted to check with you, though, give you first choice, before firming up dates with her. Do you think you'd be able to come for a week or two?"

Lily felt her temper rise. Her mother simply did not understand that she and Scott had businesses to run and holidays were, by necessity, a very rare treat.

"Lily? Lily? Are you there?" The voice was irritable, sharp. "I haven't spoken to her yet, but maybe you and Adele could come together? I know you two don't get much opportunity to see each other, it would be an excellent chance to catch up."

Lily would love to see her sister, but not with their mother around, who would constantly interrupt and interfere and spoil everything, especially if their dad wasn't there to rein her in. He was a workaholic and rarely took off more than a week at a time.

"Mum, you know that we're moving house on Friday. We'll be very busy with that, and I'll have to take too much time away from the shop as it is. And Scott certainly can't leave the garage, he's got far too much on."

"Well, surely your help... Maggie, is it? Surely she could manage your little shop for a week, darling? And you could come on your own, couldn't you? It'll do you good to have a break. I'll arrange it so it'll just be family: you and Adele, your dad and me."

And there it was. Lily just had a 'little shop' to worry about and Scott, despite being the hard-working co-owner of a garage with his brother that employed two other people, still wasn't good enough because he got his hands dirty fixing engines. She would never forget nor forgive how her mother, on being introduced to him, had fingered the pearl necklace that lay against her coffee-coloured silk blouse and said in her most withering tone, "So you're a mechanic? How interesting." She'd then turned away and talked to someone else.

Through gritted teeth Lily said, "Have a good time, mother. I'm sure I'll see you before you go." She pressed the button to disconnect the call and counted slowly to ten.

"I gather your mother was being her usual difficult self?" Maisie said, taking a duster from the drawer beneath the counter to start doing the glass and chinaware.

Lily rolled her eyes and relayed what her mother had just said.

"I'm afraid your mum's a snob, dear, and that's never likely to change. I've always thought it's why your dad travels so much for business."

Lily sighed. "You might be right, Maisie."

41

They worked on through the morning, cleaning and arranging stock and serving customers, until Maisie left at 12.30.

The afternoon passed quietly enough for Lily, with just two customers coming in. This was normal for a Monday, and she managed to sort through the bills and make payments and do a stock check on the cards and wrapping paper. Her mind, though, was constantly on what still needed to be done for the impending move, and she was relieved when it was time to close up and she could go upstairs.

Chapter 6

"She's busy, mum! A new house, running her shop. She can't afford to take the time away, and nor can Scott."

"That's as maybe, Adele, but she should make time for her family. We'd be happy to pay for her flight and she could come on her own for just a few days, surely? And now you're telling me that you can't come either?"

"No, sorry, I really can't. I've got far too much on work-wise."

"Oh, darling! You and Lily are both as bad as your father. When did you last have a holiday? Surely you can take some time off?"

"Mum, you'll never understand, will you? Just like Lily, I can't simply take off when I please. Look, I have to go. I'll call you Sunday."

Adele had to resist throwing the phone across the room. She could take a holiday, she was her own boss after all, but she wanted to go away somewhere really exotic with Rob, not spend it with her parents in Italy. Especially after having listened for the last ten minutes to her mother rant on about Lily's failings as a daughter, how she never visited her, and was now refusing to go out to the villa. It saddened her that her mother and sister could not get on. In her mother's eyes, she, Adele, was the golden girl, the one with a university degree, who had followed her father into banking. Now she had a very successful financial consultancy business, and these days she was comfortably well off.

Whereas Lily... Well, she had always been a rebel. Their mother was not at all happy that Lily had chosen to give up school at 16, leave home at 17, and had worked in a variety of shops until she got married and eventually found herself in a position to open up her own premises. Nor was she pleased to have as a son-in-law someone who worked on oily engines every day.

Oh, but she loved Rob. Not nearly as handsome as Scott, but he worked in a prestigious office, owned an amazing apartment in Bath, and drove a fancy car. What's more, he had soft hands and manicured nails, whereas Scott never quite managed to get every speck of grease and grime from his hands. Her mother flirted outrageously with Rob, and he loved every minute of it.

Two years Adele had been seeing him, and, although they'd never talked about it, she hoped Rob would soon suggest they move in together or even, though she hardly dared to dream, get married. Seeing how happy Lily and Scott were together made her hanker for such a partnership, but she would not be the one to suggest it.

Adele made a mental note to call her sister later to see how the impending move out of the flat above the shop and to their new home was going. They didn't see much of each other because, she had to admit, she was so busy and time just got away with her, but they spoke often on the phone.

But right now she had work to do, so she pushed all thoughts of her family to the back of her mind, put on her glasses, and started to read through the portfolio of one of her most important clients.

After ten minutes the ringing of her mobile interrupted her. Seeing it was Rob her very important client suddenly became totally irrelevant and she answered with a soft and, she hoped, sexy voice. "Hi."

"Can I come round?"

"Of course!"

"I've only got an hour. Be ready for me?"

"You bet."

With her stomach fluttering in joyous anticipation, she clicked off and raced upstairs, shedding her clothes as she went. A speedy shower, a fluffing up of her short, precision-cut hair, a liberal spray of scent, and she was in her bed.

Seconds later, she heard Rob's key in the door, and his footsteps hurrying up to where she lay waiting.

Chapter 7

Beth yawned and stretched her arms above her head. "I really need to get to bed. Are you coming?"

"Not yet, you go on up. I'll have the monitor down here, so if Amber cries, I'll see to her, okay?"

Beth was so exhausted she could only nod, and Alex watched with sympathy as she dragged herself out of the living room to go to bed. Amber was teething and Beth had been up with her for several nights running.

He turned the volume down on the television and settled himself on the antique-red Chesterfield armchair, relishing as always the comfort and smells of the deep-buttoned leather. He laid his head back between the gently curved wings, and rubbed the scrolled and padded arms with the palms of his hands. As a young boy, and before his dad's illness had become so bad he couldn't get out of bed, he'd loved to climb onto his father's lap for a story, the two of them snuggled up on this very chair, until he fell asleep. Then his father would carry him upstairs to his room, and he'd wake in the morning not remembering how he'd got there.

Are you here, dad?

Yes, I'm here. Thought you should know that your little angel is awake.

As if on cue, a little whimper came through the baby monitor.

Thanks. I'd better get up there in case she starts crying.

He was already at the top of the stairs when an anguished wail came from Amber's room.

She was lying on her back in the cot, her little face contorted and smeared with tears. But as soon as she heard

Alex's crooning voice, the crying stopped and she rewarded him with a chuckle and a beaming smile. He reached in and gently picked her up. "Are you wet, baby?" He positioned her against his shoulder so he could check. "Yep, you need changing."

Amber gurgled as he changed her and put her light cotton sleep suit back on, but as soon as she was laid down in her cot, her bottom lip wobbled in a clear sign that she was working herself up again. It always amazed him how something so small could make so much noise.

"All right, you win. You'll have to come downstairs with me." He gathered her up again and gently rubbed her back.

On the way past his bedroom door, he peeked in to make sure Beth hadn't been disturbed. She was sprawled across the metal-framed bed, the bed that he had made himself as a wedding gift to her. Her silky hair was fanned across the pillow, her long legs, brown and oh so smooth, had kicked the sheet away. He wanted to join her there, inhale the scent of her skin, kiss her awake. But no, he couldn't do that; she had been so desperate for sleep, and Amber wouldn't give them any peace anyway.

Nuzzling Amber's cheek, Alex whispered into her ear, "Do you have any idea of the impact you're having on my love-life?"

He tiptoed away and back down to the living room.

He gave Amber a pacifier from the fridge, a useful trick Beth had discovered for soothing sore gums, then sat on the sofa holding her. He tickled her tummy. "You are a little minx, Amber Kelburn. It's a good job mummy didn't wake up, 'cos you know how grumpy she is when she's tired."

Looking into her wide, innocent baby eyes, Alex wondered how long it would be before he would be able read her inner feelings. At the moment she only radiated her instinctive wants: feed me, cuddle me, make me warm, cool me down.

With adults it was easy. Something in his psychic brain was able to analyse and understand people way beyond the words they used and how they acted. It was a skill very few people knew he had, because he was well aware how unnerving it must be.

But it had served him well with Beth, as he'd known long before she'd told him that she was deeply in love with him. She'd known from the beginning that he was a medium, but he'd only told her about this other aspect of his psychic senses on the night he proposed.

She had gone very quiet for a while.

"You mean, then, that I could never lie to you? Not even a white lie?"

He'd shaken his head. "Nope. I call it my seventh sense, and the mediumship is my sixth. I can control them, in that I can close them down temporarily, else I'd go mad with people in the afterlife trying to talk to me and other people's emotions swirling around me."

She'd snuggled into him and said, "So you knew before you asked me that I wanted to marry you, and you know without me telling you that this rather startling piece of news makes no difference to me?"

He'd given a wry grin, and Beth had laughed and joked that he should offer his services to the government as a human lie detector.

"You'd be far better than a machine, Alex. Just a little chat, and bingo! You'd know if they were or weren't telling the truth."

Beth coming into the room brought him out of a deep sleep of confused dreams. He was lying awkwardly on his back, legs over the arm of the sofa, with Amber on his stomach. Her body was totally relaxed, her breathing soft and even. One of her tiny fists grasped his t-shirt, and there was a round wet patch where she'd drooled.

"Oh, I'd love to get a photo of that," laughed Beth. "But I know she'll wake up before I get the camera."

"And I can't lie here any longer. I've got pins and needles in my legs."

"Here, let me take her." Beth gently disengaged Amber and carried her up to her room to change her and put some day clothes on.

Alex followed them up, took a quick shower and, smelling fresh coffee wafting up, threw on shorts and t-shirt and went eagerly to the kitchen. Amber was in her high chair. Beth handed him a bib and a bowl of cereal.

"Here you go. Help her so most of it goes into her mouth and not in her hair. I made a right mess of it yesterday and I'm not sure how much she actually ate."

Alex tied the bib round Amber's neck and offered her some cereal. She opened her mouth, showing the peaks of two teeth in her bottom gum, and grabbed the bowl of the spoon. Trying not to laugh, Beth handed him a towel to wipe Amber's sticky fingers and the front of his t-shirt.

"What time did she wake you up last night?"

"About an hour after you'd gone to bed, I suppose. Dad warned me she was awake, so I was up there before she started to scream for attention. I brought her down, and we both fell asleep."

"And very cute you looked, too! Now, I've got to pop out and get some stuff for tonight's meal, so I'll take Amber with me and you can get started on her room."

He groaned. "Yes, and on what looks set to be the hottest weekend of the year. What are you going to do when you get back from the supermarket?"

Beth wiped round Amber's mouth and playfully tried to do the same to Alex before kissing him. "I am going to lie out in the sun, and watch our beautiful daughter play on the rug."

"You'll fall asleep, so I hope you're going to tie her to something. Is there any other baby who can crawl as fast as she does?"

"Tie her to something? She's not a dog, Alex. I thought you could bring the playpen out?"

"So let me get this straight," said Alex, with a wry expression on his face. "You get to lay out there in the sun, our beloved daughter gets to play in her pen, and I get to inhale paint fumes in one of the tiniest rooms on the planet?"

Beth patted his cheek. "That sounds about right, dear husband. But first I have to go traipsing round a busy supermarket, and later I have to prepare a fancy dinner for my gourmet brother and my soon-to-be-famous husband. I'll get your favourite pastries and make fresh lemonade as soon as I get back, how about that?"

While Beth cleaned Amber's high chair and tidied everything away, Alex wrestled with the playpen. He tried to get it outside in one piece, but it wouldn't go through the door, so he had to remove a few screws and collapse it. He reassembled it on the large picnic rug, and positioned the large parasol over it so Amber would be protected from the sun. Beth, he knew, would slather herself in oil and simply bask, topping up what was already a deep, golden tan.

He went into the garage and gathered up all the decorating materials he needed, including a borrowed pasting table and brush, and was soon hard at work. There wasn't enough space in Amber's tiny bedroom, so the table was set up on the landing, and Alex quickly got into the rhythm of measuring, cutting, pasting and hanging, striding from bedroom to landing, from landing to bedroom, whistling and humming to himself.

He was aware of Beth leaving in the car, and of her coming back from shopping about an hour and a half later. Another half hour passed until she came up with a tall glass and the promised jug of freshly made lemonade, rattling with ice cubes. An apricot and custard pastry was on a plate, and he devoured that in just a few bites.

"That should keep you going. I'm taking Amber outside now, and I'll call you when lunch is ready. I got some cold chicken and salad."

Alex watched from the window as Beth stepped out into the back garden. She set Amber in the playpen and put into her chubby little hands her favourite toy, a fluffy cube of red and yellow with little bells inside. She went back into the house and came out again with her arms laden with sun creams, sunglasses and magazines, which she laid on the grass beneath the lounger. Finally, she slipped off her robe to reveal a very small pink and white checked bikini. It brought to mind a delightful memory of the last time they'd made love, two days before, when he'd traced with lips and fingertips the lines on Beth's body where sun-browned flesh met creamy white. For once, Amber had allowed them a glorious twenty minutes of intimacy.

Beth looked up then and caught him at the window. She raised an eyebrow and called out, "Haven't you got work to do, slave?"

Alex toiled on, soon getting through the large jug of lemonade and crunching the last remaining tiny chunks of ice. By 1 o'clock the papering was finished, and the room that had been rag-rolled pale yellow and white was now decorated with fat pink ponies that had white manes and tails and impossibly large blue eyes. The pasting table and paste brush were cleared away just as Beth called him for lunch.

They had their picnic, and Amber was given a slice of bread cut into small squares spread with mashed banana. She managed to get some smeared into her fine fringe so that it stood on end in spikes, and he and Beth creased up at the sight of her. She giggled back at them, waving her sticky hands in delight.

"Well," he said, groaning as he stood and stretched. "I have work to do. Got to get painting."

"Alex, it just occurred to me, wouldn't it have been better to do the woodwork first? You're likely to get paint on the wallpaper."

"Oh, damn, you're right. Why didn't I think of that? Oh well, too late now. I'll just have to be extra careful."

It was a real wrench to leave them out there and return to work in Amber's room, now even more stifling in the afternoon heat.

Even with the window wide open and an electric fan on full pelt, Alex felt that he was being roasted alive. His grey shorts had damp, charcoal-coloured patches where the material clung to his sweaty skin. He peeled off his t-shirt and threw it onto the landing, where it settled on the floor in a crumpled heap.

Laughter drifted up from the garden and he couldn't resist peeping down on the lovely scene in the garden below. Beth was sitting with Amber on the tartan rug, rubbing sun cream all over her plump, protesting legs. Amber, so cute in the white cotton dress and frilled bonnet that now covered her fawny banana-free hair, squealed with delight and kept trying to grab the bottle. He knew that if she managed to get hold of it, it would go straight into her mouth.

Beth spotted him and blew him a kiss, taking Amber's hand so she could wave to her daddy.

Alex waved back before reluctantly turning away to get on with the woodwork. Squinching his long body down so that he was just about eye level with the skirting board, he wondered how long it would be before the smell of the gloss made him feel nauseated.

Beth started to sing Old MacDonald, and Amber chuckled at the silly animal sounds. There was a distant tinkling noise, and Alex could picture Amber shaking the fluffy cube in her dimpled hands, as if in accompaniment to the song.

He could hardly bear not being part of that wonderful scene in the garden. Another hour of this, two at the most, and he'd be finished and could go down and play with her.

Perhaps Beth would make some more of her fabulous lemonade, the perfect summer drink, and they could stay outside and let Amber sleep in her carrycot beside them. Then, as evening fell, they'd open a bottle of chilled white wine and relax in the garden.

As Alex painted on, extra careful not to daub the wallpaper, his mind split into separate compartments of thought, so that he was able to concentrate on the job at hand, while at the same time listen to the happy sounds from the garden and think about the heavy work schedule he had lined up. His business was thriving, with new orders coming in virtually every day, and, thanks to Paul, he was on the brink of having a second career that would surely bring big changes to his and Beth's lives. Eselmont were really pleased with the pilot he'd recorded a couple of months ago and were keen to get started on a series. Paul was even suggesting that he get started on his autobiography, and Alex had been rather thrilled with the concept. He had lots of ideas about how he would go about it, and even had a working title for it: *A Different Kind of Life*.

He began to imagine all the wonderful possibilities of his future as he dipped the brush and spread paint onto the narrow skirting. Shuffling along on his knees until he reached the doorway, he exhaled noisily, relieved to be able to straighten his back and legs to paint round the doorframe.

Somewhere out on the street a car engine revved and the driver hit the horn twice before accelerating up the road and away.

A neighbour's dog barked, a frantic sound, probably caused by someone merely walking past the garden gate.

But Alex was scarcely aware now of what was going on outside. Even the sounds from his own back garden were mere background noise. He was working to a deeply satisfying rhythm, dipping and painting, thinking and planning, lost in a world of his own as he finished the door frame and got down on his knees again to continue round the last bit of skirting board.

Suddenly, there was a pain at the base of his skull, fierce enough to make him catch his breath. He felt sick, something that always happened when he had to breathe strong, chemical smells. Deciding he needed a drink, he laid the paintbrush down so that the bristles rested on the tin lid, and picked up the large bottle of water he'd brought up with him. The water was unpleasantly warm now, but he didn't care. As he tipped the bottle to his mouth and drank, voices suddenly started clamouring for attention, and he fetched his iPod to drown them out.

"I'm off duty," he said, as he pushed the earphones in and selected some loud music. "Please go away."

He returned to the painting, working steadily, sometimes singing, sometimes humming, until it was done.

At last, he stood with his back to the door so he could admire his handiwork.

But his head was pounding now, and he was suddenly aware of his father calling to him.

Alex stood stock-still at the urgency in his father's voice, an urgency that cut right through the pop song he was listening to.

He pulled out the earphones.

For God's sake, Alex, MOVE.

But his feet were rooted to the ground. He heard his father's words but not their meaning. What the hell was going on?

Amber's laughter suddenly seemed to be right behind him.

He whipped his head round, fully expecting to see that Beth had crept upstairs with Amber in her arms to see how he was progressing with her room.

There was no-one there.

The chuckle came again; there was no mistaking that sound, and it was as if she was giggling right into his ear. The voices started up again, a cacophony of sound that made him wince, but above them all was the voice of his father, yelling at him in a way he'd never done before.

His scalp prickled and he put one hand over his solar plexus as the feeling of unease suddenly flared into a full-blown fear that felt like he'd been slammed with a breath-stealing punch. The pain in his head was a dull, sickening ache, and he cursed himself for dismissing the voices when they had first started, for he should have known something was wrong.

ALEX!

Wildly, he spun in a full circle, scanning the room. He felt certain that Amber was there, yet could see that she was not.

He ran to the window. Beth was lying on the rug, asleep. Amber was in the playpen, also asleep, her colourful toy beside her, just out of reach from her outstretched arm.

His father's voice in his head grew more insistent, wilder, and it was precious seconds before he took in what he was being told.

"NO!" His shout seemed to ricochet round the room.

Still clutching the paintbrush he started to run.

Knocked over the tin, and stepped into a fast-spreading pool of spilled white gloss.

Out of the door and onto the landing, almost tripping on his scrunched-up t-shirt.

Didn't notice and didn't care that sticky white footprints marked his trail across the almost new pale green carpet.

Took the stairs two at a time.

Almost tumbled halfway down, wrenching the ligaments in his arm and shoulder as he belatedly grabbed the banister to keep his balance.

Smacked the hall table with his hip, dropping the brush and causing the vase of yellow and rust-red chrysanthemums to teeter then crash to the tiled floor.

He made it as far as the kitchen door when Beth started screaming.

EIGHT MONTHS ON

Chapter 8

As darkness fell, Alex carried the last box into the house and returned to lock up his van. He could see the figure of a woman silhouetted at the window of the house opposite. Was she watching him, curious about him?

What would she think if she knew that a psychic medium was moving in opposite her? A medium whose baby daughter had died last summer, the consequence of which had led to the selling of the family home because his wife could not bear to live there with the memories. And that had been swiftly followed by the complete breakdown of his marriage because Beth could not bear to live with him anywhere at all. And why? Because he was a psychic medium who could still see their daughter, and she could not.

So maybe he should refer to himself as an *ex* psychic medium, because he had made the choice not to do that any more.

But, God, how he missed his dad and Amber. The last time he'd seen them, the day he'd agreed to the sale of his and Beth's house, he had been standing in what should have been Amber's room, when he'd felt the familiar dull ache at the back of his skull.

Alex?

No, dad. Please go away. I've explained to you over and over why I can't do this any more.

But your decision has changed nothing. Why go on depriving yourself of Amber, and of me? What about all the people who need you?

I have to try! I have to prove to Beth that I will do whatever it takes to win her back. Please dad, please try to understand.

He'd waited, half hoping that his dad would argue with him just as he had since Alex had first told him of his decision.

But his father had wordlessly looked long and hard at him before fading into the mist, and Alex had not seen him since.

Someone called out to him, breaking into his thoughts. "Hello there! Do you need help with anything?"

A man and a woman, well muffled in padded jackets against the cold, stood on the pavement by the rotted wooden gate that marked the boundary of this newly rented property. He'd agreed with the owner to make a metal replacement to his own design, but all in good time. He closed the van doors and walked over to the couple.

"Er, no, I've just about finished, but thank you for offering." He paused, and then stuck out his hand. "I'm Alex Kelburn, hello."

The man stepped forward, smiling, and grasped Alex's hand. "Of Kelburn Engineering in Ellison Road. I recognise you now. I'm Scott Miller. I've got the garage on the corner. We service your vans."

"Oh, yes, of course. I recognise you too." For a moment he was a little unnerved, but unless this couple were into psychic matters, it was unlikely that they would know about his other business. For a moment he was tempted to open up his seventh sense to see what he could gauge from them, but he quickly dismissed the thought and shoved the temptation away.

"And this is my wife, Lily."

He shook her hand. She was wearing stripy woollen mittens, like a child's.

"Hi. We live next door."

Scott was looking at him with an expression of sympathy, a look Alex dreaded to see on people's faces when they talked to him, and he braced himself for what he knew was coming next.

"I heard what happened to your, um, to your daughter. I'm so very sorry."

"Yes. Thank you."

Did Scott also know that he and Beth had separated?

Lily was studying his face, concern and something else in her eyes. Had she or hadn't she known about Amber? He was sure Scott would have mentioned something to her, even if just in passing. Perhaps he'd come home, and as he'd shrugged off his jacket had said something like, "Heard some sad news today about a bloke who works near the garage."

Not long ago he would have been able to tell just by opening up his senses.

Alex decided to wrap things up before they all got too ill at ease. "Thanks again for offering to help, it's very kind of you."

Lily said, "Well, just make sure you and your wife come round if you need anything. Anything at all."

Ah. He'd better clear this up. "Thank you, but my wife … well, there's just me."

After another awkward silence, they said their goodbyes, and Alex went into his house.

In the hall he leaned his back against the door and closed his eyes. As he pictured how that young couple had stood there hand in hand, radiating happiness, he remembered how he and Beth had once been just the same. The memories crowded in, invading his body as well as his mind with dark emotions, and he felt the bitter tears threaten because he and Beth had now lost each other as well as their beloved daughter.

He missed them both so much, thinking about them brought a hideously painful ache to his throat and his heart and he wished he could simply run away from himself.

Why had Beth done this? Why couldn't she see that they needed to be together? That holding on to each other was the only way they could even begin to come to terms with what had happened?

Every hour of every day since Amber had died had been a nightmare, and it seemed it would go on and on being a nightmare.

Chapter 9

"Someone's moving in next door to Lily and Scott."

"Mmm?" Jack didn't look away from the early evening news on the television.

"There's a young man over there, unloading some boxes from a small van. Doesn't seem to have much, and I can't see anyone with him."

"Maisie, how many times do I have to ask not to peer round the curtain like that? They might see you." His voice wavered between exasperation and affection.

"I never *peer round* the curtain. I stand in full view because I don't care if anyone *does* see me. What's wrong with being interested in what goes on in our own neighbourhood?"

But she came and sat on the sofa opposite Jack's high-backed armchair. "I'm surprised anyone wants to rent it in its current condition. I had hoped it would be done up first to bring it up to date and more in keeping with the rest of the street."

"So you've said, Maisie, many times."

"Well, that house could be really attractive! Think what Lily and Scott have done to their place. It's absolutely gorgeous!" she cried. "I just can't understand why Evie's son did absolutely nothing to make her home more comfortable for her."

This had long been an affront to Maisie while Evie Harrington had been alive. In her view, the old lady had been in dire need of a new kitchen and bathroom, not to mention better insulation and more modern central heating, because the place tended to be cold and damp. Evie had always insisted she liked things the way they were, but in her last years she was constantly getting ill with chest infections, and had ended her days laid up in her bed, suffering from a weak heart. Maisie blamed the son for not taking better care of his elderly mother.

She sighed. "And now he's got tenants already I don't suppose he'll bother to do much to it."

"You don't know what the arrangements are, and it's nothing to do with us anyway. But please give whoever they are a fighting chance before you go over there and take over their lives."

She flapped her hand at him. "I do *not* take over people's lives." She fiddled with the two gold bangles on her wrist. "I know Lily cared very much for Evie in the few months she knew her, but I expect she'll be glad to have someone of similar age next door. Oh, I wonder who they are!"

"It's a bit early, but how about we have a glass of something?"

"You're trying to change the subject, but it's a lovely idea, so, yes, let's. What would you like?"

"Whiskey, please. And have we got any peanuts?"

When she returned to the sitting room with the drinks and a bowl of salted nuts, Jack muted the TV, silencing the weather forecast.

"Do you mean to tell me you haven't already slipped over there to invite them over? You were gone so long I expected you to come back shepherding our poor unsuspecting new neighbours in front of you."

"Oh, you! I'm not that bad, and I was gone all of five minutes. Anyway, I know you'll be keen to meet them as soon as possible too, so don't make out it's just me." She sipped, shivering with pleasure at the first hit of the earthy alcohol. "Do you think we should invite the new people over next weekend? We could invite a few others and do wine and nibbles. It would be a lovely way for them to meet everyone."

"I don't think that's a good idea. I'm sure they'd be embarrassed by such an invitation so soon after their arrival. Why don't you just let them establish themselves in their own way in their own time? Maisie? Are you listening?"

Reluctantly, Maisie conceded that Jack might have a point. But then again, maybe he didn't. If it were her and Jack that were newcomers to the street, she'd be delighted and grateful to be invited to meet the neighbours in a friendly atmosphere. She'd really like to ask them over sooner rather than later.

Well, much as she'd love to, she wouldn't go over tomorrow. To please Jack she'd give them a couple of days to settle in.

"Maisie, I can see you're plotting something."

Before she could answer, the doorknocker sounded.

"Who can that be, I wonder?"

Jack laughed, "Maybe it's the new neighbours come to borrow a cup of sugar!"

Maisie, secretly hoping Jack was right, hurried to find out.

"Hi, Maisie, it's only us. Hope we're not interrupting dinner or anything?"

"No, my dears, you're not interrupting anything. Come on in, Jack and me are having a drink, you can join us." She led the way into the living room. "Jack, it's Lily and Scott. I've talked them into having a drink with us."

"Nothing alcoholic for me, please. Just juice or something would be lovely."

"And a beer for Scott," laughed Maisie. "I know!"

Lily said, "We only popped round to tell you that we have a new neighbour next door."

"We know," said Jack, "Maisie's been at the window watching. Have you met them yet? No, you said *a* new neighbour, didn't you?"

"Yes," said Lily. "His name's Alex Kelburn. Scott knows him. It's such a tragic story. His baby daughter died, and it seems his marriage has broken down, so he's over there on his own. Honestly, I've never met anyone who looks as sad as he does."

"Hardly surprising, going through all that," Jack said. He looked at Scott, "How do you know him?"

"His place is on the industrial estate, a metal engineering works. Not far from the garage, actually. We take care of the cars and vans. In fact, it was when one of his workers brought a van in for service that we found out about the tragedy."

Maisie noticed that Lily was stroking her stomach, obviously thinking about her own baby.

How would that poor man feel, grieving for his baby girl and his marriage, when he learned that the blissfully happy couple next door were expecting their first child?

What was he doing now, behind the closed door of that horrible little house?

Maisie didn't think she'd be able to wait beyond tomorrow before going over there after all.

Chapter 10

Alex sat slumped on the stairs, digging his fingers into his scalp and then tugging on handfuls of hair, trying to use physical pain to drive the emotional agony away. Pinprick lights blinked on and off at the edges of his vision until his head started to swim, and he forced himself to take deep, even breaths until his heartbeat steadied and he could focus properly again.

His mobile bleeped and he pulled it from his pocket to check who was calling, even though he had no intention of talking to anyone. Whoever it was could leave a message. But filial duty kicked in when he saw the name on the screen and he took another deep breath before pressing the answer button. Leaning sideways against the wall, he brought the phone to his ear.

"Hi, mum." He was relieved to hear that his voice sounded calm, normal.

"Have you moved in? Is everything all right?"

The soft Scottish lilt lifted Alex's spirits a little, and he pictured her in the brightly painted kitchen of her cosy stone cottage in Inverness. She'd be holding the receiver with one hand while she moved things with the other – the fruit bowl slightly to the left, the picture on the wall of a shaggy-haired Highland steer straightened although it wasn't crooked, a pen centred vertically on a notepad. His mother was always fidgeting, never still, even in sleep, so said Alex's stepfather, shifting position and kicking out all though the night, and he had the bruises to prove it

"Yes, I've just finished unloading the van. Haven't unpacked any boxes yet, though." He winced at the tenderness of his scalp as he raked his fingers through his hair, and made a short, bitter sound at the back of his throat. "Won't take me long, of course."

"Alex, I...I could come over...stay with you for a bit. Help you get settled."

"You've done more than enough for me already. I'm fine, mum, honestly. I'll come up and see you as soon as I can, I promise."

"Well, if you're sure? I worry so, I-" her voice broke.

"Mum, please." His tone was pleading. "Look, thanks for calling and offering to come, I really appreciate it, but I've just got to get on with it, haven't I?" He hesitated. "We all have."

Listening to the silence that came from over 500 miles away, knowing that she was searching for the right words to say and that she wouldn't find them, Alex gently brought the call to an end before it got too painful for both of them. His mother's tears at this point would be his undoing.

"Bye, mum. Give my best to Frank. We'll speak soon."

Alex clicked off before she could say anything else, and immediately missed the connection with his mother, her gentle, loving voice. He stood up so that he could push the phone back into his front pocket. His jeans were loose at the waist, evidence that he hadn't been eating enough.

But it wasn't food he wanted at that moment. He looked with exasperation towards the dimly lit kitchen because there was no wine on the rack and no beer in the fridge – in fact there was no rack or fridge either. Apart from an ancient electric cooker, a stained sink and a range of old fashioned cabinets, he only had a rickety gate-leg table pushed up against the wall and two folding chairs. He was sure that the little grocery store in the village would be closed, and he couldn't bear the thought of making the twenty-minute drive to the supermarket. Coffee would have to do.

Four large cardboard boxes and half a dozen smaller ones were stacked in the narrow hallway, and he had to flatten himself against the wall to get past them to the kitchen. He switched on the kettle and swallowed a chocolate biscuit in two bites as he tipped coffee granules straight from the jar into a blue stoneware mug that bore the words 'World's Best Dad'. As he added boiling water, he tried to convince himself that by unpacking those boxes he would magically feel at home in this house. Looking at the space where the new fridge would go when it was eventually delivered, he tutted with exasperation as he remembered that he hadn't brought any milk with him.

He carried the steaming mug into the living room and sat on the only piece of furniture in there, his treasured Chesterfield armchair. Unable to bring himself to sit in it, though, Alex sank to the floor instead, his back against the wall.

As random thoughts ran round and round in his mind, he chewed the inside of his cheek, an annoying and sometimes painful habit he'd only recently become aware of. Not wanting to think, not wanting to remember, and with no alcohol in the house and no energy to go out and get some, the only way through what was left of the day was to work on. Hopefully exhaustion would numb his body and his brain so he might have a chance of sleeping for at least a few hours.

Abandoning the mug of untouched milkless coffee, he went back out into the hallway.

The streetlight shone through the stained glass panels of the front door, casting faint blocks of red, green and violet on the tiled floor. The house was getting warm. When he'd first arrived it had actually been colder inside than out, so he'd switched on the heating and set the thermostat as high as it would go, setting the old radiators clanking as if in protest at having to work so hard.

For the next hour he worked steadily through the boxes, going up and down the steep stairs, in and out of the few rooms, opening and closing cupboards and drawers, putting his few possessions in their new places. Despite occasional pain in his shoulder, an ongoing legacy of the ligaments badly torn when he'd hurtled down the stairs that dreadful, unforgettable day, he was beginning to feel a mild satisfaction at getting things done.

But he was brought up short when he spotted an envelope of photographs at the bottom of one of the smaller cartons. The rectangular package felt heavy as he held it flat on the palm of his left hand. He stroked it with the fingertips of his other hand, remembering the day he'd chosen these pictures from the large collection gathered over seven years of marriage.

It was the day he'd packed up all of their stuff to go into storage.

Just weeks after Amber's funeral, Beth had gone to stay with her mum and dad. Their meetings had been fraught, with him pleading with her to come home, until Beth asked him to stop coming. Her father had called Alex after another month had passed and advised him to sell the house, as Beth could not bear to go back there. "She can't stand the thought of it, Alex. Better to sell and start again somewhere new."

Hoping this would be a solution, Alex had put the house up for sale, and they'd all tried to encourage Beth to look at other properties with him. But she would not leave her parents' house. In despair, Alex had had to pack up their house on his own and put everything into storage. He'd then stayed in a bed & breakfast until he'd found this house to rent, and then he'd retrieved from storage only his precious chair and a few essentials.

Almost against his will, he ripped the envelope open and tipped the contents onto the floor, thinking as he did so that it was the behaviour of a masochist. He picked up snapshots at random and studied them carefully. Here was Beth, her pretty head coquettishly tilted to one side, her left hand extended in a typical engagement pose, proudly showing off her diamond and sapphire ring. The next one had been taken on their wedding day, him looking self-conscious in tailcoat and top hat, Beth looking radiantly beautiful in a simple cream dress, star-like flowers woven into her long honey-coloured hair. Here were the two of them at a garden party, he with his arm across her shoulders and she with her arms around his waist, gazing up at him, neither of them aware of the camera. He tried and failed to remember where that party had been held and who had taken the picture.

Then there were photographs of Amber. He picked up two and held one in each hand, as if weighing one against the other. In his right hand she was just hours old, her screwed-up face looking bewildered at her new, bright world. In his left hand she was in her carrycot, sleeping, one tiny fist curled against her cheek.

So tiny. So beautiful.

He selected another picture and felt nausea rising as he studied Amber's baby-plump body held in the arms of her slender mother, her fair, fluffy hair like down. Beth's back was to the camera, but her head was turned so she could plant a soft kiss on the baby's cheek. Amber, her large blue eyes framed in long, pale lashes, gazed over Beth's shoulder, straight into the camera.

Alex put the pictures down and picked another photo from the pile. In this one Amber was sitting on their tartan picnic rug in the park, looking with wide-eyed wonder at a grey squirrel that had crept to the edge of the rug. She was wearing a blue and white gingham dress and tiny white socks with matching gingham frills around the tops. Alex's vision blurred as he remembered sliding those socks onto her delicious feet and clumsily doing up the tiny daisy buttons of that dress. She had squirmed and giggled and tried to take the socks off again. Her luscious skin had smelled of baby lotion and talcum powder.

Then the mental images started, unbidden, unwelcome, but unstoppable. Flashes of Beth's white, stricken face. Amber, limp as a rag doll in Beth's arms, held out to him like an offering.

Cursing, he hurriedly stuffed the photographs back into the torn envelope and threw the package into the cupboard under the stairs. The pictures spilled out with a dry, sandpapery rush onto the dusty floor, but he didn't care. He slammed the door on them.

Blindly, he grabbed another box and tore the tape off the top. When his vision cleared he could see that he'd labelled this one 'Bedroom', and knew that it held nothing to evoke more painful memories. It only contained a duvet, bed linen and a couple of pillows, two bedside lamps with silk shades and a few books. He took these things upstairs, put one of the lamps on the bedside table and plugged it in, then quickly and carelessly made up the bed. Next, he carried the books to the second bedroom and piled them haphazardly on the floor with others that had been unpacked earlier.

His mobile bleeped again, and he swore under his breath when he saw the name on the screen. No good ignoring this one either, his brother-in-law would keep redialling until Alex answered.

"Hi, Paul."

"Got those boxes unpacked yet?"

"Nearly. I'm-"

"Got any food in the house? Any booze? No, of course you haven't. I'm coming over."

"Paul, thanks, but-"

"No argument, Alex. See you in half an hour."

Defeated, as he'd known he would be as soon as he'd seen Paul's name on the display, Alex decided he would simply have to make the effort to be amenable to his self-invited guest as he was, at least, bringing food and something decent to drink.

By the time Paul arrived, the hallway was cleared of boxes.

"Christ, Alex, you look bloody awful. Your eyes are bloodshot."

"It's your overpowering aftershave."

Paul handed Alex two carrier bags, one containing two large flat boxes that felt hot, the other holding two bottles that clinked as they joggled against each other. Hands now free, he shrugged off his cashmere military-style overcoat and hung it carefully over the banister.

As always, Paul was smartly dressed. His two-piece suit was beautifully tailored, his open-necked white shirt without a crease, as if he'd only just put it on, and his ox-blood brogues gleamed with polish. Alex self-consciously tugged at the old, faded rugby shirt that was unravelling at the hem and frayed around the collar.

Paul noticed the gesture. "Yes, and so you should be ashamed. You look an absolute wreck. I know suit and tie are hardly suitable clothes for moving house, but what you're wearing should be in the dustbin, mate."

They went into the kitchen. Paul retrieved one of the bottles and removed the dark green tissue paper it was wrapped in, trying not to tear it. Once it was off, he

71

meticulously folded it until it was a small, neat square on the table, another post-smoking habit that saw him do this with anything made of paper.

"Got a corkscrew? Oh, don't need one."

"Whoever came up with the idea of doing away with proper corks should be roasted over hot coals. I suppose it'll be plastic bottles next. Not that philistines like you would care." Holding up the open bottle, he looked in vain for wine glasses.

Alex fetched two unmatched tumblers from a cupboard and placed them on the table. "Not lead crystal, I'm afraid, but they're all I've got."

Paul's face took on a pained expression, but he filled the glasses as he said, "So, now you're here, and totally against my advice I might remind you, where are you going to start? This kitchen is truly hideous and I bet there's not one decently decorated room in the house. The whole place is a relic of the fifties. You'll have to strip it bare and start again."

Alex raised his eyebrows. "I'm renting it on a month by month basis, remember? I'm keeping the furniture to a minimum so I can pack up and leave at a moment's notice when... *if* Beth wants me back."

"It will be *when*, Alex; it's only a question of how long. But surely it doesn't stop you making a few improvements, does it?"

"There's no point. I happen to know the owner pretty well, and he plans to do this place up eventually. When he heard about my predicament, he offered it to me for a ridiculously low rent provided I'd move out when he was ready to start renovating. Does that satisfy you?"

Paul snorted. "Hardly."

"It gives us both space, Paul."

"Space to do what? Not only are you throwing away a wonderful marriage, Beth isn't getting any better, you're wasting your true talent, and-"

"Are you going to attack me all night?"

But Alex knew that Paul wasn't being heartless. Being like this was his way of dealing with an emotional situation. Paul could be short-tempered and cutting in his business world, but he felt things deeply and covered his emotions by being harsh or sarcastic, or using dry humour.

Alex was different; he coped simply by keeping quiet.

Paul looked contrite. "I'm sorry."

There was a short silence, until Paul said, "Alex, can I ask you something?"

Alex waited.

"Well, you're psychic, so...didn't you see this coming? And can't you see what's going to happen?"

"I *was* psychic. I-"

"Oh, come on! You can't tell me it's something you can choose to be or not to be. Okay, you've closed down that part of your brain, or whatever it is you've done, but it's dormant, Alex, not dead. Anyway, that's now. I'm talking about back then, when you were firing on all cylinders."

"All right. I'm not going to argue the semantics with you. When I was firing on all cylinders, as you put it, clairvoyance was not one of my strong points anyway. I could sometimes see future events for other people, but never anything relating to myself. A defence mechanism, maybe, because how could I live my life if I knew what was going to happen in every little detail? No, Paul. What I could do was get past any outward signals and read people's inner emotions, which I have explained to you."

"And which I have experienced first hand many times! But now you can't do that?"

"No. So I have to muddle through just like everyone else."

Paul frowned and shifted in his seat. "I see. No, actually, I don't see. But let's not go there any more tonight. It'll do my head in."

Paul pulled the flat boxes out of the bag and picked at them with a perfectly manicured fingernail until the lids were open. "Good, they're still hot. I got just about every topping there is. Knives and forks?"

"Nope. Only got a few spoons and a bread knife."

"Right."

Alex almost laughed at Paul's pursed lips as he delicately pulled off a chunk of pizza, trying but failing to avoid smearing some of the sticky sauce on his fingers.

"I should have gone to the Chinese, at least then we'd have chopsticks. I only bought pizzas because I know you like them. How about a napkin? And why is it so bloody hot in here, it's like a sauna!"

Alex left the kitchen, turned the thermostat anti-clockwise until it clicked, and returned with a toilet roll. Paul tore off four sheets and wiped his fingers, cursing as the thin paper disintegrated into damp and useless shreds.

He took a small sip of wine and pronounced it acceptable, then fixed Alex with a fierce look. "Right," he said. "You've lost too much weight. Eat. And while you eat, I'll tell you what's happening with Beth."

"I know what's happening with Beth. She's living with your parents and refusing to see or talk to me."

"And that's it? You're just going to let her go on avoiding you? Look, I can understand why she insisted on selling the house, but not why she then demanded a separation. Is there... I mean, I hope you don't think I'm prying, but... well, I have to ask you: was the marriage in trouble before you lost Amber?"

"No. We waited a long time for Amber, and the gruelling treatments followed by disappointments dragged Beth down a little further. But it never, not for a moment, drove a wedge between us."

"Okay. So if you've been strong together through all that, surely she'll turn back to you eventually?"

"I hope so, Paul. Given time and distance, I really hope so."

Paul nodded. He was about to speak again, but Alex forestalled him.

"Can we talk about something else now?"

As they worked their way through the pizzas, Paul told Alex about his latest clients, some of them really famous, and what they were up to. When they'd finished the first bottle of wine, Alex immediately opened the second, but Paul put his hand over his glass: "I'm driving, remember."

Alex realised that Paul hadn't actually drunk much of the first bottle either, and smiled ruefully. "Getting me drunk won't help, you know."

Paul leaned back in his chair. "Yes, I do know. And if you were working I wouldn't let you touch the stuff. But for now it might help you sleep, which, from those suitcases under your eyes, you apparently don't manage too well. And if not to sleep, just to relax a little. Being around you makes me feel like an antelope that's strayed too close to a stalking lion."

"It's usually lionesses that do the stalking. Lions lie about in the shade until the hard work is done."

"Sensible lions." Paul fiddled with his glass, turning it round and round, and asked with a conspiratorial wink. "Want to hear about my latest conquest?"

So now Paul was going to try to lighten the atmosphere with humour. Alex shook his head and managed a weak smile. "I don't think I could take it tonight. If this one lasts longer than a week then by all means tell me next time."

Paul looked rueful as he replied, "Okay. I suppose it's hardly tactful of me to talk about my rampant sex life when your life is so spectacularly falling apart."

Alex laughed, but it was a laugh tinged with sadness. Paul really was only trying to help. And usually the tales about his love life made Alex laugh until his face ached, but even that wouldn't work tonight. He watched as Paul struggled to come up with a new topic.

"Look, why don't you call Beth? Right now."

"Paul, did you hear a word I said earlier? She's not ready to talk to me yet."

Paul held up his own phone. "I could call her and then hand it to you, then she'd have to talk to you."

"I thought we agreed not to go into this any more tonight."

"Well I'm sorry, Alex, but it's impossible not to talk about your situation. I did hear what you said, but I can't see how staying apart is the answer. Call her!"

"No! I keep telling you, she needs time and space, and that's what I'm giving her. It's what she wants."

Paul glared and his voice rose as he exclaimed, "Oh that's utter bollocks! She hasn't a clue what she wants, and neither do you. But you can't go on blaming each other for what was an unavoidable tragedy. You have to accept that what happened was no-one's fault. And you should be *together*. Why the hell you two can't -"

Alex looked steadily at Paul as he interrupted. "Have you had this same conversation with her?"

Paul glanced away.

"Thought so. Then you must accept that this is the way she wants things. And I can understand why."

"Can you? Really? Then please explain it to me, because I really don't get it."

"Okay. If it'll stop you going on at me, I'll try." He took a gulp of wine. "When Amber died, Beth was desperate for me to tell her that she was okay, that she was safe with my dad. But then she got... I don't know... obsessed. She'd demand every five minutes to know if I could see her, was she all right, was she being taken care of. She'd wake me up through the night and we'd go through it all again. Towards the end, she kept flying into dreadful rages, furious that I could see Amber and she couldn't. She said it wasn't fair, and I'd never understand how she felt unless I was the same as her. In other words, not a medium. I offered to stop. Beth said I'd never be able to do it, not even for her. So I'm trying to prove something here, Paul, prove to her how much I'm willing to give up for her."

"She doesn't really want you to stop, Alex. She's just not thinking straight. But the crazy thing is, you're both hurting and you need each other more than ever." Paul's anger lashed at him. "And why did you rent this bloody awful place instead of coming to stay with me, like I offered?" He slammed his hand down on the table. "Dammit it, Alex-" Paul choked on the words. "Sorry, mate. Sorry. I'm watching you and my sister tear yourselves apart. I think of little Amber..." He choked and had to swallow hard to continue. "I just... I really don't know what to do."

Alex made no response.

"I'm sorry. You know I'm no good with the emotional stuff. Some friend that makes me, huh?"

"You're a great friend. But you can't fix Beth and me, that's down to us. And she's made it clear she needs time away from me. I don't think she'll even begin the recovery process if I keep hassling her." Alex's tone was weary.

"So she'll stay with my parents, hiding in her room and driving them to despair because they don't know how to help either, and you'll stay in this ghastly place, and then what?"

"I don't know. But I have to believe that she will come round, and then we can buy a new place together. Start again. But until she's ready..."

Paul opened his mouth to say something more, but Alex forestalled him with a raised hand. "I'll make some coffee." He stood up then sat down again. "Sorry, I haven't got milk or sugar."

"How many times have we said sorry to each other tonight? I don't want coffee. Nor do you, it'll keep you awake. I'll go now. I didn't come here to fight with you, Alex, or upset you. I just wanted to see if I could get through to you any better than I have with my sister, but I see that you're still as pig-headed as she is. My parents are trying to get her to see a bereavement counsellor."

"It's a good idea. I hope they succeed."

"Yes, and perhaps it's something you ought to consider for yourself? God knows, Alex, there're enough people who would help you if you'd only ask. *I* want to help you, but I just don't know how." Paul waited and stared at Alex with a mixture of compassion and challenge in his eyes, but Alex had nothing to say.

"For God's sake! You're holding it all in, and that's not good. *You*, of all people, know that's not good. Hell, we've been friends for years. I know what you're capable of. I've seen you in action hundreds of times, talking to people who are in the situation you are in now. I know what you say to them, and that's why I'm finding it so hard to understand your attitude now... *Alex*, what the hell are you going to do?"

Alex merely stared, exasperating Paul even more.

"Look, Eselmont want to do the series. We had a plan to get you on more national tours, to write self-help books, your autobiography. Your website is inundated with messages asking where you are, and why you're not demonstrating anywhere or taking appointments. You were going to hand over the day-to-day running of Kelburn Engineering. Is none of that going to happen now?"

He looked to Alex for a reaction.

When he didn't get one, he placed his hands on Alex's shoulders and shook him gently. "Look, I know you've made your choice to shut down in the hope of getting Beth back, and I understand it, of course I do. But like it or not, there are people out there who need you to be doing what you were born to do. You *need* to get back on the platform."

Alex wrenched himself away. "Do I? Do I really? So that my tragedy continues to get splashed all over the place? And who'd have me after all the cancellations? You don't have to tell me, Paul, that the reason Eselmont wants a series out of me is because I'm such a good story: the bereaved psychic medium, Alex Kelburn, returns to the stage."

"Okay, let me straighten you out here. Nowhere in the press have I read an unsympathetic article. When I cancelled your tour appearances not one theatre complained, they all said they'd rebook you in a heartbeat when you're ready. And as for Eselmont, they'd made the decision to go ahead with a series even as you were filming the pilot. You're that good, Alex!"

"Well I can't do it, Paul, not now. Maybe not ever!"

Shaking with anger, Alex went to the sink to wash his hands and ran the tap too fast, so that steaming hot water splashed and soaked the front of his shirt. He searched in vain for a towel. "Shit!"

"God, have you got *anything* useful in this house?" Paul handed him what was left of the toilet roll. "Surely you could get some more of your stuff out of storage?" Paul stopped at the venomous look on Alex's face.

"I'm taking nothing else out until Beth and me are together again."

"Okay, okay. Well I'm glad you said *until* you're together again. So make a list of what you need to make this place habitable." He marched out into the hall and pulled his coat on, calling back. "I'll take you shopping."

Alex grimaced at the thought of shopping for household stuff, or any kind of stuff, with Paul. His expensive tastes would bankrupt him. "Look, thanks for coming over. I appreciate it, I really do, and I'll see you soon."

"All right, I'll go. But you can't pack it in, Alex, and you know it. And once my sister starts to see sense, she'll tell you the same."

Five minutes later Alex found himself once more leaning against his closed front door. The mingled aromas of garlicky pizza sauce and Paul's aftershave filled the hallway, and images of Beth and Amber filled his mind.

The house was cooling now, and would soon be uncomfortably cold again. He wondered what Beth was doing right at that moment. The heart-searing memories stirred again, like a sleeping monster with razor-sharp teeth rudely awoken, and he braced himself for the sickening impact of sights and sounds he'd never be able to forget.

Chapter 11

"Have you seen any more of Alex Kelburn?"

Lily looked up at Maisie, who was standing in the middle of the shop floor with a duster in her hand. "No, not to talk to."

"The poor, poor man. And his wife. Excuse me saying such a thing to you, pet, but it's the worst thing, losing a child."

Lily put a protective hand on her stomach. Every day of the first vital weeks after she'd discovered she was pregnant had been filled with worry that she might miscarry. And when she continued to have no signs of morning sickness, she fretted that she was pregnant at all. But she was, and she was so fiercely protective of the little life she carried and was longing to hold, she found Alex Kelburn's tragedy beyond comprehension.

"I've seen too many parents at the church over the years," sighed Maisie. "They're so desperate to hear that their lost little ones are safe."

"Oh, Maisie, you know I find all that stuff hard to believe."

"Yes, pet, I do know. Just like Jack and my children and just about everyone else I know. But, you really have to see it to understand the comfort it brings."

Lily laughed. "You know you won't get me there!"

"And you know I've given up trying! But if you ever change your mind..." She bustled away into the greetings card section of the shop to tidy up the displays.

Lily watched her go, thinking about Alex Kelburn. When they'd seen him, the day he'd moved in next door, even before she'd known about his tragedy, she had thought he looked beyond sad. He'd looked... deflated. Yes, deflated and defeated. She wondered where his wife was, and how she was. How did you get over something like that? She supposed you didn't; you just learned how to live with it and got on with things the best you could.

Maisie was back, leaning on the counter. "I was going to ask him round for drinks. You know, to introduce him to the street. But Jack doesn't think it's a good idea."

"Mm, I think I have to agree with Jack. The man is grieving, and what with the collapse of his marriage, you can understand him wanting to keep to himself."

"Couldn't you and I at least go over and say hello? Jack has practically banned me from going over on my own; he insists I'll say something inappropriate. As if I would!"

Lily had to hide a smile.

"But we could go together Sunday morning, after breakfast? He'll have been in a week by then, and I'm sure he'd at least like to know his closest neighbours. After all, he might be living there for some time."

Lily thought about it. She knew she needed to be neighbourly, but how would he react when he saw her baby bump up close? His child had died, and here she was, looking forward to the birth of her own child.

"What will I say to him, Maisie?"

"You will say how sorry you are for his situation, and that's it. You can't hide your pregnancy from him, you know. It would be silly to try. He might even have noticed already."

After a lot of discussion, with Lily trying and failing to discourage Maisie from going over so soon, they agreed to go and see him on Sunday at 11 o'clock. At least she could kick Maisie under the table or something if she did come out with one of her outrageous or insensitive comments.

"I'll make something that we can take over," said Maisie. "A cake, I think, and I'll take a jar of my raspberry jam."

"Okay. I'll take some chocolates from the shop."

"Do you think I should mention the church to him? He might like to come with me one evening. It could help him."

Lily couldn't help herself; she laughed. "Oh, Maisie, only you would think of barrelling up to a complete stranger and inviting him to a Spiritualist church. I can hardly insist that you don't mention it, but I would strongly advise against it. It's rather a contentious subject, and he may be Catholic or Jewish or atheist or something we've never even heard of. Remember how I reacted when you first told me? And Jack's feelings about it, for that matter."

Maisie shrugged. "People of other religions do seek out mediums, you know. But I suppose you're right. I'll get to know him better first. I do wish you would at least come to the church with me, though. Just once, so I can show you how special it is."

"Didn't you say just moments ago that you'd given up trying to get me there? I don't want to go into *any* church, Maisie, you know that, but especially one that claims to speak to the dead." She shivered. "It gives me the creeps."

Chapter 12

Alex woke from a deep sleep, his dreams shredding and dissipating like cirrus clouds in the wind. He stretched and yawned, feeling good for having slept more than his usual three or four hours.

He rose slowly, feeling a welcome ache in his muscles from the hard work he'd put in at the workshop yesterday. He didn't do so much of the heavy manufacturing these days. Nor the bringing in of orders, come to that, as he'd hired a manager to run the business at the time he'd had plans to make more of his career as a psychic medium. But he had promised his landlord a new front gate for the house, and he wanted to make it himself.

He knew his staff understood why he needed to put in some hard, physical work. They had all been wonderful after Amber's death, though it had taken a while for them to stop treating him like he might break at any moment.

And then his marriage had imploded, he'd had to sell the house, and the bewilderment and grief had doubled, and the return of the pitying looks on his employees' faces had been almost too much to take.

After taking a long, hot shower and pulling on jeans and his faithful old rugby shirt he stood staring out of the bedroom window, having a half-hearted debate with himself whether to do some things around the house to make it more homely. The alternative, which would be far more satisfying, was to go into the workshop again and keep himself busy working on the gate.

A woman in a bright red coat, a basket over her arm, left the house opposite and crossed the road. He was amused as thoughts of Little Red Riding Hood popped into his mind, but then he tensed as it looked as if she was heading over to him. To his relief, though, she went next door instead.

But he groaned just seconds later when he saw his young next-door neighbour, whose name he couldn't recall, and the brightly dressed woman striding up the garden path towards his door.

The older woman saw him at the window and waved, so there was no pretending to be out. He didn't yet feel capable of being sociable with strangers, even his near neighbours, but as he hadn't dodged out of sight in time, he'd just have to try.

He descended the stairs slowly, wary of the dangerously loose, threadbare carpet on the treads which he knew he ought to remove. As he opened the door, he belatedly realised how dreadful he must look with his uncombed hair and two days growth of stubble.

His next-door neighbour was tentatively smiling at him. She was nervous, Alex could see, but of course she would be, knowing about Amber and his broken marriage. Seeing her for the first time in daylight, he noted that she was very pretty, with a fine dusting of freckles on her nose and dimples in her cheeks when she smiled.

The older woman was more than a foot shorter than him. Her face was deeply lined, which made Alex think she might be in her seventies, but he wasn't good at guessing ages. Her attire was quite a contrast to her companion's simple short coat and black jeans. Wrapped round her head was a white scarf shot through with fine strands of silver, just showing a fringe of rich auburn hair. Her coat had large shiny black buttons and a jewelled brooch in the shape of a dragon on the lapel. The coat reached to her ankles, seeming to swamp her. Below the hem of the coat Alex couldn't help but inwardly smile to see a pair of pristine white trainers with thick, red laces tied in double bows. In the basket he could see a sponge cake, four heavenly-smelling bread rolls and a small glass jar with a cloth lid held in place by an elastic band.

His stomach growled.

"Good morning, Mr. Kelburn! I'm Maisie Fanshawe, from over the road."

"And we've already met, of course."

Damn, she didn't give her name.

Maisie held out the basket. "Chocolate cake, bread rolls and a jar of jam. All home made. I hope you like raspberry jam? Some people don't like the pips."

"And I've brought you some liqueur chocolates. I didn't make them myself, I'm afraid, but they are hand made locally, and I sell them in my shop."

Three visitors to his new home so far, first Paul and now these women, all of them bearing food. If this kept up maybe he wouldn't have to go to the supermarket for several more days.

He thanked them, took the chocolates and the basket, and invited the two women in. He could manage a quarter of an hour of polite conversation, surely? And, thanks to a quick trip to the local convenience store yesterday evening, he could offer tea or coffee, milk and sugar.

Maisie looked utterly delighted at the invitation, and swept into the hallway, quickly shrugging off her huge coat and draping it over two of the four coat hooks on the wall. Her head swung from side to side as she took in the detail of his short occupancy. His other visitor hung back a little, and he dearly wished he could remember her name.

"Tea would be lovely," she said. "Thank you." She didn't take off her jacket, the same padded one she'd been wearing when they'd met the first time.

86

Alex led the way to his kitchen, feeling a little ashamed about the state it was in. He'd unpacked all the boxes, but that's all he'd done. It looked more like he was camping out rather than living here. Still, nothing he could do about it now. He must be the gracious host.

He was more than a little amused by Maisie's bizarre appearance – the scarf and trainers topped and tailed an ankle length skirt in swirls of red and deep pink, and a red mohair sweater that was almost but not quite the right shade to match. A pair of glasses on a fine gold chain hung round her neck.

He indicated that the women should sit at the rickety kitchen table, and Maisie hardly paused for breath as she pulled out a chair and made herself comfortable.

"Cold, isn't it, but I love days like this when the skies are clear blue, don't you? They say it isn't going to last, of course. Rain is on its way, which could well turn to sleet and snow." Half a dozen narrow bangles on her right arm jangled as she gestured to the window. Then she fixed her shrewd eyes on him and said, "Mr. Kelburn, Lily told me about your loss, for which I am truly very sorry."

He was so relieved to be given Lily's name that it took a second to realise that Maisie was offering her condolences.

"Oh. Thank you. It's been a dreadful time, as you can imagine. And please call me Alex."

"And you must call me Maisie. I thought that was a hint of Scottish accent when you first spoke! Where are you from, dear? My grandparents, my paternal grandparents that is, were from Aberdeen, and I often stayed with them when I was young. I'm named after my grandmother, in fact."

Alex wondered if it was a habit of hers to ask someone a question and then follow it with a statement about herself. He replied, "I was born in Inverness, but lived most of my childhood in Edinburgh. I came south with my mother and stepfather when he relocated for work. They moved back to Inverness as soon as he retired, but I decided to stay here because by then I'd started up my metal engineering business."

That was more information than he had intended to give. He changed tack, trying to bring Lily into the conversation.

"Won't you take off your coat? I've got the heating on full pelt, you're going to get very hot."

Her face flushed crimson, but it was Maisie who gave an explanation.

"She doesn't want to take off her coat, Alex, because she is expecting and she thinks it might be upsetting for you. Not that it shows much yet."

"Maisie!"

Lily looked furious, as well she might, thought Alex. The situation was yet another reminder of how much he missed about people without the use of his seventh sense. Had he been his old self, he would have sensed this the first time he met Lily, even though she was well wrapped up in a thick coat.

He smiled at her and hoped he could put her at ease. "I understand where you're coming from, Lily, but please, there's no need worry on my account. Is it your first?"

"Yes."

"That's wonderful. Congratulations. Now, give me your coat and I'll hang it up for you."

Cheeks aflame and eyes blazing at Maisie, Lily unzipped her coat and handed it to Alex. As he carried it out into the hallway he could hear an angry whispered exchange between the two women, but they fell silent when he reappeared.

He said to Lily, "I see there's been a lot of work done on your house. That's a very impressive extension at the back. Have you and Scott done it all?"

"The extension was already half built when we bought the house, but we've done most of the work to the rest of the place, with quite a bit of help from Scott's dad. There was a lot to do when we moved in, it's been a huge project in fact, and I honestly wondered if we were ever going to finish it."

"They've done wonders," said Maisie. "It's absolutely stunning."

"You must come round, if you're interested in seeing it." Lily insisted. "Come for drinks one evening. Are you staying for a while, or is it temporary?"

"I really don't know. As I told you, my wife isn't with me. We... we split up, and I... Well, I really don't know what's going to happen."

Maisie touched his arm. "Oh, my dear. How very sad for you, on top of everything else. I'm deeply sorry."

"Yes, I'm so very sorry, too," said Lily.

Alex decided to get off the subject. "So, you live opposite, Maisie? Have you been here a long time?"

"Oh yes, years and years. But it's just my husband, Jack, and me, since the family flew the nest. You'll meet him, of course, but I warn you, he's very shy. Not at all like me." She grinned and her lively eyes darted round the room, taking in, Alex was sure, the dingy kitchen and the few things of his that were visible on the worktops. With her red sweater and dark eyes, she reminded Alex of a robin, curious and ever alert to her surroundings

"I knew Mrs. Harrington, the previous owner. It was so sad when she-."

She stopped talking abruptly, and Alex knew that she didn't want to finish the sentence. But he was fully aware that the elderly and infirm Mrs. Harrington had died in the front bedroom, because his landlord had told him. He often wondered if he'd see her and have a little chat if he was to open up his psychic senses.

"I thought her son might do this place up a bit before renting it out. Though why I thought that, I don't know, as he did absolutely nothing for his mother."

"Actually, he sold the house, Maisie. I'm renting it from the new owner, a local builder who will be renovating it some time in the near future."

Alex's stomach growled again, so loudly that they all heard it and laughed. At least it lightened the atmosphere that still existed between Lily and Maisie after the older lady's lack of tact.

"I think you'd better tuck into that food, dear," she said. "Enjoy those rolls while they're fresh and warm."

Alex put a dinner plate on the table and sat down. He opened the jar of jam and scooped some out with a bent-handled spoon, explaining that he needed to buy some crockery and cutlery. When some jam dropped onto the tabletop, he grabbed a piece of the toilet roll that was still standing in for kitchen towel and mopped it up. He sighed ruefully to himself, thinking that he'd hardly needed to say that he was living on his own, the clues were right here in his kitchen.

While the two women watched him eat, Maisie chattered on about her family, Alex had to concentrate so much on not opening his senses to explore her mind, he missed most of what she said. An uncomfortable pause alerted him that she was waiting for an answer to a question he hadn't heard.

"I'm so sorry, what did you say?"

"I asked if you've met any other neighbours yet."

Alex replied that he hadn't.

Lily joined in the conversation. "Well, you'll soon meet everybody, it's a very friendly street. The Woods at Number Twelve are very nice, and George and Helen Jameson next door to Maisie are great fun. They always have a sausage and mash party in the winter, and a tremendous barbecue in the summer."

Maisie interjected. "Did you know that Lily owns the gorgeous little gift shop, The Lilac Tree, in the High Street?"

"Um, no, I didn't. I don't get much of a chance to get to the shops, I'm afraid."

"Well if you ever need anything – cards, a gift – you make sure and come to us. I work there part time. Bless her, Lily lets me more or less pick and choose the hours, which is a tremendous help, what with Jack …"

"Maisie, I think we should go now. I'm sure Alex has a lot to do."

Maisie grinned. "In other words, I'm talking too much, as usual." Her dangly earrings swung and her bangles jingled as she rose from the table. "Anyway, I need to get lunch under way. Both daughters are coming today with their broods. Alex, I don't suppose you'd like to join us? You'd be most welcome."

Alex balked at the mere notion of sitting through a Sunday lunch with a close-knit family he didn't even know, and was grateful to catch Lily shake her head at Maisie. He declined the invitation as politely and gently as he could, pleased that Maisie didn't insist.

"I'll pop back for my basket, dear. Or perhaps you'd come over with it and meet Jack some time in the week? He can't get out much, and he so loves to have new people to talk to."

As he helped her with her coat, he replied, "I'd be delighted to meet your husband."

"Excellent. But if you don't come of your own accord, then be sure that I'll come across and fetch you! Well, goodbye for now, dear."

He saw them to the door. Maisie squeezed his hand and peered up with narrowed eyes at his face, saying, "You know, you seem familiar, and I'm sure your name rings a bell. I can't think where I've seen you before, though."

"Maisie, Alex has a business here, you're bound to have seen him around."

"Well, yes, but it's something more…" She wagged a finger at Alex. "It'll come to me. I never forget a face. I'll tell Jack you'll be visiting, he'll be so pleased."

"And you know you'll be welcome at our place any time, too. I know Scott would be pleased if you came round."

Alex exhaled his tension as he shut the door on them. That had been hard. But not too hard. They were nice, both of them. Kind. But he could well imagine that, just as soon as they were out of earshot, Lily was going to lay into Maisie for revealing her pregnancy the way she had.

He wondered what was wrong with Jack that he couldn't get out much, and thought he should have asked. Oh well.

Chapter 13

Lily cleared the table, still marvelling at the comparative size and luxury of her kitchen to the one they'd had in the flat. The fixtures and fittings had been found by Scott's father on the internet. The sellers, people Lily presumed had more money than sense, had had a new kitchen fitted, had disliked the result, so had it all ripped out and replaced. Fortunately for Lily and Scott, they'd then sold on the discarded stuff at an unbelievably low price.

Scott came up behind her and took her in his arms. His forearms were strongly muscled, his hands rough from the years of manual work. She leaned back against him and sighed as he lifted her silky honey-brown hair and nuzzled the nape of her neck.

"Mmm, you smell wonderful," he whispered. "Shame we can't go back to bed." He stroked his hands over her stomach. "You become sexier and more beautiful with each passing day."

She turned and put her arms around his waist, laid her cheek on his broad chest. His skin smelled faintly of limes and she could feel the tickle of the dark hair visible in the V of the open neck of his shirt. She loved to run her fingers across his naked chest when they lay together in bed, following the dense curly hair as it narrowed to a fine line leading down to his belly button and beyond. She would alternatively stroke with the tips of her fingers and lightly scratch with her long nails, loving the way it made him catch his breath with anticipation.

She looked up at him and smiled into his grey-blue eyes. "You always say the loveliest things. Here I am, feeling fat and unattractive, and you can't keep your hands off me."

"You're not fat, you're delicious. And gorgeous."

She laughed with delight. "I hope you'll still think so when I'm absolutely huge! You won't be late home tonight, will you?"

"Shouldn't think so. Hey, I didn't tell you. We've got an old Mercedes coming in this morning – a real classic, been in a garage untouched for years. The other guys want to work on it, but I've decided to claim the privilege for myself."

"So the adverts are working, then? You're getting more interest from classic car owners?"

"Yep. I'm really glad I decided not to go into selling. Duncan's having a ball, but I'm much happier fixing and doing up. And I'm also glad we decided to stretch ourselves and buy this house, aren't you?"

"Of course. I love it here. And I love you. And our baby is going to love both of us so, so much." She kissed him. "Let's have a romantic evening." She put a teasing note in her voice as she slipped her hand inside his trousers. "Candlelight, beer for you, sparkling water for me that I can pretend is champagne. Does that sound good?" She licked the centre of his top lip with a quick flick of her tongue and enjoyed the way his body jerked with pleasure, as if hit by a surge of electricity.

He moaned as she stroked and kissed him, then groaned louder as she took her hand away.

He swallowed hard. "And having teased me like that, you're going to make me wait until tonight? How am I going to concentrate on carburettors and brake linings with that thought in my head?"

She dodged his arms, and went into the hallway for her coat.

"I know that once you've got your head under the bonnet of that Mercedes, all thoughts of me and my *delicious* body will just fly from your mind."

"That is absolutely not true!" He looked a picture of innocence, but she stared him down until he admitted, "Well, maybe you're right. But it wouldn't do for me to make mistakes on such a valuable car because I'm thinking about you, now would it?"

She laughed. "Come on, sexy beast, time to go to work. You've got cars to fix and I've got gifts to sell."

Scott helped Lily into her long navy blue coat before picking up his jacket from the banister and shrugging it on.

She checked her bag for purse, mobile, keys and telescopic umbrella, then wound a pale blue cashmere scarf round her neck and pulled on her favourite knitted mittens.

The cold blue skies of the weekend had been replaced with low grey cloud that held the threat of rain.

Scott looked up at the sky. "It's not looking good. D'you want a lift?"

"No, it's okay. You know I love the walk, and I've got my brolly. See you later."

She tapped on the window before Scott started to drive away. He wound it down and she leaned in and whispered, "Ring me when you leave so I can have the bath and an icy cold beer waiting."

***

Vincent waited until Scott had pulled away in his car before walking to the end of the path where he could stand and watch Lily stroll away up the road. Except for her most intimate moments, he watched her all the time when she was in the house, learning, observing, fascinated by how much she reminded him of his wife. He whiled away the long night hours watching her as she slept, wondering what dreams were taking place behind her closed eyelids.

She was a restless sleeper, curling her legs up then stretching them out, lying on her right side, then her left, and back again.

Last night she'd rolled onto her back and flung a slender arm above her head. The bed covers had slipped from her shoulders, revealing the top of the little vests she favoured as nightwear, and her swollen stomach was visible. He could see all the little blue veins beneath her skin.

As he did so many times, he'd reached out to brush her fringe back from her face, but as there was no sensation in his fingers it was a pointless gesture. He'd jumped back when she'd suddenly shifted onto her side and curled into a foetal position, her hands under her cheek, and then inwardly laughed at himself because, even if she opened her eyes, she wouldn't see him.

He'd been a poor sleeper, too; had spent many nights on the chair in the bedroom, wrapped in a quilt if it was cold, so as not to disturb Rose. She had been like Lily's husband, falling asleep within seconds of settling beneath the covers, peaceful through the night, barely moving, her breathing soft and even.

Oh, how he missed his beloved Rose.

His reminiscing ended when Lily turned the corner at the end of the street and was gone from sight. He hoped she'd have a good day in the shop. He'd heard so much about it, and wished often that he could go and see it for himself. But it was outside his boundaries, so he was stuck inside and around the house.

The kitchen was not his favourite room, far from it, but he was always drawn there when Lily was out. When the house had been his and Rose's, it had been poky and dark. The sink had only had a cold tap; hot water came from the spout of the boiler on the wall. A green and white checked curtain had hidden the space beneath the sink, where Rose kept the bleach and things like that. The reddish-brown floor tiles had been uneven, and Rose complained that they never looked clean no matter how hard she scrubbed. Those tiles were long gone, so too the old sink and boiler. The glass-fronted cupboards had been replaced and even the pantry, so useful with its tiers of shelves covered in waxed cloth, had been removed.

The gas cooker was gone, too, taken out a long time ago.

There was nothing left of his and Rose's kitchen; only his memories remained.

What would Rose think of it now, if she could see it? Scott and Lily had demolished the original wall, to expand the kitchen into the extension, making it so big and light. There were two electric ovens, one above the other. The hob looked like a piece of black glass, and when Lily turned it on, she pressed the surface with her fingertip and circles within the glass quickly glowed red. There was a huge double-doored fridge with a freezer beneath. All this, as well as the electric kettle with lights that changed colour as the water boiled, and a noisy machine that produced a frothy coffee that Lily loved, fascinated him. There were so many appliances and tools and utensils, things that Rose probably never even dreamed of.

And then there was the bathroom. All shiny tiles and chrome taps. Glass shelves covered with all sorts of products for washing and shaving. He and Rose had made do with a bar of soap and a tin bath. And their toilet had been outside, freezing cold in the winter, full of flies in the summer.

Not for the first time, Vincent shook his head in wonder at it all, and decided to go upstairs to what had been his and Rose's bedroom. Lily and Scott had stripped this room back to bare walls and woodwork and painted it white, intending it to be the nursery when the baby came.

He stood before the fireplace, trying to remember which of the previous owners had bricked it up, and why. He'd been around long enough to know that these things went in and out of fashion, but couldn't understand why anyone would want to cover up something so lovely.

He'd been delighted when Scott had worked out that there was a fireplace there, and had torn down the false wall. Scott and Lily had

*both been over the moon when the Victorian cast iron fire surround
had been revealed and dusted off.*

*"Shame about the tiles, though," Lily had said. "I'd guess they're
1940's or 50's; we'll have to track down some Victorian ones and
replace these."*

*Although it had been Vincent who had bought and fixed the
offending brown and cream tiles, he agreed with Lily. When he and
Rose had moved into the house, the few remaining original hand-
painted ones had been so badly chipped, he'd had to replace them with
what he could afford at the time.*

Chapter 14

"Hello Alex." The strong Scottish accent was heavy on the first letter of Alex's name, drawing it out. "Hope I'm nae disturbin' ye."

"Frank! Hi." He hesitated. "I'm looking over the workshop accounts. There's nothing wrong with mum is there?"

Frank laughed, "No, nothing's wrong, I didn't mean to gi' ye a fright."

Alex swung his chair away from the columns of figures on his computer screen, trying hard to figure out why his stepfather would be calling him. That was usually left to his mum, and the two men passed their regards to each other through her. He waited for Frank to explain.

"She does nae know I'm callin'. It's just that she's been gettin' hersen into a wee spin about Beth's birthday. Do we send her a card, Alex, or no?"

He almost laughed with relief. Was that all it was? But it was just the kind of thing his mother would worry about.

Frank continued, "Y'know how she is. Since she spotted it on the calendar she's been worryin' and worryin', drivin' me mad."

Alex could imagine the scene at home, and felt a little sorry for Frank. His mother liked to do things *right*. Even the possibility of making a mistake or being late for an appointment sent her into such a spin it wasn't even worth trying to convince her that these things happened all the time and the sky would not fall in.

He said, "No doubt she's scrubbed the house from top to bottom, defrosted the fridge and cleaned the oven?"

A loud guffaw made Alex snatch the receiver from his ear for a second.

"Not only that, Alex, the poor wee dog got a bath and a haircut too!"

"My, my, that is serious. Well, I'm sure Beth would appreciate a card. Got a pen handy? I'll give you her parents' address."

Frank's voice was quieter as he said, "It's real sad that it's come to this, Alex, real sad. Breaks our hearts, that it does."

Having said his goodbyes, Alex pondered what he should do for Beth's birthday himself and decided he should at least follow his mum's example and send a card.

Before he could change his mind, he pulled on a waterproof jacket, placed his wallet in the inside pocket, his keys in one of the outside pockets, and set off for the High Street. Unless he drove into town the only place to buy a birthday card was, of course, The Lilac Tree.

Wind buffeted him as soon as he stepped outside, and fought him all the way, but at least it stayed dry.

The shop was quite busy. Lily was on her own, serving a customer with another waiting, and an elderly couple were browsing. She glanced up when he opened the door and gave him a quick, rather shy smile.

He smiled back, and turned left in front of the counter where Lily was wrapping some purchases, ducking his head as he went through the archway and down the steps into the section where the cards were kept.

The selection was fairly extensive, but Alex was at a loss as to what would be a suitable message from him to his estranged wife.

"Hello, Alex. Are you okay in here?"

Lily was beside him. The elderly couple could be heard bickering and Lily leaned forward and whispered, "They're looking for a silver anniversary present. I showed them a few things, and now they're squabbling over whether to buy a photograph frame or a pair of crystal wine glasses in a silver box. What about you, can I help you with something? You look a bit lost, if you don't mind my saying so."

He explained what he needed.

"Ah," said Lily. "I see the difficulty." She looked sad for him, but only for a moment, and he was grateful. "You might like to look at these. They all have lovely photographs on them, and have simple, straightforward greetings. I'd better go and help out over there before they come to blows." She laughed and walked away to speak to the couple, who had decided to buy a frame but were now arguing because he favoured a plain design and she preferred an ornate one.

Alex flicked through the cards, taking his time over them, before deciding on one that showed a delicately patterned orange and black butterfly on a bright green leaf. There were no words on the front, and as it was in a cellophane envelope, he had to take on trust the label that informed him that 'Happy Birthday' was printed in dark green curly script on an inner sheet of thin, pale green parchment. He knew he'd agonise over what message to write, but he could worry about that later.

By the time he reached the counter, the old man and his wife were going out of the door clutching a gift-wrapped box.

"Thank goodness for that!" exclaimed Lily. "They were hard work. I take it you found something?"

"Yes I did, thanks. Which frame did they decide on in the end?"

"Neither! They bought the crystal glasses."

Alex put the card on the counter and Lily turned it over to check the price before sliding it into a paper bag. She rang it up, took Alex's proffered five-pound note and counted out his change.

"I hope you manage to work things out, Alex."

He walked home thinking about Beth, wondering what she was doing right at that moment. Was she thinking about him? Wanting to contact him? It seemed impossible to think that she wasn't missing him; they'd always been so close, and she'd often said that she could endure anything as long as he was by her side. Of course when people said things like that, they didn't really imagine the worst ever happening to them. It would be impossible to live like that.

But they had been through a great deal of heartache before Amber had come along. Month after month he had known simply from Beth's white, stricken face that she wasn't pregnant. And when – finally – that miraculous morning when her period didn't come; when they'd waited an agonising week before buying a test; the joy, the all-dancing joy, when the line had turned blue; dreadful morning sickness that lasted all day; the last months she'd spent almost bedbound; the hours and hours of agonising labour; the devastating news that there could be no more babies. Yet at the end of all that, there was Amber. Tiny, perfect, beloved Amber.

And Alex had dared to believe that their world was complete.

Almost choking with grief, he just made it to his own front door when the clouds finally burst. His mobile started to ring as he was turning the key in the lock. He managed to extract it from his pocket and see who was calling as he stumbled into the hall.

"Hi, Paul."

"Alex, listen." He sounded out of breath. "I ran into Linda earlier. She's demonstrating in Devizes tonight. She said she's not heard from you in a while and she asked how you are and, well, she wants to talk to you. Insists on it, actually. Will you go and meet her? I think she'll be able to help you, I really do."

Taken completely by surprise, as he had assumed that Paul would be calling to nag him about talking to Eselmont, doing some demonstrations or mediumship, or agreeing to write his autobiography, Alex frantically searched for an excuse not to go. "It's a bit short notice, Paul."

"Bullshit!" The word exploded into Alex's ear. "What are you doing but sitting on your behind contemplating the bloody awful woodchip wallpaper and the manky plaster cherubs in that bloody awful house? You might *say* you don't want to be a medium any more, but we don't believe you and we all think that you *need* to get back to it. Let Linda help you. Please, Alex, just go, will you? It doesn't start until 6.30 and it's only a twenty-minute drive, for Christ's sake."

"I don't feel like sitting through a service."

"Then don't bloody-well sit through the service!" Sighing with frustration, Paul softened his voice and spoke slowly. "Linda said that if it's too much for you to go into the church, she'll wait for you outside at 8.00, and you can go for a drink at her hotel."

Alex didn't respond, and Paul broke the silence after a few long seconds, speaking harshly again. "For Christ's sake, she's only there for tonight, so just *do* it, Alex. Go and talk to her."

He started to argue, but Paul swore and hung up.

Dry-mouthed, he sat at the table in the kitchen deep in thought. Should he go? Unless he worked very hard to block them, just walking into a place like that might make him vulnerable to the voices that would whisper and call to him.

Whether to allow it or not was a constant battle that raged in his mind. Maybe Paul was right; he was being selfish in withdrawing from his work. He'd helped hundreds, if not thousands, of bereaved people. Maybe he should be back out there now, helping more people to come to terms with the physical loss of loved ones. Surely, his own bereavement would serve to make him a better medium? But then Beth would hear of it, and that would be the end for them. Or would it? Did she really want him to let his gift lie dormant?

Exasperated with himself for the constant warring of his confused thoughts, he wondered why he hadn't thought of contacting Linda himself. She was on a national tour, but they could have talked on the phone at any time. It didn't matter where she was, Alex knew that she would always find time for him.

Without giving himself any more time to think, he ran upstairs, stripped off and took a very hot shower and shaved quickly and rather carelessly, leaving a little circle of stubble under his chin.

He knew where the church was; he'd demonstrated there himself a few times in the very early years of his career, and if he timed it right, he'd get there when Linda had finished and she would be waiting for him.

Chapter 15

"I'm off now, love, see you later." Maisie planted a kiss on Jack's cheek, wiped off the lipstick print with her thumb, and left the room.

She called goodbye to the other members of her family, who were still clearing up in the kitchen after their long, cheerful, noisy lunch. The chill of the early evening air and the light rain that seemed to hang motionless in the air made her shiver and quickly button up her coat.

As she hurried to the car, a gust of wind caught at the blue and orange scarf tied around her newly dyed hair, and she tugged it forward over her fringe. As soon as her grey roots had started to show in her salon-coloured hair, Maisie had gone back to using shop-bought dyes. The deep auburn promised on the box had actually turned out a bit gingery on her hair, but she didn't really mind. Anything was better than the shades of grey nature cruelly thought her hair should be.

She started the car and reversed carefully out of the drive, feeling keen anticipation in her stomach as she always did when setting off for the Spiritualist church.

Her Sunday routine rarely wavered. Up early to make a full fried breakfast for her and Jack. An hour reading the papers followed by a little light housework. Preparation and cooking of a traditional roast dinner for whichever members of the family had said they'd be there for the three o'clock meal. After dessert and coffee, the others would clear everything away, insisting that she relax with her feet up for a while. Then she'd set off for the church to attend the 6.30 service, leaving them to chat and make sure Jack was comfortable and had everything he needed before they returned to their own homes.

Jack usually directed everyone in the post-lunch tidy up, even though the children and their spouses and even the grandchildren knew very well where everything went. But today he'd insisted on gathering up the wine glasses on a tray and carrying the tray one-handed into the kitchen, needing the other hand for his stick. He'd made it as far as the kitchen door when he'd accidentally tilted the tray and all the glasses had slid off. Before anyone could move, the precious cut-glass crystal had shattered with tremendous noise all over the limestone floor tiles.

Maisie, flaring with helpless anger, had grabbed the tray from him and shouted at him to go and sit in the living room out of the way and watch television. The look in his eyes as he'd slowly turned away from her had made her want to scream, but at the cruelty of fate, not at him. Why was this happening? What had Jack done to deserve it? She'd immediately followed him, fussing and apologising, making him comfortable in his armchair until she was certain he had understood the real reason for her outburst and forgiven her for overreacting.

The glass had been swept up and wrapped in newspaper, the floor mopped, and nobody talked about the undeniable fact that Jack's debilitating condition was getting worse.

If only he'd come to the church with her, Maisie thought as she waited at traffic lights, he could have some healing. The medication didn't seem to be improving his health, so why not try everything else available? But he wouldn't come. Out of earshot of everyone else, she had quietly begged him to go with her, but he had grown frustrated and angry and she'd had to let it drop. She'd asked Lorraine to take him some strong tea just as he liked it, in a china cup and not a mug, then she'd left the house.

She was lucky to get a parking space very close to the church, as it was raining heavily by the time she got there. She put up her umbrella and walked quickly, holding it so the wind couldn't turn it inside out or wrench it away from her hands altogether. She had to sidestep the deepening puddles that were swiftly forming on the uneven pavement.

The church was just like a typical village hall, not much to look at from the outside, being of unembellished brick and plain slate roof. There were no windows in the end walls, only narrow ones high up in the two side walls, which were frosted and not, to Maisie's constant disappointment, of stained glass.

But it had such a warm and welcoming ambience as soon as you stepped through the heavy double doors which led into a room with warm apricot walls and a scuffed but highly polished woodblock floor. And everyone was always so friendly. Maisie had quickly come to know so many people, and she had come to think of them as almost an extension to her family. It was such a pity that none of her real family would ever give it a chance, go with her and see for themselves how wonderful it could be. She deeply regretted that she couldn't get them to change their views, but she'd decided long ago not to waste time and energy wishing for something that simply wouldn't happen.

Maisie walked up the narrow aisle in the centre of the hall to take her usual seat on the left hand side three rows from the front, acknowledging several people who called out cheerful greetings to her as she passed.

This church did not smell of incense and damp like the one she'd attended as a child. In the summer it always smelled of fresh flowers – carnations, roses, freesias – and in the winter it smelled, as now, of the vanilla-scented candles that decorated the platform among some branches of evergreen foliage. Fluorescent strip lights in the ceiling lighted the hall itself, sadly a little too cold and bright for a real cosy atmosphere.

She propped her umbrella against the wall, pushed her large leather bag under her chair, then removed her damp coat and folded it, plaid lining outward, on her lap. This was her preferred place, particularly in cold and wet weather because it was next to a heater. She was settled in her chair just as the organ began to play, signalling that the service was about to begin.

Charles Hendry, the leader of the church, announced the first hymn, and there was a shuffle and rustle as everyone rose and quickly searched for it in the hymnbooks. Maisie didn't need the book, she knew the words by heart, and she sang them with her usual enthusiasm, her clear voice soaring to the high notes with ease. She sang beautifully, and always seized the chance to sing whenever and wherever she could. No special family event ever took place that didn't include a performance from Maisie, sometimes accompanied by one of her daughters playing piano, or her son on guitar.

After the hymns had been sung, and the prayers and short sermon delivered by Charles, Maisie fondled the fine gold locket around her neck that contained tiny photographs of her parents, and felt the tension mount pleasantly in her stomach. This was the part of the service she enjoyed the most. Everyone sat up straighter as a striking and smartly dressed woman, someone Maisie had seen here once before, came through the door at the back of the little raised platform and came to stand next to Charles at the lectern.

"It is my great pleasure to welcome back Linda Chase. Many of you will have seen her here before, and most of you will be aware, I'm sure, of her wonderful work all over the country. Please give her a warm, Devizes welcome."

Chapter 16

There was nowhere to park close to the church, so Alex had to drive up and down the neighbouring narrow roads until he found a space large enough for his car. It was cold and raining hard by the time he parked, and as he didn't have an umbrella he pulled up the hood of his waterproof jacket and ran all the way. He was very wet and his face and hands were numb when he arrived at the building, still wondering if it had been a good idea to come after all.

Well, he was here now; he might as well at least have a drink with Linda. A glance at his watch showed that he was early, and he could hardly hang about out here in the rain. Nor did the thought of running back and sitting in his car have any appeal. He had to go inside, where it would at least be warm and dry.

It was clear that the service had not long ended, for the hall was still full with people. They were milling about, chatting with each other, queuing for a cup of tea, some browsed the small library of spiritual books and magazines at the back of the church.

He glanced over the crowd and his eyes met instantly with the surprised ones of Maisie Fanshawe. She had been about to hand a cup and saucer to an elderly gentleman, but had comically frozen with her mouth open and her hand in mid-air when she'd seen him. There was no option but to go over and say hello.

"Alex! If I'd known you were interested in the church, we could have come together." She looked up at him with her usual open, friendly and curious expression.

He stammered a reply. "Um, yes, but, well, it was a last minute decision, and I had no idea that you came here,

Maisie." As he said it, he missed acutely yet again the use of his psychic senses, because he might have picked this information up from her earlier.

"Have you just arrived? If you have, I'm afraid you're too late for the service." She indicated the plates of biscuits on the table. "Would you like anything?"

Alex shook his head. "Oh, I didn't come for...er... Well, I came to see someone. And, um, no I don't want anything, thank you."

"Alex, I've been coming here every week for years. If you're going to be a regular, I'd be glad to introduce you to a few people. Charles Hendry runs it, he'd be glad to meet you, I'm sure."

He smiled. "I know Charles already, Maisie. I haven't been to this church for ages, though. It's been redecorated since I was last here. I definitely don't remember it being as smart and cheerful as this. I'm sure you enjoyed the service? Linda's one of the best."

"Oh," she said, excitement dancing in her eyes. "She's amazing! So you know her too, Alex? I'm really curious about you now!"

Damn! Why had he said all that? He didn't want Maisie, of all people, to know these things about him. He made a show of looking at his watch and said, "Um, well, it'd be great to go on chatting with you, but I must go now. Excuse me, won't you? I'll see you soon."

He turned from her and knew that her eyes were boring into his back as he walked down the centre of the hall to the door behind the platform. He wondered if she was still watching when Linda appeared and threw her arms around his neck.

At Linda's suggestion they went to her hotel, intending to sit in the bar to chat. But when they discovered a crowd of other people there, drinking and talking loudly, they decided to go up to her room where they could be sure of peace and privacy.

"Good job I came prepared! I've got a bottle of whisky, so let's see if they'll give us a couple of glasses and we'll go on up."

Alex sat on a padded armchair by the dressing table and Linda, once she'd poured them both a drink, relaxed on the bed, her back propped against the headboard. She'd kicked off her high-heeled shoes and removed her suit jacket, and was sitting with her long legs stretched out. Her feet were bare, her toenails painted the same deep raspberry pink as her long, almond-shaped fingernails.

He was surprised how moved, how relieved he was to be with her. She was a good friend, she would listen and she would give wise counsel. "How's Felix?"

"My husband is just fine."

"And the kids?"

"Fine, too. As is the dog, the cat and the two gerbils. Shall we talk about the weather next?"

Alex grinned at her. "It's so good to see you, Linda."

"Then why has it taken so long? I heard on the grapevine that you'd cancelled your church and hall appearances and all personal appointments, and then Paul told me about you and Beth splitting up. I'm so sorry, Alex, it's all so dreadfully sad. But why haven't I heard from you since it all happened? You know I'd do anything I could to help you?"

Alex blew out his breath, and swirled the golden liquid in his glass before taking a sip, which burned as it went down. He didn't know how to answer, but Linda would let the silence stretch out until he gave her an explanation. It was because of this that she was an excellent counsellor and always such good company when you were troubled; she let you take your own sweet time, speaking only when necessary and saying only what was needed. She was the complete opposite of Paul, who couldn't bear silence and jabbered to fill it, usually with talk about himself.

"I'm sorry. Of course I should have called you, but you were in the middle of your tour, and, to be honest, my head's been all over the place. I'm glad you contacted Paul as soon as you were in the area, though."

Linda's finely arched eyebrows rose. "He called me, actually. Said he'd checked my schedule and knew I was coming here, so would I contact you and see if I could help."

Alex sighed. "I should have called you," he said ruefully. "I'm an idiot."

"Well, that may be so, but under the circumstances I think you shouldn't be so hard on yourself." She got up and padded across the room to the mini bar. "Hmm, one tiny packet of peanuts. I know you won't want to go to the restaurant, so do you mind if I order something from room service? I can never eat before a demonstration because I'm so nervous, but afterwards I'm always famished."

"God, Linda, I didn't think about food, I should be taking you to a restaurant, or-"

"Stop apologising, will you?" She looked pointedly at his stomach. "I can see you're not eating properly, you've lost far too much weight. I'd rather stay here anyway so we can talk in private." She picked up the telephone. "I'll order a selection of things and you can take your pick, okay?"

Alex wondered, as he listened to Linda talking to the receptionist, why the hell he hadn't called her months ago.

"I suppose Paul has told you just about everything?"

"Only what he knows and sees, Alex, which isn't all that much. Let's face it, Paul's adorable, but also the most self-centred and emotionally stunted person I've ever met. But he's really concerned about you." She gave a wry smile. "I mean, above and beyond the fact that he's your manager and needs you to work so he can make money out of you!"

Alex firmly refuted that it was about money, because Paul made loads of that through his other clients. Paul had been his friend first, then his manager, and he had offered to steer Alex's career until he became one of the best-known mediums on the circuit. The other people he managed were mostly actors and writers, but Alex was the only one of his kind on Paul's list. It had been through Paul that Alex had met Beth, so along the way, they'd become brothers-in-law as well. But since becoming his client, it sometimes seemed that the manager role outstripped that of the friend and relative, as Paul focused on organising tours, book deals and television contracts. And now it was possible that all his work could come to nothing, and Alex felt guilty about that.

Linda broke into his reverie. "Are you going to talk to me, Alex? Or shall I talk *at* you in the hope that you'll listen? You know, your dad came through at the church, which really took me by surprise."

"No, Linda, I don't want-"

He was interrupted by a knock on the door.

"Ah, our food. Here, Alex, help yourself."

Linda handed him a plate and napkin from the trolley that had been wheeled in, and he stared at the sandwiches and pastries with no appetite whatsoever.

"As I was saying, your dad came through, and he's here now." She stared at a point to the left of where Alex sat. "Alex?"

Alex closed his eyes and his mind so that he couldn't see or hear his father.

When he opened his eyes again, Linda's expression was puzzled as she fixed her shrewd green eyes on Alex's face.

"My God, surely you're not shutting your dad out? For heaven's sake, why?"

Alex felt his face drain of colour, and Linda came over to him, nudging his glass of whisky out of the way so she could kneel on the floor in front of him. She lifted his hands from his lap and held them tightly.

"Your father tells me that you're doing this because you think it will bring Beth back to you. But will it, Alex? She's still at her mother's and you, and I quote Paul here, are living in a hovel. Amber's death was not your fault; it wasn't *anyone's* fault, and the fact that you can follow her life on the other side… Well, it's a gift. You know that." She squeezed his hands tighter, willing him to listen to her and accept her offer of help. "*Please*, Alex, talk to me. I know some of it, but tell me again what happened. All of it."

For one long minute Alex stared at their joined hands, then he nodded, just once, indicating that he had come to a decision to talk.

Linda returned to sitting on the bed to let him tell his story.

"I was decorating Amber's room. I wanted to shut out the voices, so I was listening to music. Amber was outside in the garden with Beth. I looked out of the window and everything looked…" He swallowed hard at the memory, then took a deep, ragged breath and continued. "Everything looked fine. Beth was dozing in the sunshine and Amber was asleep in the playpen, shaded by the parasol. At least, I thought she was sleeping. Then the voices got louder, so loud I couldn't tune them out, and I heard dad screaming my name. By the time I understood what he was telling me and I got down there, it was too late. I was just too late."

"What could you have done? The aneurysm was a time bomb that could not have been defused. Even if you or Beth had been holding Amber in your arms, you would not have prevented her passing."

"I do know that now, but... it doesn't stop me running through the what-ifs a thousand times a day. It's something that's impossible to rationalise. Beth seemed to lose her mind. She screamed and screamed, held Amber out to me, but then wouldn't let her go. She was in deep shock. We both were. Then there was the post mortem. Beth went crazy all over again, saying that she wouldn't allow them to cut our baby open. They did, of course, and after that there was the funeral... My God, Linda, you were there, that tiny, tiny white coffin... She didn't even make it to her first birthday."

He choked and had to pause to compose himself. "And after that, Beth and I just..." He swallowed hard. "We had to get through Amber's birthday, then Christmas coming so soon after. It was so bloody miserable, but as everything was so raw, what could we do? Beth wouldn't let me near her. I couldn't comfort her. I realised then that it was just a matter of time before we completely fell apart. She blamed herself for falling asleep. She blamed me for not being open to dad straight away. Actually, she blamed me for not *knowing* that something was wrong with Amber. And I'm so angry at myself, so angry I think I'm going to explode sometimes. What bloody use is this ability I've got if I can't protect my own daughter?"

"Alex, come on, now." Her voice was soft with heart-felt sympathy. "It was one of those things, those bloody awful, inexplicable things that have no rhyme or reason. There are some things we are not meant to know, because such knowledge would make our lives impossible. You'd tuned out because you wanted a rest from the voices, like we all do. We can't be open all the time, we couldn't live that way. But I say again, and your dad confirms it, you could *not* have prevented Amber's death. And some things are just fated. You know that, too. For whatever reason, it was her time. When the aneurysm ruptured she was taken over to your dad instantly; he already had her with him when he first called to you. He was yelling at you to get down there to help Beth."

Alex squeezed his eyes shut and pinched the bridge of his nose. The inside of his cheek was sore where he kept chewing on it. He knew Linda was right, but it was still so hard, just impossible to accept.

"I thought you and Beth were so good together, it seemed such a strong marriage..."

"I thought so too. I thought we could survive anything. But, of course, you never think of the worst thing, do you? Turned out our marriage wasn't strong enough for that."

"You and I know that the loss of a child can bring couples together, even strengthen their relationship, but all too often it drives them apart. We've dealt with such crises often enough in our work."

"Yes, that's true. I knew of course that it would be immensely hard, but I didn't think we'd break up. I thought it might heal her pain a bit when dad brought Amber through for me, and it did at first. But something... something inside Beth couldn't deal with it, and it only made matters worse."

Alex repeated what he'd told Paul, about Beth's obsession with what Amber was doing, how she was being looked after, then her anger that Alex could see the baby and she couldn't.

"So I offered to shut down the mediumship so she and I could be on an equal footing and grieve together, heal together. Then we argued over whether I should or

117

shouldn't close it all down, until I didn't know who was arguing for what. Beth's emotions were so confused, her thoughts and actions so irrational, I simply couldn't fathom what she wanted me to do. Even my psychic senses were no damned use, and it seemed to me I was damned if I did, damned if I didn't.

"In the end, when she told me she simply couldn't stand that I could see Amber and she couldn't, I asked dad to stop communicating with me. I made the choice to stop the mediumship." He shook his head. "It didn't do any good, though. She moved out of the house and went to stay with her parents, because she said the memories were too painful. I put it on the market when she said she wouldn't come back and live there, hoping we'd find a new place together. But when our house sold, she asked for a separation. And here I am."

He took a shuddering breath, but he couldn't look at Linda. Shame and guilt enveloped him like a pall of smoke.

"I'm so sorry, Alex. Truly. I've thought about it so much ever since Paul told me you and Beth had split up. I, well, I've been trying to work things out in my mind. Trying to find the right way to help you, even if it's just a little bit, because you are somewhat different to my usual clients.

"Losing a grandparent or a parent is painful enough, but we cope because it's the natural order of things, right? But losing a child is the worst thing that can happen, and I can understand Beth being undone by grief. But you shouldn't have to feel the same way she does in order to help her. Bereavement is different for people like us. Of course it's agonising, but we should be more capable of dealing with a tragedy like that, because we don't really lose our loved ones, do we? We *know* they survive. What would you be saying to someone in your place?

118

"Look, I know this might not come out right, so please don't misunderstand me, but I think you'll suffer even more if you shut your dad and Amber out and stop working. You've worked so hard to make your reputation, and you're *good*, Alex. You know that! Now you've made a wonderful pilot for a television series that could be the start of a truly fantastic career for you, and you'll be able to do so much to spread the truth. You have the ability, the gift, a special presence, and that, I think, means you also have a responsibility. A duty, even. There are millions who would give anything to be able to do what we do, so why walk away from it when you can't even be certain it will fix things with Beth?"

Alex's head dropped onto his chest and his shoulders heaved. He let the tears come. Linda was so right, but he knew he had to try living without his psychic senses if it gave him the slightest chance of saving his marriage.

"I have to try. If it's really over with Beth, then I'll reconsider everything, but for now… I'm just not up to it anyway, Linda, so it's not all for her, not any more. I need a break for the sake of my own sanity. I'm no bloody use to anyone while my life is in such a mess."

Swirling the whisky in her glass while she considered everything he'd told her, Linda eventually said, "Look, you're exhausted, and no wonder. Go home and rest. Call me whenever you want to talk." She put up her hand as Alex started to say something. "Let me just say this. You're too good a medium to walk away. Just promise me you won't make any drastic long-term decisions for a while."

Chapter 17

Maisie exclaimed. "You'll never guess who I saw at the church last night! I spotted him right at the end, as I was helping out with refreshments. It was Alex."

Lily raised her eyebrows in surprise. "Really?"

"Yes. He seemed a bit embarrassed when he saw me, actually."

"Maybe he was there hoping to hear something about his baby? That's what happens there, right?"

"Well, that's the odd thing. I'm pretty sure he didn't come in until the service was finished, and after talking briefly to me he disappeared out the back of the church. He told me he knew the medium, and from the hug she gave him, I'd say he knew her very well indeed. As I was driving home I remembered how I'd felt when we went round to his house that first time. He seemed familiar. I think I said as much to him. Now I'm wondering if I've seen him in the church before, even if it was years ago, but he did say he hadn't been there in a while. Anyway, the service was fantastic." She sighed, then said, "Oh I wish Jack believed in it and would come with me, but he won't even discuss it with me any more."

"Any more?" Lily smiled, imagining poor Jack trying to fend off a never-ending stream of Maisie's beliefs and ideas.

She was sitting in the chair behind the counter, and Maisie had brought a stool from the back. It was 2 o'clock, and the hour and a quarter until the primary school finished for the day was usually quiet.

Maisie's face took on a faraway expression. "I think I've told you that we both come from very strict families? Our

120

parents were extremely religious. I was sent to a convent school, and they were so narrow-minded there. We were force-fed their kind of religion, but I always thought there were other ways, other things we should be learning about. Once Jack and I were married we only ever went to church for the usual reasons."

"Yes," said Lily, "Christenings, weddings and funerals, like most of us."

"Exactly. And even then under sufferance sometimes. But I discovered the Spiritualist church, and I've been going there ever since."

"How did you find it? I mean, something must have happened to lead you in that direction?"

"Well, yes, dear. It was when my mother died." Maisie sipped her tea, then wrapped both hands around it, her thumbs through the handle, to rest it on her lap. "Are you sure you want to hear about this?"

Lily nodded, for even though she had little time for Maisie's strange beliefs, she was curious now about what had led her to them.

"I was in the hospital cafeteria, having just visited my mum. She was dying, we knew that, so me and my sister Pam were taking it in turns to sit with her. Mum was barely conscious most of the time, but when she was awake she kept looking past us, and saying that my dad was there, waiting. He'd died three years earlier, and mum kept on and on about how she wanted to join him.

"Anyway, so there I was, having a cup of tea, and this woman came and asked to share my table. The café was practically empty, so she needn't have bothered me, but I was too upset and worried about mum to care. She was hugely fat and she wheezed like an asthmatic, but she was very young. Before I'd even acknowledged her, she'd drawn out a chair and flopped down with a grunt. The chair creaked so much under the strain of her bulk I was worried she'd end up on the floor. Her hair was thin and greasy, she smelled of unwashed clothes, and her fingernails were caked with dirt."

"You seem to remember her very well," commented Lily.

"Hard to forget someone like that, considering her appearance and what she told me. I'd recognise her even today." Maisie tilted her head in thought. "But of course this was seventeen years ago, so perhaps I wouldn't. Anyway, she sat down, though she didn't have a drink or anything to eat. I had the feeling that I was being intensely scrutinised but I didn't look up; I just continued to fidget with the handkerchief in my lap, trying not to cry.

"After a while, the woman leaned forward and said my name. How had she known my name? I looked her full in the face for the first time, and found myself unable to look away. Her eyes were huge, and this weird topaz colour. Hypnotic. She spoke in a very soft, rather musical Irish accent, which didn't at all match her appearance.

Maisie's face took on a faraway look. "She told me that she had a message from my dad. She said he'd come to take mum over, and that it wouldn't be long. He wanted her with him, and she wanted to go. He didn't want Pam and me to grieve, but to be happy for them."

Lily shook her head at this. She almost wanted to laugh at what Maisie was saying, but it was hardly appropriate. "Gosh, Maisie! What did you do?"

"I wanted to tell her to go away. But I couldn't look away from her eyes, and then she totally floored me by saying that mum wanted me and Pam to take a piece of her jewellery each from her musical box – we knew that, because mum had told us this many times. And then the woman described the little ballerina inside the box that turned in front of a mirror when you opened the lid, and named the tune it played."

Maisie sipped her tea. "I was too stunned to speak, as you can imagine. But she wasn't finished with me yet. She told me things that only my dad could have told her."

"It's unbelievable. I don't know what I'd do if that happened to me."

"Well, pet, I could only sit there, my mouth opening and closing like a fish, as the woman practically ordered me to call Pam and get back to mum so we could say our goodbyes. 'Tell her it's okay to go,' she said. Then she heaved herself up and waddled out of the café without looking back. Well, of course I phoned my sister then I ran back to mum's bedside. Mum held on until Pam got there, and, Lily, you would not believe the look of wonder and joy on mum's face as she whispered my dad's name and took her last breath."

"Did the woman ask for money?"

Maisie shook her head. "She did not, even though she seemed in need of some. And that's why I was so convinced by her. Why go to all that trouble and ask nothing in return if you weren't genuine?"

"But psychics do charge as a rule, don't they?"

"Of course. They have to make a living, just like the rest of us."

"Did you ever tell Pam about her?"

"Yes, I did, but she didn't believe me. No-one believed me, and Jack practically *ordered* me to stop talking about it. I searched for that woman for months, asking everywhere, until someone suggested I try the Spiritualist church. But no-one knew her there, and I never found her." A gleam came into her eyes and she grinned. "But that visit to the church changed my life, I can tell you."

123

Lily found herself fascinated, though she still could not really credit what Maisie had told her.

Someone coming into the shop interrupted the story, so Lily stood up to serve and Maisie quickly carried the stool out to the back.

They didn't get a chance to discuss it again, but what more was there to say? Maisie seemed pleased to have told her story, and Lily had to admit she found it intriguing. When Scott joined her at home in the early evening, she told him what Maisie had said.

"And that's it. What do you think?"

Scott raised his eyebrows. "I think she's worked up a harmless encounter into something entirely different. I mean, she was in a state over her mum, so she might genuinely believe it happened, but it was really her imagination in overdrive. I agree with Jack, all that stuff is plain hokum."

Lily, standing at the stove stirring a fragrant tomato, mushroom and basil sauce with a wooden spoon, looked thoughtful. "I agree. But Maisie's no fool, you know, although she sometimes gives a good impression of it. She told me about the service she went to yesterday, too. You know that she goes to the Spiritualist church in town every Sunday evening?"

She tipped some bow-shaped pasta into a large pan of boiling water. "There was a medium called, um... I don't remember her name, but no matter. Anyway, she was able to give accurate names and dates and all sorts of information. Oh, and get this! Alex was there."

Scott took a beer from the fridge. "So he must believe in all that psychic stuff, too?"

"Well, we don't know that, do we? Grief makes people do desperate things, maybe he's just... you know... looking for answers." She tasted the sauce and added some

124

freshly ground pepper. "Okay, this is ready, could you bring the plates over please?"

"Would you go?"

"To the church? Maisie kept asking me when she first starting working at the shop, but you know I don't believe in any of that so I've never even been tempted. But listening to her story about her mum... I don't know. It makes you think, doesn't it? Maybe I'd go once, just to see what it's all about. What about you?"

Scott gave a dismissive shrug. "Doesn't appeal to me in the least. It's all rubbish, no matter what Maisie says. When you're dead, you're dead."

Lily frowned at the morbid direction their conversation was taking and decided to change the subject.

***

When you're dead, you're dead.

There had been times when Vincent had wished that were true, because he was so lonely. Death, in the way Scott meant, would mean oblivion, and that would mean he would just be... nothing at all, and that would surely be better than this half-existence he endured now.

But he knew that Scott was wrong. Oblivion did not follow death. Wasn't he proof of that?

So where was his Rose? Had she made it to the Other Side? Was she still waiting for him, or had she gone on without him?

Or had they got it all totally wrong, and she was in limbo somewhere, just like him, because they had chosen to end their lives rather than wait until the bitter end?

No. That couldn't be. In the end she had had no way of stopping him, so he was entirely to blame for the manner of their deaths.

And what of poor Mavis? Frantically searching for Rose, he had inexplicably found himself back in the house just as Mavis had let herself in. She'd torn the note off the front door and read it and then, instead of calling the police like Vincent had told her to do, she had carefully opened the door and rushed in. What if her key in the lock had sparked? What if she'd switched on a light? She could have caused an almighty explosion and killed herself and injured goodness knows how many others.

The thought still made him shudder.

He'd been forced to witness her horror and all the awful scenes that followed. The eventual arrival of the police and the fire brigade. All the questions poor, distraught Mavis had to answer. The removal of the bodies to an ambulance parked outside, where people had turned up to gawp.

Only then had he realised that it had been wrong of him to leave her to clear up the mess.

She had never returned to the house after that day. Some men had come to clear out the house, completely stripping it bare, and it had, eventually, been sold.

Vincent had no way of knowing if Mavis had carried out their funeral wishes. Had there even been a funeral?

So many times he had tried to escape and he still he went on trying. But he got no further than across the street from the house, or, sometimes, he found himself held fast within a thick, sticky fog. When that happened he would call for help, try to propel himself upwards, sideways, any way but back into the house. But eventually the mist would roll away and here he'd be.

Again.

He had no idea what had gone wrong, could only think it was punishment for what he'd done, but he clung on to the hope that one day he would find a way to be released from his earth-bound state. And when that time came, he would not rest until he found his Rose and knew that she was safe.

Chapter 18

At home having dinner with Jack, Maisie tentatively said to him, "I told Lily about the strange lady in the hospital today, the one that talked to me just before mum died."

Jack's face immediately took on the set expression of disapproval that Maisie hated.

He said, "Why do you want to stir all that stuff up again? I hope you're not trying to talk Lily into going to the church with you?"

"No, pet, I'd not do that. She has no interest in it, and I respect that. But why can't I even talk about it? I don't push it onto anyone else, I-"

Jack interrupted, "Except me. You've never given up trying to get me to go back; you went on about it after I broke the glasses, remember? All that nonsense about healers?"

Maisie sighed. It was perfectly true.

"And you must remember what happened when I went the first time?"

Maisie could hardly forget it. It had taken a lot of pleading to get Jack to accompany her, and he'd only agreed to go that one time in the hope she'd shut up about it from then on.

At first he'd been surprised at how similar the proceedings were to an Anglican service, and he'd whispered this to Maisie. She'd asked in return what had he expected, a high priest sacrificing a goat? It had meant to be a whisper too, but Maisie spoke too loud and many people around them heard her and laughed, much to Jack's obvious embarrassment.

But aside from that, he admitted that he had actually enjoyed the atmosphere of the little church and the cheerful service, right up until the medium appeared on the platform. What followed had been, Maisie thought, a very good demonstration during which the medium had given accurate information to several people, so she'd had high hopes that Jack would be convinced by what he was hearing. Unfortunately, he hadn't been.

Back at home she'd tried to have a reasonable discussion about it during supper, but the conversation had soon become heated. Jack had acidly told Maisie that he had watched and listened in mounting disbelief and simply couldn't credit that all these people, his wife included, actually believed that the medium was communicating with the dead. He accused all mediums of being charlatans, who took advantage of the gullible and, worse yet, conned the bereaved.

Maisie had passionately countered his argument by saying that charlatans were soon rooted out, and those who really had the gift genuinely brought comfort to people who had lost loved ones, and that could only be a good thing.

"Even if it isn't real - and I'm not saying it isn't, mind, this is just for the sake of argument - but if people believe in it and they go home with a peace of mind that no-one else has been able to give them, then that can't be a bad thing. And remember, Jack, they don't get paid for church services, they just get a share of the collection. And I know some of them take nothing at all, they have jobs so they can do it for the love of it. That must mean something, surely?"

Jack had snorted angrily. "But in all the years you've been going there, you haven't had a single message from your mum or dad, have you?"

"I know," she'd declared passionately. "But it's enough to see the joy on the faces of those who do get messages. And remember how it all started for me, Jack, with that woman at the hospital-"

But Jack had not let her finish. "Enough, Maisie. Please. Let's not go over that again. You keep on going to the church if you want to, but I will not come with you again, and I do not want to hear about it."

So she'd tried really hard to keep it all to herself. She went to the church every Sunday without fuss or ceremony, and she came home saying nothing more than she had enjoyed the evening.

There was no point in trying to discuss it with Jack now, and she regretted even telling him that she'd told Lily about the hospital lady. Not wanting their meal to end on a sour note, she apologised for bringing it up.

Jack's face softened. "And I apologise too, love. I know how much it means to you, and I'm sorry it's something I can't agree with you on. This is delicious, by the way."

Knowing this was Jack's way of holding out an olive branch, Maisie smiled and fondly patted his hand.

Later, as she was getting undressed to go to bed, she thought again about seeing Alex in the church. Why was he there? He obviously knew the medium, Linda Chase, very well, which meant...

Meant nothing, really. She could be a family friend, even a relative.

Or maybe Alex had booked a one-to-one session with her, in the hope of getting some comfort in his bereavement?

Oh, how she longed to know!

Chapter 19

Alex spotted Scott Miller jogging up the road, and hoped to catch him up so they could run together, but by the time he got his trainers on and was out of the house, Scott was nowhere in sight.

As he didn't think he could possibly catch up, he decided to turn right onto the main road, run all the way to and around the sports field, loop back and come along the High Street and through the little industrial estate where his workshop was, then home. It was a distance of just a few miles, but he felt it was all he could manage after so much time not doing much exercise at all.

He ran the first part of his chosen route quite easily, but it started to get harder as he came out of the sports field and started the next leg. By the time he was at the bottom of the steep hill leading up to the High Street, his lungs were burning and he suspected his face was the colour of a ripe tomato. "I bet Scott ran up that as easy as anything," he muttered, as he was forced to slow his pace to a walk to make it up the hill. He'd been pretty fit once, but that was back in the days his life had been happy and normal, the days before the world had tilted and cruelly tipped him into a place he didn't want to be.

He hadn't eaten before setting out, thinking it might give him a stitch, but now he wished he'd had a little something because his stomach was growling. It dawned on him that he was really not enjoying this run/walk, and the overcast sky looked like it might open up at any moment and add to the misery.

But he decided not to give in, turn round and go home. What was there at home, after all?

Once over the brow of the hill, Alex could see all of the pretty High Street laid out before him. The road dipped into a hollow before rising up again and ending at a T-junction, but he would be turning off before that point.

He jogged past the little redbrick primary school on his right, and then on past the shops on either side, all closed except for the ever-reliable newsagent. He spotted the shining black door of The Lilac Tree and recalled how helpful Lily had been when he'd bought a present for his mother's birthday, for she had beautifully gift-wrapped it for him and then provided a box and some foam chips so he could safely mail it to Scotland.

He waited at the kerb while a couple of cars went by, then crossed over and ran down the narrow side street that led to the industrial area where he had his engineering works. As he neared Scott's garage, he spotted Scott standing outside, hands on hips, looking at some obscene graffiti that had been sprayed on the wall.

"Hey, Scott. Did that happen last night?"

"Oh, hi, Alex. Yes, must have done. I've got a broken window, too. I'm going to have to sort this out before my customers see it in the morning. Good job I had my keys with me. I don't usually run with them, but I wanted to pop in for some paperwork."

"Well, if you need a hand, I'd be happy to help. I'll just go and check my own place out first, make sure I've not been targeted as well. Back in a sec."

"Thanks a lot. I'll get some things together."

Alex walked the perimeter of his premises, checking that the office, warehouse and workshop doors were all secure, relieved to find no broken windows, no graffiti and no sign any other kind of vandalism.

When he got back to the garage, Scott was coming out carrying a tin of paint and a large brush in one hand, a hammer in the other, and a small sheet of hardboard tucked under his arm.

"Any damage to your place, Alex?"

"No, nothing. I glanced at a few other places, too, and it looks as if you've just been unlucky. Shall I do the painting while you board up the window?"

"Are you sure? That'd be great. Do you want some overalls? I've got some clean ones in the office."

Alex indicated his jogging gear and shrugged. "These are very old clothes."

"Okay. Hey, have you got plans for lunch?"

"Um, no, I don't." He pointed to the paint, grinning. "Why, are you planning on having me paint the whole building?"

Scott laughed. "Tempting, but no, just covering the graffiti will do. I'm about to call Lily, she'll be wondering where the hell I've got to, and I'd like to invite you to lunch, if you're free to come?"

Alex said he'd be delighted, as long as it was okay with Lily, and set about his task while Scott went back into the building to get some nails. He'd been working steadily for just a couple of minutes when his hand stilled in mid-air.

The smell of paint.

The feel of a brush in his hand.

The rhythm of dipping and sweeping the brush from side to side.

As the unwelcome images rushed to fill his mind, beads of sweat broke out on his forehead, and he felt himself starting to hyperventilate.

"Alex? Hey, Alex! Are you all right?"

Scott was taking the tin from him, examining Alex's face with concern.

Alex made the effort to steady his breathing and forced a weak smile. Scott knew about Amber, of course, but not the detail, not that he'd been decorating her tiny room when she died. "Sorry about that. I'm all right now. Probably the paint fumes on top of the exertion of the run, as I'm out of condition. Plus I haven't had breakfast." He took the tin back. "I'll have this done in no time."

"If you're sure?"

"Absolutely. I'm fine."

Scott disappeared and came back with a mug of coffee and a battered tin of biscuits. "Do you take milk and sugar, Alex? Help yourself to biscuits."

When he'd successfully covered over the graffiti, Alex stepped through the door into the brightly lit garage. The smell of oil, grease and petrol was incredibly strong, and that, on top of the paint, made his stomach heave.

Scott had asked him to put the paint in the storeroom diagonally opposite the door, and he would find there a large plastic container of white spirit for cleaning up.

As he crossed in front of the service area he could hear Scott on the phone telling Lily they were about to leave. Looking at a vehicle that was up on hydraulic jacks, he thought to himself that he wouldn't want to have to work underneath a ton of car.

.

Chapter 20

As soon as Scott had left for his morning run, Lily pulled the huge floral maternity dress over her elastic-waisted trousers and t-shirt ready to start decorating. She'd bought it from a charity shop earlier in the week specially for the dirty jobs around the house. But looking at herself now and seeing that it was far too big for her and the huge white collar was ridiculously twee, she wondered if she'd made a mistake. Scott would find it hilarious when he came back and saw her, that was for sure.

Humming happily, she went into the room that was going to be the nursery. In the far corner was a lovely white cot on rockers, and she set it in motion for a couple of gentle rocks before covering it with a dustsheet.

The plan for today was to re-tile the little fireplace, so while Scott was out on his run, she planned to remove the old brown and cream ones and get the surround ready for Scott to put on the new ones. They'd found some beautiful hand painted tiles in a reclamation yard a couple of weeks ago, and she couldn't wait to see them fixed on.

Lily selected a chisel with a slim blade and a small hammer from the toolbox, and set about levering the first tile away from the cement. It came off easily, bringing the next one with it, and she had the left hand side cleared within minutes. The other side proved more difficult, though, with one of the top tiles being particularly stubborn. Carefully, she tapped round it, easing the chisel further and further under it, until it cracked and she could work at the pieces until they fell off.

Something had been carved into the cement.

She got a dry paintbrush to clean away the dust until she'd uncovered a heart with an arrow through it. On one side was the initial V, on the other an R.

"Oh, how lovely," she breathed, feeling excited that she had something interesting to show Scott.

Wondering who 'V' and 'R' might have been, and if there was any way of finding out, she swept up the old tiles and the dust, piling everything into a strong bag ready to be carried downstairs.

She glanced at her watch. Scott had been gone for ages. He'd said he was going to stop off at the garage to get some papers, though, so she guessed he'd be about another half hour yet. That gave her time to get cleaned up and make a start on preparing lunch.

As she made cuts all over the chicken with the point of a sharp knife and pushed in slivers of garlic, Lily ran over in her mind exactly what they had accomplished, bringing them to this exciting point in their lives: a lovely home and plans to start a family.

When she and Scott had announced their engagement, Lily was still sharing the rented house she'd lived in since leaving home at 17. It was a nice place, but she and Scott were not in a position where they could get a mortgage.

Her parents had wanted to buy them a brand new two-bedroomed house on a small and exclusive development as a wedding present. Scott, though, had wanted them to get there through their own hard work, and she'd wholeheartedly agreed. They had politely but firmly refused and had started married life in Scott's tiny flat that had been up four flights of stairs with no lift. Besides, Lily believed that her parents' offer hadn't been made so much as a gesture of love, but to save her mother the embarrassment of having to admit to anyone that her daughter lived in what was, to her way of thinking, abject squalor. After three years of hard saving, the sale of Scott's flat and her car, plus a small mortgage and a loan from her father (she had insisted it be a loan rather than a gift and she was still paying it back), they'd been able to buy the shop and the lovely little flat above. They'd been happy there until the opportunity for this gorgeous house had come their way.

Lost in her reverie, she was surprised to find three quarters of an hour had passed. Maybe Scott had met someone and got chatting.

She fetched the bags of potatoes and carrots and stood at the sink peeling them. Once they were in salted water on the hob, she peeled, cored and sliced some cooking apples and made a crumble topping for Scott's favourite dessert.

Another fifteen minutes. Where had he got to?

Lily wiped down the surfaces and put the used utensils and dishes in the dishwasher, then went into the dining room so she could see out onto the street. There was no sign of Scott.

She decided to try his phone. He didn't always take it with him when he went running, but sometimes…

An electronic rendition of *The Entertainer* came from his jacket pocket hanging in the hallway, and just as soon as she hung up, the house phone rang.

"Lily, I'm so sorry. I know I should have called ages ago."

She sagged with relief at hearing his voice. "I was just starting to get worried! Are you at the garage?"

"Yes. It's a good job I needed to get those papers, because the side window has been smashed, and there's graffiti on the wall."

"Oh no! Has anything been taken?"

"No, nothing seems to have been touched, so I'm not sure anyone even got in. It's a small window, hard to see how anyone could fit through it. It was probably kids out causing Saturday night mischief."

"Have you called the police?"

"No, there's really no point. It's just a bit of mindless vandalism, no need to claim on insurance or anything."

"Well, can Duncan come and help? Or shall I come? I can paint the wall, or something."

"Actually, Alex happened to come by and he's helping out. Lily, I wondered-"

Lily interrupted before he could finish. "Why don't you invite him to lunch then? It'll be a thank you, and a chance to get to know him better."

"Are you a mind-reader, Lily Miller? That's what I was about to ask you."

Lily laughed. "There's no end to my talents. You should know that by now. Is an hour enough time for you to finish over there?"

She returned to the kitchen to prepare some more vegetables and set an extra place at the table. She was glad she'd invited Alex, as they'd only met socially a few times, and she felt that they didn't know him very well yet.

As she peeled back the foil and skewered the chicken to see if it was cooking through, Lily wondered how Maisie would react when she found out Alex was having lunch with them, because ever since she'd seen him at the Spiritualist church, she'd been bursting with curiosity. But spiritualism was hardly a subject likely to come up over a Sunday lunch. Nor did she think he would talk about the tragedy of losing his daughter and then separating from his wife, so she wondered what they would talk about. She hoped Scott wouldn't offer to show him round the house, because seeing their nursery-in-progress would surely be too painful.

After more than the hour had passed with no sign of Scott, Lily began to feel anxiety fluttering in the pit of her stomach. He should have been back by now. What if Scott had been wrong, and someone *had* got into the garage? He might still be there, hiding, but if discovered…

The place was full of potential weapons – wrenches, spanners, chains – what if Scott had been attacked? But no, she was being silly. Alex was there, too. Something must have held them up, that's all.

She rang the garage, but there was no reply. Surely, then, they were on their way.

***

Vincent stared at the initials carved into the cement. To him it felt like yesterday that he had carved that heart and his and Rose's initials. Rose had called him a silly old thing when she'd seen what he'd done, but he could tell from the faint blush on her cheeks and the light in her blue, blue eyes that she was touched by the gesture.

This had been their bedroom, and they'd had a high double bed with a springy mattress and there they had cuddled up, made love, slept. It had been covered winter and summer with a colourful patchwork quilt Rose had made before they had married. What had become of it? They'd used it for years and years, but he vaguely recalled Rose wrapping it up and putting it away somewhere to stop it fading any more. They'd bought another one from a shop, the one he'd used to cover them both in their final moments. He didn't care what had become of that one.

Opposite had been the wardrobe, a heavy, dark old thing that neither of them had liked very much. But they'd never replaced it. In those days you made do, and buying new furniture was a luxury they'd simply not been able to afford.

It wasn't like that nowadays, he knew. The successive owners of this house had replaced things without even seeming to think about it,

138

and what they simply threw away amazed Vincent. What had happened to frugality, thriftiness, prudence?

Rose had made clothes last by turning the collars and cuffs of his shirts and patching torn pockets of his trousers, and by adding trimmings to her dresses to make them look newer and fresher. Leftover food had gone into making other dishes. Nothing was wasted in their household, not even the slivers of soap, string or paper. Everything was reused.

Oh Rose, Rose! I miss you so much.

Chapter 21

Having left the garage a little earlier than they'd thought they would, Alex strolled companionably with Scott along the High Street as they chatted about their respective businesses. He'd have time to nip home for a quick shower and change, and he was really looking forward to a home cooked roast dinner.

Scott said, "I saw what looked like a sculpture outside your place. I thought you made things like gates and railings?"

"Oh, we do. If it's something made of metal you want, from railings to spiral staircases to oil tanks, we can make it. That's the main part of the business. But I make metal sculptures too, for sale in garden centres and places like that mostly, but I also take commissions. It's my hobby as well as my job."

"Yeah, like me and engines. Never happier than when I'm tinkering with cars. Best way, isn't it, to do what you love and make money from it? Couldn't stand working in an office. Are they expensive, your sculptures?"

"It depends. Size, materials. Why, are you interested in something? For the house, maybe?"

"Hmm, it's just an idea that came to me when I saw that piece outside your place. We're thinking of having a fishpond, and I thought a kingfisher would be a great present for Lily. She loves kingfishers; they're on everything at our place: tea towels, cushions, pictures on the wall. You'll see."

"Well if you decide, let me know and I'll give you a good price."

They left the High Street and started down the steep hill.

Alex heard the sound of a racing, roaring engine and he and Scott turned at the same time to see what it was. A large delivery van crested the hill at that moment, and Alex could see that the driver's head was lolling, as if he was asleep at the wheel.

As it started its downward journey the van began to veer from side to side, clearly out of control.

For a moment, both men froze, hardly believing what they were seeing, until Scott shouted and Alex felt a violent shove in his back that sent him sprawling. The roar of the engine grew louder as it got inexorably closer, and Alex felt the beginnings of terror as it became obvious they were in the van's path.

Chapter 22

The first thing Alex remembered as he started coming round was hearing the horrendous roaring sound of an engine revved to its limit, followed by a heavy blow that had winded and felled him. Unable to prevent himself, he shouted out in panic.

It jolted him to full wakefulness, but the light hurt his eyes, making his pupils contract in protest. He closed his eyelids again, his mind racing at what could possibly have happened. His head, face and arms throbbed, and he felt he might throw up at any moment.

Darkness took him back into itself, and he slept dreamlessly until a soft voice woke him.

He opened his eyes to see a young nurse adjusting the sheet across his chest. "Hello, Alex. I'm Lara."

Fragmented memories flowed back into his confused brain. Jogging through the village. Out of breath. Hungry. Scott with a hammer in his hand. A broken window. Feeling ill as he painted out graffiti on the garage wall. Had it been words or a crude drawing? He couldn't recall.

Gingerly, he moved his head from side to side on the soft pillow, relieved that he could do so because it meant his neck wasn't broken. There was no pain this time, but he couldn't seem to move anything else. Had his spine been damaged? Was he paralysed? The mere thought made him want to yell out with fear and rage, but as he opened his mouth, a warm hand touched his forehead briefly and the same soft voice murmured, "You're quite safe. I'll be back soon."

All panic flowed away to be replaced with a feeling of utter serenity. I'm drugged, he thought, of course I'm drugged. Everything's going to be fine.

When he came back to consciousness again, it all felt different. The first time, he'd felt damaged, scared, and somehow... heavy. The second time he'd felt just scared and heavy. Now he felt unafraid and light as air.

So light his body lifted from the bed and started to float and rise upwards. He reached the ceiling and looked down. There he was, lying on his back in the hospital bed, his face stark white on the pillow. A light, cool breeze blew across his skin and he started to move again. He had no control as he floated sideways through walls and ceilings until he was hovering beneath the ceiling of another room. Was this a dream? Hallucination? Or was it an out of body event, like he'd known about but never before experienced?

Once again he was looking down on a pale-faced figure lying perfectly still on a bed, but this time it wasn't himself. It was Scott.

The room was stark white. Everything white. Floors like gleaming marble. Walls that glowed as if lit from within. No furniture other than the bed. Just like the room he had mysteriously floated out of a few minutes ago.

A steady beeping was the only sound, but Alex could see no monitoring equipment, no wires or tubes connected to Scott's body.

Scott's eyes were looking straight at him, but after a moment Alex could tell that Scott did not see him. He tried to call his name, but had no voice.

The cool breeze sprang up again and he felt himself being pulled back through the wall, growing smaller and smaller, until there was just a tiny atom of thinking, feeling mind. And even that winked out as he slid back into an unconscious state for a matter of seconds.

Wide awake again and terribly confused, Alex explored his teeth and lips with his tongue, then carefully moved his jaw, and reached up to explore his face with his fingers. He felt no pain at all.

He found he could move his upper body, but his legs still wouldn't obey him and the thought of being paralysed still gnawed at him.

Frustrated, he studied the room, trying to get some clues to what was happening, but there was definitely nothing in it but his bed. No cupboard, no washbasin, no pictures on the walls. Nor was there a window, so he had nothing else to look at but clinical white. It made him feel exhausted and he slipped effortlessly and gratefully back into sleep, wondering as he drifted away how the drugs were being administered to him, if not by intravenous drip.

There was no way of knowing how long he spent between waking and sleeping, sleeping and waking, because he began to feel that he was dreaming even when his eyes were open, so he could no longer tell the difference between the states of awareness and unconsciousness.

At first the dreams were pleasant, and in them he was a child again, playing and laughing, then he was older and there was a young woman with shining conker-coloured hair and laughing eyes, and he was in love with her and they were getting married and planning their future. There was a baby. A beautiful, giggling little girl, who mashed food in her hair and always pulled her socks off as soon as they were put on her tiny feet.

He felt himself coming awake, and fought against it, not wanting to come out of the dream. Lara was standing beside his bed again, regarding him with dark, serious eyes fringed with long lashes. Her hair, pulled back from her pretty face into a ponytail, was a glossy blue-black that gleamed in the soft light like a raven's wing.

Finding it difficult to speak, he swallowed a couple of times and eventually managed to whisper, "Which hospital is this? Why can't I move my legs?"

The young nurse smiled, showing small, even teeth, and patted his hand. "You're being well looked after, Alex, but you must wait for Grace, and then all your questions will be answered."

Alex opened his mouth to ask about Scott, but Lara had already left the room. He looked around for a door but could not see one. Of course there's a door, he told himself, how else could the nurses and doctors get in here, unless they could walk through walls. The thought made him laugh, but hearing himself sound on the edge of hysteria, he took deep breaths and calmed himself down.

After that, variations of this scene seemed to happen many times. Lara was there when he awoke, but he never actually heard or saw her come in. He would ask: Where am I? What's happening? Does my family know I'm here? To each question Lara would reply gently but firmly, "You must wait for Grace."

At first he thought she meant he had to be in a state of grace, and wondered why a hospital would expect such a thing of its patients, and how the hell he was supposed to achieve it when no-one was telling him anything. But after the fourth or fifth time of hearing Lara say it, it dawned on him that she must be referring to a person. Perhaps Grace was the Senior Consultant or something, but he was sure nurses did not usually refer to doctors by their first names. Determined to demand that someone in authority come and talk to him, he opened his mouth to shout for attention, but before he made a sound he was

145

overwhelmed with exhaustion and fell back against the pillow, hoping to return to his dream…

…He was lying on a pavement, the smell of petrol so strong, a horrid metallic taste in his mouth. He was fighting a roaring blackness that seemed to seep in from the air around him, blinding his eyes and muffling all other sound. Scott was shouting something, but he couldn't make out the words.

He turned his head, looking for but not finding a call button to summon Lara, somebody, *anybody.*

He stared around the room wildly, and almost cried out when it started to shift and change around him. He saw the solid, white walls begin to shimmer, the light brightening until hurt his eyes with its fierce brilliance. "It's the damned drugs," he said aloud, reassured to hear his own voice. "That's all it is. This won't last much longer."

A musical but firm voice said, "No, Alex, it won't last much longer." A woman, older and taller than Lara, was beside his bed. "I am Grace," she said.

Alex studied her, reassured by her steady gaze and the spotless white coat she was wearing, and waited for her to explain where he was, and what was being done for and to him. But she didn't speak. Her stillness and unwavering, dark-eyed gaze were so like Lara's, but Grace unnerved him in a way that Lara did not.

"All right, Alex. Let's go."

"Go? But…" The sheet lifted away from his body, and some unseen force pulled him into a sitting position as it rolled down to his ankles. Lara helped him to stand up and he stared at his legs, flexing them, bending each knee and rotating his ankles. "Thank God," he whispered. "I thought I was paralysed. How long have I been here? I haven't seen anyone but Lara until now, and she's told me absolutely nothing. Please. I need to know."

146

Grace's expression did not change. It was as if he hadn't spoken at all.

"Come," she commanded. "Let's go and see your friend."

Chapter 23

Adele sat on the hard chair, hollow-eyed and hollowed out after the hours of waiting for news. The families had gathered quickly: her parents, Scott's mum and dad, his two brothers, the grandparents.

A woman had arrived at the same time as them, weeping against a young man whose skin was aflame with acne. Adele wondered if that was the wife and son of the van driver. They didn't yet know what had happened to him.

A nurse came to the double doors leading into Intensive Care and let the woman and the young man in. At the same time, another nurse came out and suggested to Adele's group that they all follow her to a family room, where they could wait in private. In a tense, silent group, they followed the nurse along a short corridor. She turned a sign on the door so it read 'occupied', and said gently, "Someone will bring you all some tea."

Adele wondered what the nation would do without tea in times of crises. But much as she'd like something to quench her thirst, what she – what they all wanted – was information.

Scott's parents had been to his bedside, but had come out so Lily could be alone with him. She'd now been in there for a long time, and the rest of them were waiting in agony to hear if he was showing any signs of coming out of the coma.

Just as an older woman wearing a wrap-around apron brought them the tea, Adele heard loud sobbing coming from the corridor and she peeked out, expecting to see the woman and young man again. But it was a different couple that passed her, a very pretty woman and a tall, handsome man wearing a camel overcoat. The woman had the look of someone in deep, deep shock.

Lily appeared then, looking like a ghost. Adele ran to her and hugged her hard as the others surrounded her, firing questions at her: "How is he?" "Is he awake?" "Has a doctor spoken to you yet?" "What's happening?"

Lily stammered, "He's still in a coma." She pulled away from Adele and went to Scott's parents, hugging them both. "Why don't you go back in and sit with him? I'll just be a minute."

She watched them leave, before sinking to the floor as if her bones had melted.

Adele knelt down beside her, supporting her, and held her tight as she cried out the pain and anguish.

So far she hadn't dared think it – probably none of them had – but, Oh God! What if Scott didn't make it? He was strong and fit, yes, but he'd suffered severe head injuries. What if he lived but had permanent brain damage? Would Lily have to raise the baby on her own?

As Lily cried against her shoulder, Adele glanced around. The two sets of grandparents were sitting together, all holding hands and murmuring encouragement to each other. Scott's mum and dad had not let each other go since they'd arrived here, constantly touching each other and hugging. At one point, Scott's dad had brushed his mother's hair from her forehead and kissed her before pulling her into a tight embrace.

And what of her? Where was Rob?

She had tried to call him several times and had been forced to leave a message in the end telling him where she was and asking him to come as soon as he could. Then she'd sent text messages. But that had been hours ago, and she'd heard nothing from him.

All sorts of scenarios were running through her mind as she sat there on the floor with her sister sobbing against her shoulder. He'd gone out and left his phone at home. He'd lost it. It had been stolen.

Or her messages had not gone through. Sometimes there were long delays between messages being sent and being received.

She didn't think any of these things were likely, but clung on to them anyway, because to think he was ignoring her pleas for him to come was too much to take right now.

Chapter 24

"Alex! Oh, thank God you're all right. I've been going frantic in here wondering what the hell's happening."

Alex walked forward and grasped Scott's shoulder in a tacit gesture of sympathy and solidarity.

"Why don't you take a seat, Alex?" Grace indicated the chair next to Scott's bed that he was sure had not been there one second before, and he sat down, feeling a prickle of unease as he did so. Doctors known by their first names, doors and furniture that appeared as if from nowhere, no machines in sight, except he could hear that infernal beep beep beep.

He felt he must be dreaming or hallucinating because nothing felt right in this place, but at the same time he was sure he was totally awake. He wanted to ask questions, demand answers, but something about Grace kept him silent.

Her attention was now fully on Scott.

"Scott, I need you to concentrate and work with me. Will you do that?"

Scott gave a wry grin. "Do I have any choice?"

Without returning his smile Grace asked, "Do you like this room?"

"What do you mean, do I like this room?" He glanced from Grace to Alex, his face showing first confusion, then irritation. Grace displayed no emotion at all.

Alex was surprised by the banality of the question too, but intuitively he knew that Scott would get no explanations until Grace was good and ready to give them. He squeezed Scott's shoulder again to offer some reassurance, and Scott replied, "It's all right, I suppose."

151

"What would you prefer? What would make you more comfortable?"

"Apart from answers about my health, you mean?"

Grace did not react.

For a long moment, Scott and Grace regarded each other, until Scott seemed to deflate a little, and he said, "Well, if you insist on playing this game. It would be nice to have a room with a view, and a cupboard for my things, assuming I have anything here. A jug of water would be nice, I seem to be very thirsty all the time. Oh, and a telephone so I can call my wife."

Without moving any other part of her body, Grace swung her eyes from Scott to look at Alex with her unblinking and unnerving gaze. Her large eyes were a deep, deep pansy-purple, the pupil indistinct from the iris. He felt he was being drawn into their indigo-flecked depths, that he would find secrets there, and laughed somewhere at the back of his mind that the drugs were still making him fanciful.

But she was intriguing and he studied her impassive face, the high cheekbones, the full lips, the unblemished skin, until she indicated something with her hand and he turned his head to see where she was pointing. There was a window. He could see a cloudless blue sky framed in a pristine white rectangle of glass, the glass so clean and clear it took effort to see that it was actually there. He blinked slowly and swallowed hard.

Scott looked equally stunned.

"Here's a small cupboard, and there, as you see, is a jug filled with water and a glass." Grace's voice was quiet, patient.

Alex looked and found himself transfixed by the white paper doily beneath the tall glass.

152

He knew his bewildered expression matched that of Scott, and thought it was their obvious and utter confusion that made Grace smile at last, an unexpected and beautiful sight.

Needing desperately to be reassured, Alex said, "It *is* the drugs, isn't it?"

She didn't respond by word or by movement.

Scott squirmed and then blurted, "Look, I can't stand any more of this, you *must* tell me what's going on. Why haven't I seen my wife? Or any visitors, come to that? And why haven't I seen *you* until now?"

His voice rose with each question, and Alex could understand perfectly why he was so agitated. He felt the same way, and he wanted to say so. But as he opened his mouth to support his friend, the walls seemed to shift in the periphery of his vision and he saw silvery sparks dancing and flickering in the outer corners of his eyes. He gripped the seat of his chair until they disappeared.

"You have had visitors, both of you, you simply haven't been aware of them. Now then." Grace took two paces forward so she was beside the bed, directly in front of Alex. She touched the centre of his forehead with the fingertips of her right hand, and Scott's forehead with her left. "It's time."

His forehead burned where Grace's fingers touched his skin.

"Time? What for?"

Had he said that, or had Scott?

She removed her hand and gripped his fingers, interlacing them so their hands were palm to palm. Heat flowed from her into his body, and he felt it like a river of molten metal flowing in his bloodstream. It frightened and perplexed him in equal measure, until he realised the sensation was actually pleasant, calming, and he begged her to explain what was happening.

"Just support Scott, that's all I ask of you."

"Support him how?"

Grace did not answer. She let go of his hand and turned to Scott.

"I need you to think very carefully," she said. "Think about everything that has happened to you since you woke up here. Think about your dreams. This room. Look around you, and concentrate on my words."

Scott looked so confused, so desperate, that Alex felt a sick sensation in his stomach as he was forced to be a helpless, silent witness. Grace hadn't ordered him to stay silent, but he instinctively felt that he must not say a word. Whatever was about to happen would happen, and nothing he said or did would change the outcome for Scott.

He knew with every fibre of his being that he was about to go through something that would profoundly change him. But what of Scott? A man he hardly knew, really, but someone he liked and with whom he was now sharing something so... so deeply intimate.

Grace lowered her voice, leaning in close so that her lips almost touched Scott's cheek, yet her voice filled the room. "Do you want to get up?"

Scott scrambled up and stood in front of Grace. Like Alex, he was wearing a thin hospital gown with ties up the back. A totally undignified garment as far as Alex was concerned, but hardly worth worrying about right now.

"Both of you, go over to the window," she commanded. "Alex, tell me what you see."

Alex joined Scott at the window. When he spoke, his voice sounded husky and unfamiliar. "I see an area like any other hospital garden I've ever seen."

"Describe it. The details."

"Describe it? Okay. Well, there's a neglected patch of grass, a few untrimmed shrubs, some straggly marigolds in the border, a couple of scarred benches for patients and visitors to sit on, cigarette butts and sweet wrappers scattered around them."

"Scott? What do you see?"

"The same as Alex."

Grace said, "Let me tell you what I see. Out there is a typical English cottage garden, filled with roses and hollyhocks. There are fruit trees in the distance – a small orchard of apples, cherries, plums - and a magnificent oak tree. There's a stream running through the middle of the garden, with a wooden bridge going across it."

As she spoke, Alex could see everything as she described it, and knew that Scott could too. How was this possible?

Where there had been sad marigolds the flowerbeds were now filled with glorious roses of all colours and tall deep pink hollyhocks that swayed in a breeze he desperately wanted to feel on his face. A fairly wide stream, spanned by a beautiful Japanese-style bridge, sparkled in the sunlight. The bridge was covered in wisteria, its heavy lilac blooms dipping into the water. The oak tree looked ancient and magnificent. Alex knew that if he could step out of this sterile room and into the garden he would smell the flowers, hear the music of birdsong and the flowing water of the stream.

Scott suddenly cried out: "Look, there's a kingfisher perched on the bridge." He lowered his pointing finger and said slowly, "Oh, Lily would love to see this. Remember, Alex, I told you how she loves kingfishers?"

The brightly coloured little bird rose from the parapet of the bridge in ultra-slow motion, spread its iridescent wings then pulled them in tight and flew down like a dart into the stream. A crown of water rose up and sparkled in the sunlight before separating into silvery beads that fell gently back into the stream. The bird disappeared into the depths, and then rose up and out of the water with gracefully flapping wings. It returned to the bridge with a small golden fish wriggling in its beak and droplets cascaded from both creatures. A hundred shimmering rainbows hovered in the air until Scott sighed and the world outside returned to normal speed.

Alex, watching this yet not believing his eyes, swallowed hard.

All this time Grace was standing between him and Scott, holding their hands, looking out of the window with them. The silence between them stretched into minutes, hours, eons.

Alex felt the change in his friend even before Scott broke the silence with, "Why was Lara dressed like a nurse? And you, white coated, like a doctor? Why the whole hospital scene?"

"Because it's where you expected to be and your physical body *is* in a hospital."

Alex realised that the beeping sound, which he'd always been aware of in the background since coming into this room, was no longer keeping a steady rhythm. He wondered if only he could hear it.

Scott was gazing at Grace, intently studying her face, and Alex felt his mouth go dry and his throat tighten.

Scott's voice was hardly audible as he asked the question, "My *physical* body? Is that what you said? I'm dreaming, right?" He challenged Grace with an unflinching stare, but her expression gave nothing away.

Alex could sense that Scott was fighting the truth.

"I want my wife," Scott exclaimed. "Why isn't my wife with me?"

"She is with you."

The floor beneath their feet seemed to change to clear glass, and beneath them they could see Scott lying on a hospital bed. Lines and tubes snaked from his body, hooking him up to all sorts of machines.

Beep beep beep.

Lily was clasping his hand, pleading with him to open his eyes. On the other side of the bed stood two older people, holding each other, both crying. Alex supposed them to be Scott's parents.

Scott was so still, Alex wondered if he'd gone catatonic with shock. But then Scott seemed to shake himself and he squared his shoulders before speaking. His voice was so quiet Alex had to lean forward to hear him.

"So this is death, Grace? Me and Alex, we're both dead?"

"It is *your* death, Scott."

"I don't understand."

"Alex must go back."

Utterly stunned, Alex kept his eyes fixed on the kingfisher, which was in motion again like something in a time-lapse sequence. If he wasn't to go with Scott he didn't feel he should be a part of this.

But why did he have to go back?

Why wasn't he allowed to stay, when he wanted to so much?

He jumped as Scott suddenly cried out in anguish. "My God, Grace! I have to leave Lily? And my parents, my brothers? Lily is *pregnant*, Grace. We're about to have a *baby*!"

Feeling too shocked to move or say anything, Alex could hardly bear to look at Scott's stricken face.

Grace reached out and cupped the back of Scott's head with one hand and placed her other hand gently on his

157

forehead. Her voice was steady, reassuring. "I'm taking away the emotions, Scott, just until you get used to being here. You need to concentrate on yourself now, just yourself. Everything will work itself out, believe me."

Her melodious voice was hypnotic, and Alex felt a calmness seep into him, just as it seemed to be seeping into Scott.

All at once, Scott seemed to go limp, and Grace steadied him. The room was filling with people, lots of people, smiling, laughing. They surrounded Grace and Scott, pushing Alex back and away into shadows. He frantically searched for his father, for Amber, but they were not among the crowd. These people were there only for Scott.

"No! Wait!" Alex shook himself from his stupor and fought his way back into the light of Scott's room. "Send Scott back and take me instead! I have little to go back for, yet Scott has everything. Grace, you must know that my baby is here, in this place! She's with my dad, but she needs me. Let me stay and be with them. Please, Grace, keep me and send Scott back to his family. *Please*."

In his desperation to be heard, he had grabbed Grace by the upper arms and was shaking her.

"Let me go, Alex." Her features remained totally impassive, and her voice was soft, yet it was a command that Alex could not disobey.

Devastated, he dropped his hands to his sides and stared at the floor.

"Look at me."

He lifted his head. Grace seemed taller and her eyes were now so black, he could not see the pansy-purple irises of before. There were no whites, either. It was as if her eye sockets were filled with orbs of darkest obsidian.

"This is how it must be, Alex. It is Scott's time and it is not yours."

It was such a relief when she blinked those fathomless eyes and looked away from him, he almost fell to his knees.

Grace was speaking to Scott now. "Look who's come to help you build your new world. Do you see them all? Do you see how beautiful it is?"

Alex watched helplessly as Scott was drawn into the crowd of excited, happy people. He wanted to beg again to be taken instead of Scott, but he was boneless and had no voice. He had been dismissed. His place was not here, no matter how he longed to stay, and the bright light was fading now.

Alex could still hear the beep beep beep of the machine monitoring Scott, but it was slowing down and he could no longer see his friend. Only Grace was visible as he felt himself being pulled backwards, sucked inexorably away from her and all she represented. Then her image became fainter and smaller with distance until he could see only the darkness of his own eyelids and hear only the roar of his living blood in his ears.

Chapter 25

The first face that Alex saw when he came round again was Paul's. A nurse was just leaving the room, and she turned and told Paul not to tire her patient out. It wasn't Lara.

"Paul?"

"At last! Bloody hell, mate, you've been out for the count for hours. And dreaming some strange dreams, too, by the sound of it?"

"What?" his voice was a mere croak.

"You've been talking in your sleep. Something about gardens and kingfishers and God knows what else."

"There's not a bit of me that doesn't hurt."

"Not surprising. Your shoulder was dislocated. You've got concussion, a couple of broken ribs, massive bruising. You got off lightly, mate, considering. I've brought some stuff for you: pyjamas, toothbrush, that kind of thing."

"Thanks." He felt around his head, wincing when he found a bruise at the back. "Hey, did you say I've been out for hours? Feels more like a week. Have you called my mother?"

"She's here, Alex. With Frank. At my insistence they've just gone down to get some breakfast."

Alex shook his head, immediately wishing he hadn't. "There was no need for them to come."

"That's what your mother said you'd say. Come on, Alex, wouldn't you go rushing to her bedside, if she'd been in an accident?"

He hardly dared voice the question, but he had to know. "What about Beth? Is she coming?"

Paul dropped his gaze to his hands. "Um. She's been here, yes. Actually, she sat by your bedside and held your hand all through the night."

"Really?" Alex felt joy and hope surge through him, immediately numbing the pain of his injuries. "So where is she now? Having breakfast with mum and Frank?"

Paul looked stricken. "Mate, I don't know how to… well, the thing is…"

He looked so discomfited Alex's high spirits immediately plummeted. "What is it? What's happened, Paul?"

Paul rubbed his hands over his face, and Alex noticed for the first time the stubble on his cheeks and chin.

"Alex… you need to stay calm, okay? There's no easy way to say this, so I'll just come out and say it. She's had a complete emotional breakdown."

"She's *what*?" He sat bolt upright, gasping as his injuries flared.

"She was sitting beside you, as I said, and I was on the other side of the bed, next to your mum. Beth was crying and apologising over and over to your mum, saying how awful she'd been to you, how she loved you and thought she'd probably lost you forever. Then she insisted she didn't deserve forgiveness and wasn't worthy of you anyway because she could never give you the children you wanted. You muttered something about wanting to be with Amber and… well, I've heard of people falling apart, but I've never actually seen it until Beth …" He shook his head, unable to continue for a moment. "Your mother held Beth and told me to fetch a doctor."

"So where is she?"

"In the psychiatric ward. Heavily sedated."

Alex pushed the bedclothes away, intending to get out of bed. "I must go to her."

"No, Alex, you can't." Paul pushed him gently back against the pillows, apologising as Alex groaned in pain. "As I said, mate, she's sedated. No visitors allowed. The doctor will come and talk to you later."

He made as if to resist, but realised it was pointless.

"I'm struggling to remember what happened, Paul. I know Scott was with me. There was a van ... Bloody hell, yes! A van, coming straight at us. I think Scott pushed me out of the way."

"I only heard a short while ago that the driver had had a heart attack. He died in the ambulance, apparently."

"And Scott? Paul, what about Scott?"

Paul's expression gave the answer before he spoke the words. "I didn't want to have to tell you yet, on top of everything else. I'm really sorry, Alex, but he died a couple of hours ago. He never regained consciousness."

The whole thing came back to him then, all the events leading up to them walking towards Saxon Road and lunch with Lily.

Scott had saved Alex's life at the cost of his own.

Every detail of what he had experienced with Scott flooded his brain. He remembered Grace, her beautiful, impassive face, those fathomless obsidian eyes. What was she? Some kind of angel? A guide in the afterlife?

He knew that many would say that what he'd seen had been a dream or a drug-induced hallucination. But he would always know that, somehow, and for some reason he couldn't yet figure out, he had shared Scott's passing and been sent back.

He had to stop thinking about it when his mother and stepfather came back from their breakfast. When his mother saw him awake and alert she immediately burst into tears.

"Hey, I'm okay. None of that now."

162

"Oh, Alex, to see you unconscious and all bruised, and then Be-" She stopped, her hand to her mouth.

Paul said gently, "It's all right. I've told him about Beth. He knows about Scott, too."

"It's tragic. Just tragic. I've just seen Scott's family and they are distraught. Well, you can imagine. But I'm so relieved that you're awake." She started to cry again, and Frank put his arm round her shoulders and gave her his handkerchief.

"It's right good to see you," he said to Alex. "I don't need to tell you the state your mother's been in since we got Paul's call."

No, Alex didn't need to be told. He asked his mother to sit on the bed so he could hold her hand, and they stayed that way, talking mostly about Beth.

A nurse came in and asked them all to step out for a few minutes so she could take Alex's temperature and blood pressure, as the doctor was on his way to see him.

Chapter 26

Lily left her seat and walked to the front of the packed room. Every part of her body trembled, and she felt light-headed and sick. She had been crying hard from the time she'd been brought to the crematorium by her parents and sister right until this moment, when she needed, absolutely needed, to stop the tears and do this heartbreaking thing. She stood alone, a piece of thick cream paper clasped in her trembling hand. Behind was the coffin upon which rested her magnificent floral wreath. Samantha had made it, a square pillow of velvety white lilies surrounding dozens of creamy yellow rosebuds in the shape of an S.

All she wanted to do was turn and fling herself at the coffin, tear it apart, beg for this nightmare not to be true. It couldn't be Scott in that horrible box; it was all some terrible mistake.

But she had been with him at the very moment he died. She had seen him days later in the Chapel of Rest, his injuries artfully concealed. When she had planted a gentle kiss on his cold cheek it had given her the sensation of pressing her lips to a face made of wax. His life force was truly gone.

Not all eyes were fixed on her as she stood there. Some were hidden behind handkerchiefs or tissues, some were downcast. But they were intently listening, waiting for her to speak. She glanced over at her parents-in-law. Scott's mother had objected to his funeral not being held in a church, but Lily had been adamant. After this dreadful day they would probably argue with her some more about her insistence that Scott's ashes be scattered. But she and Scott had talked about their wishes a long time ago, a time when the thought of death had seemed so remote it wouldn't touch them.

Scott had told her that he would want a civil funeral service, and for his ashes to be buried or scattered somewhere beautiful, with no need for a memorial plaque anywhere. Lily had answered that she wanted the same, as long as their ashes were scattered in the same place.

He'd smiled at that and said, "Why? What will it matter? When you're dead, you're dead, Lil."

He'd said the same thing when they'd discussed Maisie's connection with the Spiritualist church.

Was it true?

Was he really just... nothing at all?

She mustn't think about these things now. She had to concentrate on the present time and deliver her tribute to Scott, even though, right at that moment, she wished her heart would simply stop beating and end the agony.

She raised the paper to her face. Her handwriting blurred, and although she had spent hours learning the words, she couldn't remember them now. She needed to be able to read it from the paper, so she might not miss out a single word.

Hesitantly, in a voice too quiet to reach the back of the hall, she started. "I want to-"

Her voice quavered and the breath caught in her throat. Just three words spoken, and she had to stop. Breathe hard. A heady smell filled her nostrils, the potent scent of hundreds of flowers and the perfumes and colognes of the mourners. It reminded her of The Lilac Tree, but brought her no comfort.

Everyone had tried to talk her out of doing this, but she had been determined that she would make a short speech and read the poem she had painstakingly selected especially for this moment. She tried again.

"I w-want to read a short poem… it describes just what Scott m-m-meant to…"

Her voice broke once more and she knew with despair that she couldn't go on. She stood there, shaking and weeping, nose and eyes running unchecked, clutching the piece of paper as though her life depended on it. Her despair caused nearly everyone witnessing it – especially Scott's mother – to cry and sob. Scott's father, dry-eyed but shoulders shaking, looked down at his hands. Duncan and Scott's younger brother, Micky, sat side by side, their faces so stricken, so lost, Lily could not bear to look at them.

She fixed her eyes on her precious piece of paper, but it could have been written in a foreign language for all the sense she could make of it, and she simply could not make her tongue form the words.

It was Adele who left her seat and came to stand beside Lily. Taking her sister's hand, she gently took the poem from Lily's frozen fingers and read it out in the clear, practised voice she used so effectively in her business presentations. All eyes were looking up now. It felt as if everyone was holding their breath as Adele spoke for her sister, delivering Lily's eulogy for Scott as Lily could not contain her grief for long enough to do it herself.

When she'd finished the reading, a collective sigh rippled through the mourners. Scott's mother all but collapsed against her husband. He put his arm around her and hugged her close, his knuckles turning white.

Adele led Lily gently back to the front pew and helped her to sit down next to their father. Held between them, Lily closed her eyes and endured, simply endured, the rest of the service. But when the music had started and the curtains parted to receive Scott's coffin, her ears started buzzing and everything, mercifully, went black.

Hours later, Lily slowly awoke in her own bedroom, dry-mouthed and confused. She'd been dreaming about Scott, a wonderful dream where he was standing in a beautiful garden with a stream running through it, but much as she tried to hold onto the wonderful images, as she so desperately wanted to hold onto them, they swiftly disappeared.

Pushing herself up to sit on the edge of the bed, she saw that she was barefoot but still wearing the simple black linen dress, now badly creased where she'd lain on it. How had she got here? She realised she had fainted at the funeral, and supposed she had somehow been brought home and put to bed.

She felt sick again. Since the accident she had hardly been able to eat, yet her stomach ached not with hunger but with throwing up nothing but bile every day. She cradled her stomach, and whispered an apology to the baby within.

Sounds drifted up from the room below, loud chatter and bursts of laughter that made her wince. How could people be laughing today of all days?

Going downstairs was the last thing she wanted to do. Far preferable to hide up here, in the semi-dark of her curtained room.

But she had duties to perform, so she must go down and do what was expected of her.

***

If only he could comfort her, thought Vincent. Who could have imagined such a tragedy? Was the house cursed?

It wasn't the first time he'd wondered this. He didn't know what had happened to the occupants who had lived here before he and Rose arrived, but he did know about those that followed.

Each family had suffered in some way, whether by illness, as his beloved Rose had, or emotionally — he'd witnessed more than one marital breakdown — or financially, like the couple before Lily and Scott.

He'd had such high hopes for Lily and Scott's happiness when they'd bought the place, especially when he'd learned they were to have a baby. They were such a wonderful couple, clearly in love.

But now this.

Vincent watched as she brushed her hair and put her shoes back on.

She was being so brave, and his heart went out to her as she slowly left the safety and silence of her room to face the crowd downstairs.

Chapter 27

The funeral had been so painful, and when Adele had taken the paper from Lily's hand and read the poem on her behalf, Alex hadn't been sure he could stand it. Why oh why had Scott died and not him? It wasn't fair that he had saved Alex's life at the cost of his own. All these people, especially Lily, could have been spared this misery if only it had been his earthly life that had ended. Lily would still have her husband; the baby she was carrying would have a father; Scott's parents would still have their son.

And he would be with Amber, his beautiful child, holding her in his arms in that wonderful place where kingfishers flew in slow motion so every detail of their magnificence could be seen and admired. He'd begged and begged Grace to let him stay and for Scott to return to his family, but Grace had fixed her black, impassive eyes on him and told him how it must be.

He took a drink from a tray carried by a passing waiter and caught a glimpse of Lily entering the room, her face pale and her black dress a little dishevelled. He hadn't yet had a chance to speak to her, but perhaps it was just as well. What could he say? Sorry Scott died instead of me? But speak to her he must, so he started to thread his way through the people who filled the room, all eating and drinking and chatting.

His route was blocked by Maisie, as she caught his sleeve and said hello.

"I always think it strange to hear laughter at a wake, don't you Alex? But I've been to enough funerals to know that this is how it works. Someone is lain to rest and then it's only natural that people want to remember the good times they'd had with the person who's gone. After death, life must be celebrated, right?"

Someone – obviously a long-standing friend of Scott's - was telling a funny story about their first chemistry lesson at school. Maisie seemed to be listening in on the story, but her attention was suddenly drawn to Lily. "Dear God," she said quietly. "Just look at her, Alex."

Alex turned. Lily, as he'd known she would, looked utterly defeated. Her frame was so skinny, he wondered and worried how she could support the extra load of her growing baby.

Lily's mother and father hurried across the room to her, and the room quieted as people slowly came to realise that she was there. The expectant hush was marked after the loud chatter and laughter. Her father reached out to take her into his arms, but Lily's eyes overflowed with tears and she turned on her heel and ran back through the door. Her mother, fighting back her own tears, watched Lily go, then followed her.

Maisie spoke again. "Oh, it's so sad. I have no idea what to say to the poor girl. Did you see her, the way she had to be held up while we waited for the hearse to arrive, and then she all but collapsed when it turned in through the gates? Oh, and when she got too upset to read the piece she'd written, I thought my heart would break. Then she fainted when the bit came for the..." She hesitated, flapping her hand in front of her face as she tried to stem the tears. "You know, when the curtains opened and the coffin... Oh, I feel so helpless!" she pulled an embroidered cotton handkerchief from her sleeve and dabbed at her eyes."

"I know, Maisie. We're all helpless at times like this."

"Yes, but listen to me going on about myself. It's not about me, is it? Or anyone else. It's about her and Scott. It shouldn't have happened, should it? He was so young, and they had such plans. The baby..." She touched his arm and shuddered. "And it could have been you as well, Alex."

"Yes. I think about that all the time and wish it had been the other way round."

Maisie looked stricken. "Oh, Alex, forgive me for being so insensitive. I do go on without thinking, I know. Jack's always telling me off about it."

He dismissed her concerns with a kind smile, but he could tell that she was bursting to say something else.

She clutched his sleeve and stood on tiptoe, so he bent down as she whispered like a conspirator. "Alex, I want to ask you something. Remember when I saw you at the Spiritualist church? Are you a believer? You know... in life after death?"

Alex looked down at her, wondering how best to answer. He knew that if he were to admit that he was a psychic medium she'd never give him any peace. But it would surely do no harm to tell her that he believed as she did.

When he said so, Maisie couldn't hide her delight and said in rush, "Lily thinks it's nonsense, but don't you think we should try and get her to go? Or maybe see someone privately, like that Linda who was at the church when you came? She was so good, and wouldn't it be a comfort for Lily?"

"Oh, Maisie, that's a tough one. You can't force anyone to share your beliefs. And if Lily has told you that she thinks it's rubbish, I really don't think it would be wise to force it on her. She needs time to find her own way forward from here. A lot of time."

Maisie was crestfallen; she'd obviously thought it was such a good idea.

171

Alex squeezed her hand. "You're a wonderful friend, Maisie, and Lily is going to need her friends. Now, where's Jack, I haven't seen him yet."

Maisie looked around, searching for him, but Alex, being so much taller, spotted him first and told Maisie that Jack was across the room, sitting in an armchair in front of the open French doors, a half-full glass of beer in his hand and a plate of food on his lap.

He went first to clear a way through for Maisie, who said when she could finally see him, "Oh, good, he's got company. That's Lily's sister, Adele; have you met her?" She sighed. "There are so many people here. Don't you find such a mass of plain, black clothes oppressing?" She swept a hand down the front of her plain black dress. "My wardrobe is filled with bright colours and cheerful patterns, so I had to buy this especially. Oh, that sounds awful, doesn't it! But when my turn comes, I'm going to insist everyone wears bright colours to celebrate my life." She heaved another sigh. "But then again, I will have lived a long life and raised a family. Scott has been taken far too soon." She tutted and smiled ruefully. "I'm sure I'm boring you with my gabbling, Alex. Jack, here you are!"

The room felt stifling, so Alex was relieved at being near the open garden doors. He shook hands with Jack and said hello to Adele.

In the small dining room behind Jack he could see the impressive buffet on the table, set out on large china platters and silver dishes.

Seeing where he was looking, Adele said, "Mum suggested that the wake be at her house where's there's more room, but that was ridiculous really, and Lily quite rightly said no. So then mum insisted she be allowed to hire caterers and uniformed staff to serve the food. Not at all what Lily wanted, she wanted to keep it informal, but there's no stopping my mother when she's set on doing something."

Adele was looking at him a bit quizzically as she spoke, and Alex worried that she had asked a question that he hadn't heard. But she smiled and said, "Does it hurt to talk? I don't think I've ever seen such colourful bruises?"

He gently touched his jaw. "My face is quite a sight, I know, but I look far worse than I feel. It's my ribs that give me the most trouble, but nothing I can't cope with."

A shadow passed over Adele's face, and Alex wondered if she was thinking how lucky he'd been, thanks to Scott. At that moment he wanted to jump up on a chair and shout out to everybody that he was sorry he was still alive and Scott wasn't, that he would have taken Scott's place if he could. But what good would that do? None at all.

It was a fine afternoon and people gradually spilled into the long, pretty garden. Small groups stood together on the patio, laid just months ago by Scott in readiness for a summer he wouldn't see. They were clutching their glasses of wine and plates piled high with sandwiches and cake. Others were wandering across the lawn, stopping to admire the profusion of spring flowers in the borders and the antique sundial. It looked for all the world as if they were guests at a grand garden party, who had been instructed on the invitation to wear head-to-toe black.

Even with so many people moving outside, the living room was still full with mourners. Alex drifted over to the fireplace, and couldn't help an audible sigh at the sight of the large framed photograph of Scott and Lily that had pride of place in the centre of the mantelpiece.

He decided he'd stayed long enough, and went to see if he could find either of Lily's parents to say his goodbyes, before going home where his mother and Frank were waiting.

Chapter 28

Lily woke and waited for the misery to overwhelm her like a black, choking cloud. Every night she forced herself to go to bed, her lonely bed, where she tossed and turned until exhaustion finally closed her eyes in the early hours, and she sank gratefully into the oblivion of sleep. But only for two or three hours. She would wake, have a blissful second of peace, and then the empty space beside her would force her to recall that Scott was gone. Everything then would blast like a nail gun into her brain, her heart, her skin.

It was becoming an effort to sit up and swing her legs over the mattress because of the increasing weight of the baby. It was pressing uncomfortably on her bladder, too. "Not long, baby," she whispered. "I'm longing to hold you and tell you all about your daddy."

Pulling on a pair of Scott's tracksuit trousers and his favourite dark blue sweater, she wandered downstairs and out through the French doors into the garden.

It was looking in need of attention but beautiful nonetheless. All the time she had spent with a sketchpad, coloured pencils and gardening books designing it had certainly paid off, but it meant nothing to her now.

From the day they'd moved in, they'd worked on the house every spare minute they had, and had been glad to get outside when the weather allowed. It hadn't taken long for them to transform the long, narrow rectangle of rough grass and overgrown borders into a lovely garden. She had dug out and planted the curved flowerbeds and Scott had created a pond, not yet populated with fish, and laid a new patio and meandering stone and gravel paths. They had filled dozens of pots with evergreen shrubs and profusions of flowers, and installed an old stone birdbath and sundial.

The outlines of the half-collapsed greenhouse and rotting garden shed that had once stood at the bottom of the garden were still visible. Scott had built a smaller greenhouse and a new shed a little nearer to the house, screened by ivy-covered trellis. Looking at it now, she wished she had the energy and the will to go down there and start up the mower. Scott had bought it second hand, stripped it and rebuilt it. He was a man who loved gadgets; if it had a motor he wanted it, so the shed was full of implements and machines. The last thing he'd bought was the power washer to keep the patio stones clean, but it was still in its box, unused.

Lily stared at the untidy hedges, the straggly grass and the empty bird feeders. The wind chime stirred in the rose arbour at the bottom of the garden, and she remembered with sharp clarity the day the chimes had arrived in The Lilac Tree.

If only she could go back to that time.

It was warm yet she shivered as utter despair threatened to completely overwhelm her. She and Scott would never again sit outside on a summer's evening and enjoy a glass of cold beer or chilled white wine. She would never hear his voice again, never feel his arms around her, never feel his lips on hers, never…

Howling, she wrapped her arms around the swell of her stomach and fell to her knees. An appointment had been set for Monday at the antenatal clinic but she didn't know how she would find the strength to get herself there. She'd missed a couple already; maybe she wouldn't bother with this one. All those happily expectant mothers-to-be, smiling and asking her questions: When are you due? Do you know what you're having? Will your husband be there at the birth? Or, even worse, those who knew she was a widow and either avoided her with embarrassed, downcast eyes or asked how she was in hushed, sorrowful voices.

At last, she managed to drag herself up and into the kitchen, where she poured out a bowl of cereal. She wasn't hungry, but the morning was passing and she knew she had to eat, for the baby's sake.

The mirrors in the house reflected how dreadful she looked, with shadowed, haunted eyes, hollow cheeks, and bloodless lips. She was tired of people telling her that she must take care of herself for the baby's sake. Tired of people saying in that bright, brittle way that everyone seemed to use these days when speaking to her, that the baby was a good thing, that it would bring something positive to her life. She knew all that, but she felt that everyone was focusing solely on the baby, and her grief for Scott was being brushed aside.

She and Scott had decided not to know the sex of the baby, wanting the excitement of finding out when he or she chose to make their entrance into the world. At the funeral, Scott's mother had sobbed and hugged her, saying how she hoped it was a boy. Her own mother had tucked a lock of hair behind her ear the way she had when Lily was a child, and launched into a litany of how difficult it was to be a single mother, suggesting just about the worst thing Lily could imagine: "You should come and live with us, darling, at least until you find your feet."

Her mouth was so dry, she had difficulty swallowing the cereal, and the first spoonful went down the wrong way. Coughing and spluttering, abandoning the rest of her breakfast, she curled up on the sofa and stared at the blank TV screen, unable to summon the energy to turn it on.

The doorbell rang.

She blinked, unfolded herself slowly from the cushions and concentrated on finding her balance as her right foot had gone numb. A glance at the clock showed that she'd been sitting there, unmoving, for almost two hours.

How could that possibly happen?

Now the doorbell was ringing again. Over and over. And then a thud-thud-thud, as if someone was kicking the door.

She wasn't expecting any of her friends. Her mother never came without calling first. She hoped it wasn't Scott's mother or brother. Or Alex. He was trying his best, and he was a really nice man, but seeing him was too hard for her. But it wouldn't be Alex, she remembered now; he'd said he was going to Scotland. Or was that next week? She was finding it so hard to remember what people told her, and to keep track of time.

Most likely it was Maisie, come to fill her in on the week's business. Such a sweet woman, Lily thought, a good friend, keeping the shop going. She went in nearly every day, insisting to Lily that she did it willingly and gladly. Business had boomed in the first couple of weeks after Scott's death, and Lily had acidly remarked that it was because people were hoping to catch a glimpse of the grieving widow, or, better still, be served by her.

She'd managed to work in the shop a few days a week immediately after Scott's funeral, until she had started to suffer from severe anxiety attacks every time she left the house. She'd known then that she had to hire another part-time assistant to help Maisie, even though it would eat it into the profits.

Lily opened the door now to find Maisie standing there, her elbow jammed on the doorbell, her hands encased in oven gloves, holding a small covered dish.

"Chicken casserole, pet, fresh from the oven. I brought it over because I know you won't come over and join me and Jack."

She ignored Lily's protests and marched straight to the kitchen. She spotted the cereal bowl, almost full of very soggy cornflakes.

"Have you eaten anything today?"

Lily stood in the doorway, biting her lip.

"You haven't, have you? Nor yesterday, I wouldn't be surprised. Well then, you'd better eat this now."

Maisie knew her way round Lily's kitchen, so she set out a place mat and cutlery, put the casserole down and doled some out onto a plate. "There you go. Just you sit yourself down and tuck in."

Lily stayed where she was. "Just leave it, Maisie, I'll eat it later."

"No, pet, you won't. It'll end up in the bin and you'll go yet another day with nothing decent inside you. Think of the baby."

Lily stopped her saying any more by raising her hand in warning.

"I'm sorry, Lily, but your baby needs you to be responsible. Come on now, love. You need something nutritious inside you and I'm staying put until you've eaten at least half of what's on that plate."

Lily put on her most mutinous expression, but it didn't faze Maisie one bit.

"It won't do any good, young lady. I am not going until I've seen you eat." She folded her arms, bracelets jangling, and leaned against the sink, her mouth set in fierce determination. Lily had never known her to look and sound so severe.

"Isn't Jack waiting for you?"

Maisie glared and said, "Yes, he is, so the sooner you eat up, the sooner I can go home."

Defeated, Lily forked up a small bite of chicken and carrot and chewed slowly. She swallowed and took a little more. But this time, just like with the cereal, her throat closed on it and she almost choked. Maisie handed her a glass of water. She sipped it and it helped get the food down. Another mouthful of meat and gravy. Another sip. She chewed and swallowed, sipped, chewed and swallowed, while tears coursed down her cheeks. She could smell and see that it was good food, she knew full well that Maisie was an excellent cook, and that she needed to eat, but her tongue gave her no sensation of taste or texture. When the plate was only a quarter empty, she glanced up at Maisie, hoping it was enough.

Maisie's arms were still folded, but she was crying too.

With a sob, Lily leapt from the chair and ran upstairs to the bathroom, just in time to be sick into the toilet bowl. As she knelt on the floor, retching and heaving, she wondered just how miserable it was possible to get.

She sensed Maisie come in and tried to wave her away, but Maisie sat on the floor behind her in the tiny room. Her gentle hands held Lily's hair away from her face and she crooned something that sounded like a lullaby, as Lily was sick and sick until she felt as if she were being turned inside out.

When at last she was entirely spent, Maisie gently helped her to the bedroom. Lily wearily lay down and allowed her friend to remove her slippers and cover her with a blanket.

"I'll leave you to rest, Lily, love. Maybe you'll sleep. Listen now, I'm going to take a key so I can let myself in later, just to see that you're okay. Or you can call me if you need me sooner."

179

When she heard the front door close, she turned on her side and pulled Scott's pillow into a tight embrace. She'd changed the sheets but not the pillow cover, convinced that she could still smell his skin, his hair, when she pressed her nose into it, even though it couldn't be possible after so long

Hugging the pillow to her face, she cried so hard she felt as if she was drowning in tears. Her eyelids burned, her throat ached, her head throbbed, but this was what misery was. It was all she knew, all she would ever know, because she didn't have Scott.

Exhausted, she slipped once more into a restless sleep, hoping to dream about him and never wake up.

But she did wake up. It was dark outside, but she didn't turn her head to look at the clock. What difference did it make whether it was midnight, or two o'clock or four? She lay on her back, feeling the baby kick, and let the tears flow unchecked.

**

He had begun to think of her as the daughter he and Rose had hoped they would have, and, now Lily was so soon going to be a mother, Vincent wished more than ever that he could comfort her. His heart ached to see her hugging Scott's pillow like that. She wore his clothes, opened his bottles in the bathroom just to smell his shampoo or his aftershave. She dragged herself round the house like a lost soul.

The first time she changed the sheets after Scott's death, she'd piled them into the washing machine and switched it on. Lily had taken just two steps away when she'd fallen to her knees and crawled back across the hard, cold tiles. She'd tried to claw open the door, but it was too late. For the whole time the sheets were swishing in the sudsy water, she'd sat on the floor, her hand pressed flat against the round glass, howling like a banshee.

Another time, she'd tried to clear Scott's wardrobe, cramming things into large black bin bags. Vincent had wanted to stop her, to tell her that it was far too soon, but he could only stand silently by. When Lily had a pile of bags heaped on the bedroom floor, she'd stood, hands on her hips, breathing hard and glaring at them. Then with a yell, she'd torn the plastic apart and shoved all the clothes back into the wardrobe.

She kept a shoebox in her wardrobe, and often he saw her bring it out, remove the lid, and just stare into it. He didn't know what it contained, photos maybe, but it always brought on another paroxysm of tears.

Her grief was unbearable to witness, and it brought back so many memories for him. Memories of the visceral pain when he found that he had lost Rose. Memories of screaming with rage at such a cruel quashing of their plans and dreams. Where was she, his Rose? Why hadn't he gone to the same place?

Helpless, Vincent stood by the rumpled bed. Lily was crying silently now, tears sliding from the corners of her eyes into her hair.

"Lily. Oh, Lily, my dearest girl," he whispered. "People will keep on telling you that it gets easier with the passing of time. But it doesn't. It really doesn't."

Chapter 29

The door of the little stone cottage opened as soon as Alex's taxi pulled up outside; his mother had been keeping a lookout for his arrival. As soon as he was out of the car, he was enveloped in a fierce, fragrant hug. "Alex! It's so good to see you."

His mother held him for a long beat before letting him go, and he leaned round her to shake Frank's hand.

"Come away in, she's prepared a wee banquet. Sunday roast on a Monday, if ye please."

Laughing, Alex retrieved his bag from the back seat and paid the driver, and then Frank led the way into the house.

The dining table was set with the best white damask cloth and heavy cutlery. The silver pepper and salt set and matching mustard pot sat in the centre, and a long-stemmed wine glass gleamed at each place setting. Wonderful smells of roasting beef wafted in from the little kitchen, making Alex's stomach rumble with anticipation.

Their dog, an elderly King Charles spaniel, came running and jumped up at Alex, scrabbling at his knees. "Hey, Tilly. Hey, girl." His hands were licked and the dog's frantically wagging tail fanned the air.

"She's looking good for her age, isn't she?"

"Aye, she's as fit as a fiddle, and so she ought to be with all the exercise she gets and only the very best of food. Fed better than me, that dog is." Frank looked at his wife, smiling fondly. "Except when you're here, Alex. I get fed right fine then."

"Why don't you take your bag up to your room," said Alex's mother, "Then we'll eat and you can tell us all the news."

Upstairs, he threw his bag onto the bed then went to the bathroom to wash his hands and face. Tilly followed him, panting, her tongue lolling after running up the stairs, but her tail still madly wagged from side to side.

Downstairs again, he found Frank already seated at the table and his mother bringing in steaming dishes. She put them down, moved them around, realigned the cutlery, picked up a wine glass and polished it with the tea towel she was carrying over her shoulder, then went back for yet more dishes. Frank winked at him, and he grinned, just as she came in with the gravy jug.

"I know, I know," said his mother, flapping the tea towel at them. "But I can keep still sometimes, you know." She sat down and folded her hands in her lap. The two men looked her, and within seconds she started to squirm and wring her hands. As they burst out laughing, she leapt up and started serving food onto their plates, piling them high with generous slices of tender beef, crisp roast potatoes, carrots, broccoli, Yorkshire pudding, almost drowning the lot in thick, brown gravy.

"Eat up, Alex, you're far too thin. Although..." Head on one side, she studied him. "A little better than when we last saw you."

Alex took the plate she handed to him. "I bet you've been cooking since the day I told you I was coming!"

"Oh, aye," said Frank. "Cakes, biscuits, bread. And me not allowed so much as a taste..."

"It's lovely that the bruises are all gone from your face," said Alex's mother. "How about your ribs, better now?"

"I get twinges, nothing major."

"And Paul, how is he? He was so kind to us when you were in the hospital, arranging our flights and sending a car to pick us up from the airport."

"He's fine, mum. Champing at the bit for me to get back to work, of course, as Eselmont have offered a full series."

Eyes sparkling, his mother beamed at him. "Well isn't that grand! My handsome son, a TV star."

Alex chewed and swallowed a piece of potato. "Actually, I'm not ready to do it yet, and I don't know how much longer they'll wait."

Frank, who didn't hold with Alex's mediumship – despite knowing and trusting his stepson, he still couldn't bring himself to believe that he actually spoke to the dead - cleared his throat and changed the subject by asking about the factory.

"It's doing just great, thanks, Frank. I found a really good manager to look after the day-to-day stuff, but I still go in to keep my hand in. I'm making a rather special garden sculpture just now, for Lily Miller. Scott's wife."

"Ah, that poor woman. How's she coping?"

"As you'd expect. I'm not sure when her baby's due, but it must be so tough for her. She's got some extra help at her shop, and I understand Scott's younger brother is going to buy Scott's stake in the garage. I go round to visit her, to see if I can do anything, but I think it's too hard for her to be around me because I'm a constant reminder that her husband died saving my life."

His mother glanced quickly at Frank, and Alex saw the warning shake of his head in the response, but she couldn't resist asking the question.

"Alex, haven't you seen Lily's husband? Couldn't you pass on a message or something?"

"I haven't, mum, no." He hadn't told her, hadn't told anybody, about how he'd shared in Scott's passing. "Sometimes, after a traumatic death like Scott's, it takes a long time for them to be able to communicate. Besides, as

I said, I'm not ready to go back to it and anyway, Lily has no idea that I'm a medium."

To Frank's obvious relief, Alex steered the conversation to inconsequential things while they ate. His mother helped them both to seconds of everything, no more for herself, and watched with satisfaction as her two men ate. The moment their cutlery was laid down tidily on the plates, she whipped all the dishes off the table. Alex heard her moving around the kitchen, stirring and whisking something, opening and closing the oven door. Minutes later, she reappeared in the dining room carrying three dessert dishes, then returned to fetch a large, freshly baked apple pie and a jug of thick, yellow custard. She set them down on the table

She saw Alex looking at the jug and offered cream or ice cream instead.

"No, it's fine. I was just remembering when I was here with Beth and Amber. Do you remember how we gave a spoonful of custard to Amber, and she just loved it?"

Flustered, his mother sliced the pie into pieces that were too wide for the dessert dishes. She adjusted the size of the slices, but messily, then splashed custard onto the tablecloth as she poured it.

"Damn!" she said, and burst into tears.

Frank was out of his chair in a second, his arm around his wife's shoulders.

"Lizzie, Lizzie, there now. What's all this, eh?"

"It's because I mentioned Amber," said Alex softly.

His mother kept her head down, dabbing at her eyes with her napkin. Alex leaned towards her and took her hand, giving it a gentle shake. "It's all right to talk about her, mum. She's with dad, and she's absolutely fine."

His mother's face went pink, then white, then pink again. She still held the napkin, pleating it now on the tabletop with her fingers, over and over. "I'm sorry, darling. It's not only Amber. I keep thinking about Beth and what happened at the hospital. That poor wee girl just broke apart in front of my eyes and I couldn't do anything to help."

Frank sat back in his chair, his face glum. Then, with a scowl, he got up and went to the kitchen, returning with a bottle of Scotch whisky and three crystal tumblers. He poured generous measures of the golden liquid and handed them round.

He raised his glass and looked first at his wife, then at Alex. "Here's to Beth getting better and our wee Amber and her dear granddaddy livin' the high life beyond the veil."

Alex, grateful and pleased that Frank would offer such a toast, raised his glass and waited for his mother to pick hers up off the table. Slowly, a little reluctantly, she did so, and they drank.

Chapter 30

Adele stopped the car in the next street, reluctant to finish her journey by going round the corner to her sister's house in Saxon Road. She didn't think for a moment that she'd be welcome, but mum had telephoned her and insisted that a member of the family, meaning Adele, should be with Lily now she was just a couple of weeks away from having the baby.

"I've tried my best, God knows," she'd said, sounding like a martyr as usual. "Lily simply will not let me help her. She rejects me at every turn. So, I think it would be best if you went to stay with her. I fear for her emotional state, I really do. She shouldn't be alone."

She could picture her mother, facing the ornate mirror above the telephone table, fingering her hair or her pearls or whatever type of necklace she was wearing that day, pulling at her eyes and cheeks, worrying about the lines on her face that no amount of expensive creams could keep at bay.

Adele wanted to help Lily, of course she did, but she felt utterly inadequate to the task. How did you even begin to help someone who had suffered such a tragedy? And although she had to admit she was being selfish, she hadn't wanted to leave her home just then because things weren't going at all well with Rob. He'd promised to try harder after they'd had a huge row about his lack of support when Scott had died, but he had been even more distracted lately, and hadn't seemed bothered when she'd told him she planned to go and stay with her sister. What if her absence brought things to an end between them?

She pulled her mobile from her bag and checked it. No message. She tried not to be too disappointed, but still she'd hoped that Rob would at least...

There was no point even thinking about it. She must put her own woes out of her mind because they were, after all, as nothing compared to Lily's.

Feeling resolute now, Adele put the car in gear and drove the remaining short distance to Lily's house. Her sister's car was skewed across the driveway, two wheels on the grass, the driver's door not quite shut. Adele looked at it and felt anxiety flutter.

Her suitcases and laptop were on the back seat, but Adele decided to leave them there. When she'd phoned to make the arrangements, Lily had been adamant that she did not want company, so Adele thought she had better gauge Lily's reaction to her turning up before she actually moved herself in.

At first she thought the door was closed, she expected it to be closed, but when she got right up to it, she could see it was open just a crack. She pushed it with her fingertips and stepped inside.

"Lily? It's Adele. Where are you?"

No answer.

The house was dimly lit because most of the curtains were closed, even though it was only early afternoon. There was something about the profound silence that made Adele's heart begin to race.

Louder this time, she called out again. "Lily? Are you okay?"

A sound. A muffled sob. Adele turned her head from side to side trying to detect where it was coming from. Moving forward warily, she made her way into the living room. Her eyes had adjusted to the gloom by now, and she could make out the slumped figure of her sister half on and half off the sofa.

"Oh, Lily!" Adele ran and knelt on the floor, brushing the strands of hair away from Lily's flushed and tear-stained face. Lily looked at her as though she didn't recognise her.

Adele was no good at this sort of thing. She couldn't cope with illness and was dismissive of people who showed weakness of spirit. But this was her baby sister, who was neither ill nor weak. She had lost a husband in one of the most horrible ways imaginable, and found herself alone, pregnant and utterly bewildered.

"I'll get you a drink." It was the only thing Adele could think of.

Going back into the hallway, Adele first closed the front door before going into the dining room, where the bottles were kept in an oak dresser. She knew that Scott had always drunk beer or wine and Lily only wine, but they kept a selection of spirits in case visitors asked for them. Plus, she thought, there was sure to be hard liquor left over from the funeral.

Searching through the bottles of gin, sherry, dark rum and port, she was relieved to find a bottle of cognac right at the back. From a glass-fronted cupboard at the top of the dresser she picked out a heavy crystal brandy glass, one of a pair that she had bought them for a wedding present, and carried it and the bottle back to where Lily still lay. She hadn't moved, though she had to be dreadfully uncomfortable in the position she was in.

It took too many seconds to get the top off the bottle, and she thankfully breathed in the fumes when they were at last released to the air. Adele splashed cognac into the glass and made Lily sit up on the sofa.

"Oh, God, are you allowed to drink? Look, just have a sip. I'm sure it'll do more good than harm."

She tipped the glass to Lily's lips, and then took a large gulp from it herself, gasping as it burned her throat and heated her insides as it went down.

She was glad it was almost a full bottle. She was going to need all the help she could get.

"I told you not to come."

"Lily, you can't possibly be on your own, and it was either me or mum. I thought you'd prefer me."

Lily gave her a wan smile at that and said she needed a hot bath.

"Then you shall have one. Can you get up? Will you need any help?"

"I'm pregnant, Adele, I'm not an invalid. I can manage a bath on my own."

Pleased to hear some fight in Lily's voice Adele said, "Okay, okay. Well, you go on up then, and I'll bring my things in. Then you can tell me what brought this on."

When Lily came back down, wrapped in her dressing gown, she seemed to have recovered a little. There was colour in her cheeks, and she looked so much better with freshly washed hair rather than the lank, greasy tresses of earlier.

"What happened, Lily? When I saw the way your car's parked, and the front door open…"

"I had a panic attack. You know I keep getting them, I told you. But when I woke up this morning I didn't feel too bad; better than I have done in ages. I went out to get some bread, because toast seems to be the only thing I can tolerate at the moment and what bread I had was mouldy. I was heading for the checkout when I started to hyperventilate. I couldn't get back here fast enough."

"Oh, poor you." Adele searched for the right thing to say. "Lily, I don't know what I can do for you, I don't know how to help you, but let me stay, at least for a few days. I can go shopping, and I'll cook us some simple, nutritious meals, because surviving on bread won't do you any good."

Lily nodded. "I'm sorry I was so horrid to you on the phone. I really am glad that you're here. Thank you."

"It's the least I can do. Look, I'm going to see what you've got in the cupboards and fridge, we'll make a list, and-"

"I can tell you that there's nothing you can make a meal from. I didn't even manage to buy the damned bread, I just dropped it and ran."

"Then we'll forget the list, and I'll go shopping right now. No, I don't want any money. Just sit tight, Lily, and I'll be back before you know it."

Chapter 31

There was a smart silver car parked behind Lily's, and Maisie wondered whether she should leave her visit until tomorrow. But she had something that needed to be sorted out, so she proceeded up the path and rang the doorbell.

She recognised the woman who opened the door, and was relieved that Lily had someone there to look after her.

"Hello, dear," she said. "I remember meeting you at the…" She couldn't bring herself to say funeral. "Adele, isn't it? Such a pretty name. I'm Maisie, in case you can't remember, and you had a long chat with my husband, Jack. He was very taken with you. But you must have met so many people on that dreadful day, and it's impossible to remember too many new names, isn't it? Is Lily up to a quick chat, do you think? I need to talk to her about the shop."

Adele led the way into the kitchen, where she was obviously in the process of putting some shopping away. Good, thought Maisie. Maybe Adele could get Lily to eat properly.

Lily sat at the table, a mug of coffee in front of her.

Maisie kissed her on the cheek. "Hello, pet, how are you today?"

Lily tried to smile. "Oh… you know."

Adele asked if Maisie would like a cup of tea or coffee.

"No, thank you, dear. I won't be staying long."

Maisie patted Lily's hand. "I'm sorry to intrude, pet, but we've had a bit of a setback at the shop."

With a groan, Lily's hand flew to her mouth and she looked stricken.

"No, no, it's nothing that can't be fixed. It's just that Celia's taken a tumble and broken her foot, so she can't come in for a while. And I can't do the shop for a couple of days next week, at least not for the whole day. Jack has a hospital appointment on Monday and I want to go with him. I don't think the drugs he's on are doing any good, and he just won't push them to do anything for him."

She hesitated, waiting for a response. She didn't get one, so continued, "On Thursday I simply have to go and visit Caroline, there's some kind of crisis. Not serious, but she needs her mum."

"Who's Celia?" asked Adele.

"She's a part-time assistant Lily hired to help us out," replied Maisie, "She's been a treasure, she's-"

"Oh, Maisie!" Lily cried, interrupting her. "I'm so sorry you have to worry about all this. Look, just close the shop when you have to; I know you have to get home to Jack in the middle of the day. Do you think I should replace Celia?"

"Well, that's up to you, pet, though she thinks she'll be mobile again in about a month, six weeks at the most. She's very good, so I think it would be a shame to lose her. You'll certainly need her when the baby comes."

"I'll be back at work myself then, Maisie."

"And how will you manage that, pet?"

"I'll bring the baby with me."

Maisie, looking doubtful, caught Adele's eye and saw she was thinking the same thing: Lily could not possibly manage to run the shop with a newborn to look after. But she knew there was no sense arguing with her, and said in a placating way, "Well then, let's cross that bridge when we come to it. Now, about next week."

Adele spoke up. "Could I do it?" She looked from her sister to Maisie, and Maisie beamed back at her with gratitude.

"Lily, what do you think?"

"Could you, Adele? It would be a weight off my mind. But what about your own business?"

"You let me worry about that. Maisie, what do you think about me working in the shop?"

"Well, I don't see why not, pet, if you're sure you're happy to do it. But we'd have to go in now so I can show you how to switch off and reset the alarm, and how to operate the till. I can't do it tomorrow because I have all the family coming."

"Okay, great, if you really don't mind? I'd better warn you though, I haven't worked in a shop since I was a teenager, and modern tills look so complicated."

"Oh, if an old lady like me can do it, a bright young thing like you will manage just fine. If Lily would give you her keys, I'll just pop back and let Jack know what's happening. Shall we meet outside in five minutes? It's a lovely evening and it's only a short walk, but if you'd rather drive?"

"No, no. A walk would be lovely."

Maisie rose from the table, and looked with concern at Lily. She seemed completely out of it now things were sorted out for The Lilac Tree, and she was desperately worried for her. Thank goodness her sister had come.

Adele was waiting for her with the shop keys when she came out of her house having explained what was happening to Jack, and they walked a few yards in silence.

Maisie heaved a sigh and said, "It's so unlucky that Celia should have an accident. Of course I feel sorry for her, don't think I'm not sympathetic, but I don't want Lily worrying about The Lilac Tree on top of everything else.

She has panic attacks, she stays in that house for days on end, and she's not eating, you know. I popped round the other day with a stew, and she couldn't keep anything down."

"So I've discovered. But in our last phone call she told me not to come because she was managing just fine on her own."

Maisie considered this. "I suppose she was trying to reassure you, dear."

"No. She was trying to stop me from coming. I'm glad I didn't listen to her, though, because anyone can see that she's depressed. She's not sleeping much either, by the look of her. When I arrived, I found her in a heap on the floor. She'd been to the shop for bread and had to leave it to rush home because of one of those panic attacks. I think she needs to see her doctor."

"Yes, pet, I think that would be a good idea. Especially as the baby could come just about any time now. She really should be having counselling, but she won't hear of it. She's very stubborn, is our Lily."

They reached The Lilac Tree, and Maisie unlocked the door.

"I haven't been here in ages," Adele told her. "I'd forgotten how heavenly it smells."

"Yes, it is lovely. I never tire of being here. It was very busy today, which is just how I like it, but I do feel bad that I'm going to have to close for an hour each day to get home to Jack. Mondays are usually quiet, though so don't look so worried! You'll be fine."

For the next hour, Maisie showed Adele the merchandise, how to switch the alarm on and off, and how to operate the till, pausing so Adele could scribble notes and instructions on a pad.

The two women walked back to Saxon Road together, Adele having to shorten her stride so Maisie didn't get left behind.

"Will you come in for a little while, Maisie?" asked Adele, and Maisie could sense her reluctance to go back into Lily's house alone.

"Well, pet, I'd love to, but I'd best be getting back and get the dinner on. How long are you staying?"

"As long as Lily will have me. I'll have to nip home from time to time, and go to a few business meetings, but basically I can work anywhere as long as I have my laptop and phone."

"Good. Then I hope you'll come over for a meal some time. I'll rely on you to get Lily to come with you."

"That would be very nice. Thank you."

Maisie patted Adele on the arm. "It's not going to be easy for you, pet, but just remember that it is Lily who is suffering. All I can advise is that you be patient with her. And get her to see her doctor."

"I will. Thank you again. And I'm looking forward to helping in the shop."

"I'm glad. It's certainly one thing less for Lily to worry about. I'll come in on Monday after Jack's appointment if I can."

"No, Maisie, please don't worry about rushing back here. Why not give me your phone number, and I can call if I really get stuck with something?"

Chapter 32

Adele's first day in the shop was, as Maisie had predicted, nice and quiet, giving her time to study her notes and familiarise herself with some of the merchandise. Customers had trickled in one by one, and the only difficulties Adele had encountered were her comical attempt at gift-wrapping an awkwardly shaped ceramic dish, and a mistake putting through a card payment. Fortunately, the woman had realised that her pin number was being added to the price, and, although a bit flustered and embarrassed, Adele had swiftly managed to correct the transaction, and the customer had taken it in good humour.

Maisie rang and offered to come in mid-afternoon, but Adele insisted there was no need. For lunch she'd brought with her a sandwich and an apple, which she was able to eat undisturbed. The time passed slowly, but she was happy tidying and dusting the shelves and dealing with emails on her laptop.

At 4.30 Adele was in the tiny kitchen, washing up the mug and spoon she'd used throughout the day, and was recalled to the shop by the bell. Three women and a man had come in and were standing in front of the counter.

"Is Maisie here?" asked the man.

"I'm sorry, no. I'm Adele, Lily's sister. I'm helping out."

"Oh, we've all heard about you from Lily. Pleased to meet you, Adele. I'm Max, I own the hairdressing salon opposite. This is Ellie, from the boutique, and Samantha, who has the flower shop."

"And I'm Thelma. Here, please take these home with you." She handed Adele a navy and white box with 'Thelma's Bakery' printed on it in curly pale blue script.

Adele peeked inside the box and saw two chocolate éclairs, a cream-filled bun and a jam doughnut nestled there. She thanked Thelma, thinking but not saying that she'd probably end up eating them all herself, as Lily was unlikely to want them.

Thelma said, "Maisie told us about Celia, so it's a relief to see you here. Is Lily okay?"

Adele shook her head. "She's struggling. We're all hoping that the baby's arrival will help."

"It's such a shame," said Thelma. "To lose Scott like that. They made such a lovely couple. Anyway, we came over with a proposal, but perhaps it's not necessary now. Are you going to be working the same hours as Celia did?"

Adele shook her head and explained that she had her own business to run. "I'll work here as much as I can, of course, but I do have meetings I have to go to, so…"

"In that case," Thelma handed Adele a sheet of paper. "We've drawn up a rota so there'll always be someone to cover through the lunch periods."

"Or other times if need be," added Max.

Astounded, Adele could only stare at them, a slow smile spreading across her face.

"Really? You can do that? I… I don't what to say! Maisie will be so relieved; I know she's been worrying about getting home to look after her husband."

"Well, then. Now she – and you – can take a proper lunch break."

"Thank you so much. I can't wait to tell Lily and Maisie how kind you all are."

The visitors stayed for a while longer, filling Adele in on what went on in the High Street, and inviting her into their shops for a chat whenever she felt like it. She was sorry when they left; they were all so nice and friendly. She particularly liked Max's outrageous sense of humour.

With ten minutes to go until closing, she wandered again round the shop, studying ornaments, handmade jewellery, candles, smelling different types of pot pourri and incense sticks. Everything was meticulously labelled, and in front of many items were handwritten cards in Lily's neat calligraphic script, explaining relevant and interesting details about them. She had to admit that her sister had excellent taste.

She picked out and read a few of the humorous greetings cards, some of them laugh-out-loud funny, then inspected the pretty rolls of wrapping paper, boxes of bows and reels of coloured ribbon.

In a wicker tray she found a selection of solid silver money clips in the shape of initials. She sorted through them, found and took out the letter R. Holding it in her hands, feeling its thickness and weight and tracing the initial through the clear cellophane wrapper, she tried to decide whether or not to buy it.

But why should she buy Rob a gift? He'd never bought anything for her. No, that wasn't quite true. In the early days he had given her the occasional present. Perfume or chocolates, usually, bought at the Duty Free on one of his frequent business trips abroad.

She walked over to the revolving display cabinet, the core of which was set with mirrors. As it slowly and smoothly turned she studied her reflection in the sparkling rectangles of mirrored glass. She and Lily did not look alike at all. She was fairer, shorter, a little rounder, but she spent money on her appearance and knew her clients and colleagues thought of her as a very elegant woman. Lily was prettier, more slender, with a vivacious face that needed very little makeup. Adele kept her hair short and spiky, a style that was expensive to maintain, while Lily's hair was long and shiny smooth, trimmed every six weeks or so in Max's salon.

It was 5.30, and she was so reluctant to leave the beautiful shop and go back to Lily's house, she decided to stay for another quarter of an hour, amongst the heavenly smells and pretty things.

She heard her phone ringing and, hoping it would be Rob, dashed over and retrieved it from her handbag, which was tucked under the counter. She had to swallow her disappointment before answering.

"Hi, mum."

"Adele, darling. Are you with Lily?"

"No, I'm in the shop. I've been working here today."

"Lily's shop? Why?"

Adele explained.

"So she doesn't have enough help?"

"Not at the moment. But Maisie is working all the hours she can, and as soon as the other lady's foot is better, she'll be back. That'll be in about six weeks, I should think."

"And what about your own business, Adele? You can't work there for six weeks, surely? I'll be there tomorrow."

Adele frowned. "Be where, mum?"

"At the shop! You can show me what to do."

"But... Mum, you've never worked a day in your life!"

There was a short, charged silence. Then: "Excuse me, young lady, I may not have worked for a wage, but I have run a home, raised you and Lily - practically on my own, I might add, to allow your father to work those long hours. Not to mention all the entertaining I do for him, those interminable dinner parties where everyone burbles on about portfolios and stocks and shares."

Adele laughed at the image of her mother having to feign interest in her dad's business. She would have done it very well, though. "Okay, mum, I'm sorry. That was a thoughtless thing to say, and I can't believe I said it. But I can't imagine you working in Lily's shop; you've never really approved of it, have you? And it's a long way for you to come."

"I want to be of help, Adele, and this seems to be a practical way that I can be. Should I be there at 9 o'clock, or earlier?"

Surprised at the softer tone of her mother's voice, and the realisation that she really did want to help, Adele confirmed she should be there at 9, and ended the call. Goodness knows what Lily would say. Or Maisie.

She realised she had slipped the money clip into her pocket while talking to her mother. Looking at it once more, she remembered with a clarity that brought pain to her chest the story of how Scott had taken Lily to the house in Saxon Road on her birthday. They had done so many wonderful, thoughtful things for each other; they had been best friends as well husband and wife. They had loved each other deeply, and shown it in ways both large and small.

It was painful to admit it, but she knew she would never have that kind of relationship with Rob. Probably she had known it for most of the past year, but had ignored the signs. She replaced the money clip in the box and considered Lily's dreadful situation.

"Adele, stop being such a wimp," she said out loud to herself. "Get out of here and go and help Lily."

Chapter 33

"Alex? It's Charles Hendry. How are you?"

"Charles! I'm very well, thanks. You?"

"Fine, fine. Look, the reason I'm calling is, well, I hope you don't mind, but I got your number from Linda. She suggested I got in touch and asked if you would be our guest medium one Sunday."

"Oh, I don't know, Charles."

"It needn't be this week, or next, but, really Alex, we'd be so pleased if you could do it. We all know why you needed to take a break, and we're all deeply sorry about what happened, but our thinking... well, Linda's thinking, is that our church would be a good place for you to start again. I hope we're not being too presumptuous?"

Alex's mind raced. On the one hand, he felt rather peeved with Linda for not forewarning him, but on the other hand, he knew she was absolutely right. And, knowing Linda, she deliberately hadn't told him that Charles would call so that he wouldn't have a refusal ready. The other thing was, was it sensible to work so close to home? Maisie was sure to be there.

"Charles, can I think about this? I'm very grateful, and I would be honoured to do it, I just need to work out when I'll feel ready."

"Of course, Alex, of course. Linda told me about your TV series, you must be very excited about that. And we'd love to have you before you're too famous to do the small provincial churches any more."

Alex laughed. "I haven't made the series yet, Charles. And if it does come off, I hope I never get too big for my boots in that way. I'll call you in a couple of days, if that's okay?"

"I look forward to it. Thank you, Alex, and God bless."

Alex put his mobile in his pocket and turned his attention back to the design drawings of the kingfisher garden sculpture he was making for Lily. He'd set himself the deadline of having it finished and ready to install before she had her baby, so there wasn't much time.

But he couldn't concentrate. Charles's invitation to give a demonstration at the church had come out of the blue, but Alex was beginning to realise how badly he wanted to do it. Time after time, usually at night as he waited for sleep to come, he'd be torn between staying away from mediumship in the hope that he could win Beth back, and wondering why he had been sent back from the other side if not to use his gift for the good of other people. That latter thought was occupying his thoughts more and more lately, and he could see Grace in his mind's eye, her black, fathomless eyes, as she'd dispassionately told him he must return.

His mobile trilled again, and Alex saw that it was Paul.

"Alex! Great news, well done! I've already been onto Eselmont, and we're setting up a schedule for you to record the series. Now, lets-"

"Hold on, hold on! What are you talking about?"

"Charles Hendry told Linda that he'd spoken to you about doing a demonstration at his church. Linda rang me to let me know. So, now you're back in harness, there's no time to waste, pal."

Stunned, Alex couldn't find his voice.

"Good," said Paul. "We've finally been able to make you shut up about not doing what you were put on this earth to do. Could you meet me at *The Beijing* at 7.30? I will treat you to a decent meal while we sort things out."

Alex, feeling that Paul would not hear him even if he yelled at the top of his voice that he was still not ready, agreed to meet Paul in his favourite restaurant. Maybe face-to-face he could make the man listen.

A waiter escorted him to Paul's table, obviously chosen by Paul to give him command of the room. As he approached, Alex had to admit that his brother-in-law was a very charismatic man. And add to the charisma his good looks, his mannerisms, his clothes, the way he wore his hair, the diamond studded watch and other ostentatious evidence of his wealth... well, it was no wonder Paul had no difficulty attracting women. In fact he went through women like... Alex couldn't think of an appropriate analogy.

He had been engaged once, but it had lasted no more than a month. Alex remembered the fiancée with fondness. She had had the typical look Paul went for: long, long legs, gorgeous face, model figure, and she'd also been clever and funny, a really lovely lady. Sadly, she hadn't been able to compete with all the other long-legged, gorgeous creatures that occupied Paul's world. The whole family had been disappointed when she'd publicly thrown the huge sapphire ring at Paul and flounced off into the arms of an American political journalist who had swiftly married her and carried her off to a glamorous life in another country.

Paul was generous and could be great company, if somewhat self-centred most of the time. And that, he had once admitted without so much as a hint of an apology, was the problem as far as relationships were concerned: he simply couldn't see himself loving anyone more than he loved himself.

Paul stood up when he saw Alex, his hand outstretched. "Hi, Alex. I knew this day would come, but I can't tell you how happy I am you've seen sense. Or maybe I should say it your way: you've seen the light! And I must say, you are looking extremely well."

Alex sat down. "Paul, shut up!"

"What?"

"I haven't agreed to do a service. I simply told Charles that I would think about it."

"But-"

"No buts. You've gone and jumped the gun, and you're going to have to tell Eselmont that I'm not ready."

Paul heaved a sigh and shook his head in exasperation. "I suppose I should have known that you wouldn't easily come out of your self-inflicted prison. I thought that since telling you that Beth is starting to recover..."

"Have you told her that I'm doing a demonstration? If you have, Paul, so help me-"

"I haven't said anything. But she'll have to know sooner or later."

Furious, Alex started to stand up, but Paul grabbed his arm and asked him to sit down.

"Okay, okay. Let's not fall out. You're here now so let's enjoy a good meal. No family talk, no business talk, just mates having an evening out. Okay? Please?"

With a deep breath to calm his temper, Alex sat down again.

A gleam came into Paul's eye. "Don't look now, but we are getting the eye from a table of lovely ladies across the room. I reckon they're out on a hen night; we'd be lucky to come out alive. I'll send something over, though."

The waiter appeared with two large menus and the wine list, which Paul immediately took control of. Opening it, he said to the waiter, "While I look this over, would you please send a bottle of Cristal champagne to that table of lovely ladies over there, with my compliments?"

Alex glared at Paul, then hid himself behind the menu, which fortunately was the size of a broadsheet newspaper. Inside, though, the thick, gilt-edged pages were half the size. He winced at the prices and was glad he wasn't paying.

"God, Alex, don't bother reading that. I'll order for both of us."

Alex put the menu down and looked in the other direction as a bottle of chilled champagne was presented to the ladies in a silver ice bucket. He heard the pop of the cork, the giggles and shrill exclamations, but did not turn his head even when all the women raised their glasses and chorused their thanks to Paul.

Paul gave their order. The wine was immediately brought over, uncorked and poured for Paul to taste and approve.

A short while later they had to sit back as various piping hot plates and sizzling dishes were placed on their table, followed by little ceramic bowls of sauces in shades of red, orange and brown.

"My friend here will need a knife and fork, thank you."

Paul removed the narrow red ribbon from his lacquered chopsticks and started expertly picking things from the dishes and piling them onto his and Alex's plates. The cutlery, tied with ribbon like the chopsticks, appeared at his right hand, for which Alex was both embarrassed and grateful. But he looked at his plate with confusion. Liking simple things such as pizza and pasta, his cuisine of choice was Italian; he never ventured into any other kind of restaurant unless he had to.

"Don't ask what anything is, just eat. Trust me, it's all delicious."

Alex picked his way through the assortment of foods slowly, only half listening to Paul while thinking about Charles Hendry's offer and Eselmont's decision to go ahead with a series. It had been many months since he'd recorded the pilot programme, and he was grateful to Eselmont for their patience. He had loved the challenge of performing in a TV studio where he was much closer to the audience than in a church hall. He'd worried that the cameras might put him off, but they hadn't bothered him one bit.

The studio had advertised for people to participate as members of the audience and they'd been vastly oversubscribed, so they'd had to put all the requests into a very large box and randomly select who could come. He supposed they would do the same for the twelve recordings that would make the first series, and Alex hoped they would get the same terrific response.

That thought brought him up short. He was thinking *when* not *if.*

Because he wanted to do it. He really did.

All it would take was one word from Beth, if only she would agree to see him.

Paul, mindful of the cuff of his white monogrammed shirt as he dipped a large prawn into the red-coloured sauce, paused with the prawn halfway to his mouth. "Alex? Alex, you've disappeared somewhere. What's up?"

"Oh, sorry. Nothing. You were saying?"

Paul gave him a sharp look, but poured more wine into both their glasses and carried on talking about a famous, headline-making new client he'd signed up that day.

Chapter 34

Adele waved to Lily, got into her car and started the engine. She needed to go home to ensure everything was okay with her house and to check her mail, but the main reason was to see Rob. She'd asked him to visit her at Lily's, but he always had an excuse: "You'll be too busy looking after your sister to worry about me as well." "I don't want to intrude." "You have enough on your plate."

She knew he wasn't too good at empathy or sympathy, but she was pretty much the same, so she had accepted it as he had so many positive attributes. That's what she reminded herself of every time she sent a text and he didn't bother to respond. But the glaring shortcomings of their relationship could no longer be denied.

Maybe he'd met someone else and was stringing her along while he made up his mind which of them he wanted. Maybe he wanted to simply end their relationship but wanted her to be the one do it so he wouldn't be the bad guy. Maybe all he wanted from her was sex, with no strings attached – she in her own home, he in his, seeing each other but not committed to each other.

She pulled her phone out of her bag and started to tap out a message. Then she paused. If she sent this, he would either be there waiting, or would arrive soon after her, and they'd most likely be in her bedroom within minutes. Even thinking about his body moving over hers brought her out in a hot sweat of desire and need. But it would be sex, not lovemaking. He wouldn't ask her how she was, or how Lily was coping. They wouldn't have a conversation at all, because he'd have some excuse to leave soon afterwards.

She deleted the words and threw the phone onto the passenger seat. She'd contact him when she'd had a chance to be alone in her house for an hour or so.

The doormat was covered with letters and junk mail of various shapes and sizes. Adele scooped them up and put them on the coffee table in the living room, pausing to read a picture postcard from a friend who was on a safari holiday in Kenya. The picture was of a magnificent bull elephant, huge ears outstretched. How she'd love to leap on a plane and forget her troubles under the African sun.

"What troubles, Adele?" she muttered to herself. "If anyone has troubles, it's Lily."

The cottage was warm and airless, so she went round opening doors and windows until a cool breeze was flowing through. The red light on the answering machine in the study was not blinking. Not surprising. Anyone who mattered knew she was at her sister's, and, besides, she conducted nearly all her business and social life using her mobile phone.

She moved from room to room, checking everything was okay. She made a mug of coffee and drank it while she read her mail and made a couple of calls. Then she called Rob.

Even though she was expecting it, the slam of his car door twenty minutes later still startled her, and when within a few seconds more a key clicked into the lock of the front door, she felt a moment of dry panic.

Rob seemed to fill the tiny hall. "Hey! I hoped you'd be back today."

Adele stayed in the living room doorway, her arms loose at her sides, regarding the man who had been such a huge part of her life for more than two years. He looked stylish and appealing in his habitual weekend outfit of cream chinos, brown leather belt and shoes, light blue shirt, sleeves rolled above the elbows. His thick mouse-brown hair was artfully spiked, and, she noticed, he had new glasses. Very trendy.

"Adele? Aren't you pleased to see me?" It was said with a slight irritableness that was quickly covered by a smile and small shrug that she once would have found totally disarming. But then he glanced at his wristwatch, and she knew he was there for just one thing and, she had to finally admit it now, it had always been this way.

The photograph that graced the centre of Lily's mantelpiece came into her mind, of Lily and Scott on their wedding day. He was holding both her hands in his, and they were gazing at each other with such love. Of course, most wedding photos included this pose, it was practically standard, but the thing was, Adele had seen Scott and Lily look at each other just that way every time she had seen them together.

"Is there someone else, Rob?"

His immediate denial seemed genuine, so she chose not to pursue that avenue further.

"Do you love me?" she demanded.

He laughed, a touch nervously now. "What? Why are you asking me that?"

"Because if you do I'd like to hear you say it."

He reached out and tried to take Adele's hand, but she pulled it away.

"Come on, Adele. What's brought this on?"

She exhaled sharply. "Where do I begin? All the time we've been together you've always been a bit distant, as if you keep some part of yourself back from me. And lately you've been distracted as well. I haven't had a single message from you since I've been staying at Lily's. You haven't once asked how she is. Or how I am, come to that. You don't really share your life with me, Rob, you never have. All you really want is get into bed with me and then leave as soon as possible."

His eyebrows shot up and he laughed. "I don't know where this is all coming from, Adele. Of course I want to go to bed with you! And you've always seemed just as keen."

He was right about that.

Catching herself staring at his mouth and longing for him to kiss her, she folded her arms and asked herself where she thought she was going with this. Was she really ready to end it? She had believed herself happy with Rob, but since spending so much time with Lily and hearing about how things had been between her and Scott, she was no longer so sure that what she had with Rob was enough.

"Look, Adele, are you going to keep me standing here or-"

"Take you upstairs? You haven't answered my question. Do you love me?"

He stared at her.

"Do you ever see a time that we would move in together? Get married? Have children?"

"Well, I- God, Adele, do we have to do this now? I've got to be across town in a couple of hours."

Adele closed her eyes and blew out her breath. "Leave your key and go."

"What? Oh, okay. I see what this is about." He pulled his phone out of his pocket. "I'll call and tell them I'm not coming. It's not important, just something I arranged as I wasn't sure if I'd see you today."

"No, Rob. That's not good enough."

"Then what? What do you want me to do?"

"I want you to *want* to be with me! Not just as arm candy at some function or other, or your oh-so-willing partner in bed, but all the time. I want you to tell me you

211

love me without me having to ask. I want you to share your life with me. I'd like it if you asked if there's anything you can do to help Lily." She was crying now. "It's taken the death of my brother-in-law to realise what's missing in our relationship. Scott and Lily loved each deeply and they were best friends too. I doubt she will ever recover from losing him. I want that kind of love, Rob. And we don't have it. We never shall."

For a while it looked as if he might try to change her mind, but then his shoulders dropped and he nodded slowly.

"I had wanted to sit down and tell you this, Adele, but you've ruined any chance of me delivering my news the way I'd hoped to. I have been distracted, it's true. That's because I've been offered a job in New York. A brilliant job. I'd be mad not to take it."

She raised an eyebrow. "I see. Were you going to ask me to go with you?"

"I'd be back often, you could fly over…"

"Then that proves my point! I'm glad for you about the job, I really am. But long distance romances rarely work, and I'm not sure that what we have can even be called a romance. Let's just say goodbye, and wish each other well."

"All right." He held out her key. "Goodbye, Adele. I hope you find what you're looking for."

"You, too, Rob. You too."

She waited until she heard his car roar away up the road, then she flung herself onto the sofa and cried until her nose ran and her eyes stung as if filled with grit. But slowly it dawned on her that she wasn't crying for herself because Rob had gone from her life. She was crying for her sister, who had lost Scott so tragically, so horribly.

She must get back to Lily.

Chapter 35

After traipsing round the shops in town looking for new shoes to go with a dress she'd bought for an upcoming barbecue, Maisie was in need of hot coffee and a large slice of cake.

She went into her favourite café and was peeved to find it full; she'd have to go to the other one further up the street, not as nice, but-

"Maisie! Over here!"

She craned her head to see who was calling her, then spotted Charles Hendry waving at her. She hurried over with a happy smile.

"Charles! How nice to see you. Isn't it busy today?"

"It certainly is. Would you like to join me? I've only just arrived and was lucky to get this table. Tell me what you'd like and I'll go and place our order."

Delighted, Maisie took off her coat and sat down. She only knew Charles through the church, but he was always so friendly and approachable, so she looked forward to having a cosy chat with him for a half hour or so.

When he came back to the table they went through the usual conventions of asking about each other's families, then Charles said, "You've been a member of our church for a long time, haven't you?"

"Oh yes. Even before you came along, in fact. Were you at a different church before then?"

Charles nodded. "A big place, in London. But my wife and I wanted to move to Wiltshire to be near our daughter and the grandchildren, so I was delighted to find this one. It's a special place, I think."

Maisie nodded her head enthusiastically. "I've never seen you do it, but are you a medium, Charles?"

He laughed. "Unfortunately not. I wish I were! My wife is and my daughter is in a development circle, but neither of them has ever wanted to do platform work. It's a big responsibility. I really do admire those who can demonstrate to large crowds. In fact I'm hoping to have a really great medium come to us soon. Alex Kelburn. Have you ever heard of him?"

For a moment Maisie thought she must have misheard and asked Charles to repeat the name.

"I know an Alex Kelburn," she said slowly. "But I... well, he's never mentioned that he's a medium." She explained about the time she'd seen Alex at the church, and how he'd obviously known Linda Chase.

"Oh yes, they're very good friends. Alex started out in our church years ago, when he was very young. He's gone on to make quite a name for himself on the circuit, and he fills some very large venues these days. He's even making a TV series. But he's not worked for a little while because there was a tragedy... his baby... Anyway, I was told he's ready to return, and it would be quite a coup to get him."

Maisie's eyes widened. And then it came to her. The feeling she'd had when she'd first met Alex that she knew him from somewhere. It hadn't been at the church, she was sure of that, but she must have read about him somewhere. If he'd gone on to bigger and better things, as Charles said, there'd probably been leaflets at the church about his tours and she might have spotted his picture on one of them.

Charles talked about needing to get more chairs in for when Alex demonstrated there, because he was sure he would attract a lot more people than the usual congregation. Then he moved on to talk about other mediums, and it was all Maisie could do to concentrate and participate in the conversation.

Why hadn't Alex said anything when he found out Maisie was a regular member of the church? How could he see Lily's terrible suffering without saying *something* that might help her? And… oh my goodness! He was actually in the accident that had killed Scott! What did that mean for someone like Alex?

Her mind reeled with questions, and she felt so excited that she actually knew a psychic medium. But she was also dismayed that he had kept this part of himself secret.

"Well, Maisie, it was delightful to chat to you. I'll see you on Sunday?"

She forced her attention back to Charles and nodded, remembering just as Charles left the table to thank him for the coffee and slice of walnut cake he had insisted on treating her to.

When she was back out on the street a few minutes later she looked right and left wondering what to do. She hadn't yet found a suitable pair of shoes, but she didn't feel like looking any more. No. She needed to think. She needed to go home.

And then what? Would she tell Jack this startling news? Lily?

Or would she tackle Alex. Her earlier feelings were starting to turn to annoyance. She felt he'd been dishonest with her by withholding this information about himself. Oh yes, she could understand him wanting privacy in some respects, but because of his connection to Scott and Lily, surely he had a responsibility towards them?

By the time she had parked the car on the front drive her temper had risen to boiling point. Forcing it down, she made herself stroll into the house and greet Jack cheerfully. She explained that she hadn't found shoes and so might have to make a trip into Salisbury another day. She prepared a pot of tea and made small talk while they drank it. And all the time she was itching, just itching, to march over the road and confront Alex.

At 6 o'clock she said nonchalantly, "I'm just popping over to Lily's, pet. See how she is. I won't be long."

But it was Alex's door she pounded on, not Lily's. When he opened it with a smile of greeting, the way his expression swiftly changed at the dark expression on Maisie's face was almost comical.

She waded straight in. "Why did you keep it a secret, Alex? All this time, what with Scott's passing and his funeral. Why didn't you say something?"

It seemed to take an age for Alex comprehend what she was talking about. "I think you'd better come in. May I ask who told you? "

"Charles Hendry. I saw him in town earlier." Her hands were on her hips now. "I know it's true; there can't be two Alex Kelburns who are psychic mediums. I just want to know why you didn't tell me."

Alex looked rueful. "It's a long and complicated story. I didn't say anything because... well, it's a hard thing to explain to people you've only just met."

"I understand that. But when I saw you in the church, and you realised that I'm a believer in what you do, why not tell me then? And what about Scott? Alex, please, I have to know - can you communicate with him? Can you help Lily?"

His eyes shadowed with sorrow and he shook his head. "I wish I could say yes, Maisie, I really do. But since my wife left me I have not worked as a medium. I've... shut it down. I did so for reasons I don't want to go into, but believe me the decision wasn't taken lightly. If you like, I can recommend others for Lily to see-"

Maisie looked long and hard at Alex and her temper and frustration immediately drained away. His deep sorrow and pain were so obvious. Lily was grieving, but so was Alex.

She put her hand on his arm. "I'm sorry. I'm sorry for barging over here and-"

"Apologies not necessary, Maisie. I know how much you care about Lily. But I think it would be better if she didn't know about me. At least not yet."

As Alex opened his front door to let her out, Adele's car swept into Lily's driveway. Maisie apologised to Alex again and said goodbye, intending to go straight home. Instead she found herself pushing through Lily's gate and ringing the doorbell.

She wasn't going over to tell Lily about what she'd just learned, she really wasn't. She just wanted to be able to go home to Jack and not lie about where she'd been.

Chapter 36

Lily heard Adele's arrival and glanced at the clock.

"You're early; I wasn't expecting you till about 11."

"Didn't see much point in staying at home. There was nothing I needed to see to. What are you watching?"

"Some nature programme. I've not really been paying attention."

Lily found it impossible to concentrate; she only had the television on for sound to fill the silence when she was alone. She glanced at the screen and then back at her sister. Adele's eyes were puffy and her nose was red.

"Are you feeling all right?"

"Um. A bit of a cold coming on, I think. I'll be fine."

"I've got some cold remedies in the bathroom. Oh, who's that now?"

"I'll get it."

Adele came back with Maisie following behind.

"Hello, pet. I just popped in for a moment to see how you are."

Adele offered to make tea, but Maisie said she'd just had some with Jack. They chatted for a while, but Lily noticed that Maisie was fidgety and her eyes were bright, a sure sign that she had something on her mind. And Lily also knew that she wouldn't have to ask; Maisie would spill before she left.

But it seemed she was wrong about that, because Maisie got up, saying she needed to get back to Jack. She even made it as far as opening the front door. Then she quietly closed it and returned to the living room.

"What is it, Maisie? You seem a little upset."

Maisie plonked down on a chair and blurted, "Alex Kelburn is a medium."

Lily and Adele simply stared at her, until Adele said, "Alex who is a what?"

With a sigh, Maisie began to explain how she had come to learn this about their neighbour.

Lily said, "But he's an engineer, Maisie. He's got a workshop by the garage."

"Yes, but he's also a medium. And a fairly famous one by all accounts. He's making a television programme."

Frowning, Adele said, "You mean a psychic medium? Is that what you're talking about? That gorgeous guy next door talks to the dead?"

Maisie nodded and Lily explained to Adele that Maisie went to a Spiritualist church where mediums gave demonstrations every Sunday evening. Adele shuddered but smiled at Maisie as she said, "Doesn't appeal to me, but each to their own, I suppose."

A couple of hours later, after Maisie had left and Adele had gone to bed, Lily sat on her bed with her laptop and typed 'Alex Kelburn' into the search box. There were pages and pages about him, some relating to Kelburn Engineering, many more to his medium work. As she read page after page she was amazed how well known he seemed to be. She looked at the Tour Dates page on his own website and read that a national tour had been cancelled due to personal tragedy. Well, she knew all about that.

He'd filled some pretty big venues, and there were hundreds of messages of condolence and testimonials from people he'd helped.

She stared at the screen until her vision blurred. Mediums claimed to communicate with people who had died.

Alex was a medium.

Scott had died.

Could Alex communicate with Scott?

She leaned back in the chair and rubbed her gritty eyes. Why was she even thinking like this? There was no such thing as life after death.

Was there?

For a couple of moments she stared into space while her mind whirled with possibilities. Then she closed Alex's website and started to search for more general information about psychic mediums. It was staggering how much stuff there was on the subject, far more positive than negative, and Lily scrolled through information until her eyes burned with tiredness.

If she hadn't known Alex she would have carried on dismissing the very notion of being able to talk to the dead, to convey messages from them. But she did know him. She liked him. He seemed a genuine, caring person and he had helped thousands of bereaved people, according to what she'd just read.

Could so many people be wrong?

She closed the laptop, switched off the light and burrowed down into the bedclothes, but she couldn't sleep.

After tossing and turning for an hour, she sat up and stared into the gloom.

"Scott? Scott, are you there? If you are, if you can hear me, please, please give me a sign. Please, Scott."

***

Vincent left Lily as she settled back down under the bed covers and went to the room that had been his and Rose's bedroom, staring at the wall that divided this house from next door. On the other side of that wall, he now knew, was a psychic medium.

A medium who might be able to see him, hear him. Find Rose for him.

He concentrated on passing through the plaster and brick construction that divided the two properties. He could go from room to room in this house and get himself across the road just by thinking about it, surely he could do this?

He could.

Blinking in surprise and relief, Vincent gazed around the bedroom he found himself in. He'd been inside this house when he'd been alive, but never in any of the upstairs rooms. It gave him a jolt to see how like his and Rose's bedroom this was. It wasn't the size or the layout, he knew after all that the two houses had been mirror images of each other before the extension had been built next door, but the décor looked to have been untouched since the 1950's. Flower-patterned wallpaper covered all four walls, so similar to the one Rose had picked out in the hardware store and he had hung one wet weekend. A busily-patterned carpet, chosen because it wouldn't show wear and tear. Heavy velvet curtains like the ones Rose had sewn by hand. A dark old wardrobe that he felt sure would have a familiar smell of mothballs inside. A small fireplace with the original painted tiles in its surround.

Only the double bed seemed modern, its metal frame unlike anything he'd ever seen before.

And in that bed was Alex Kelburn.

Vincent stepped up close and looked down at the dark-haired man, but Alex was fast asleep. He stretched out his hand, but of course he could not touch him, could not shake him awake.

Frustrated, he knew he'd either have to wait until Alex woke up, or come back and try some other time.

Deciding to return to Lily, he slipped effortlessly back through the wall and on into her bedroom, pleased to see that she had fallen asleep.

Chapter 37

"Is that what you're wearing?"

Maisie looked down at herself then faced her husband. "As it is on my body, the only answer I can give is yes, this is what I'm wearing! What's wrong with it?"

"We're going to a barbecue, Maisie, and that's... Huh, I'm not sure what occasion that dress is meant for."

"Well I like it and I'm not changing."

Jack regarded her for a long moment, then burst out laughing as he took up his walking stick and offered Maisie his arm to escort her out of the house. "Are we calling round for Lily and Adele?"

"Yes, I said we would."

Maisie was so glad to hear him laugh. Ever since she'd told him about Alex being a medium and that she'd told Lily, even though she really hadn't meant to, he'd been so cross with her. He'd told her that she really needed to learn to mind her own business, because if Alex had particularly said he didn't want Lily to know, there was probably a good reason. Of course he was right and, feeling ashamed, she had gone over to see Alex the next day to confess what she'd done and apologise for her indiscretion. He'd looked so crestfallen, so disappointed, that she'd burst into tears, and when he'd tried so hard to tell her not to worry, she'd felt even worse.

But now it looked as if the storm was over and Jack had forgiven her, and she felt better again as they crossed the road at Jack's slow and unsteady pace with their old and familiar companionableness.

When Adele came to the door, she looked harassed as she greeted them and announced that Lily did not want to go. "I've tried to persuade her, I really have, so I don't know if you'll be able to convince her to go."

Maisie and Jack followed Adele into the living room, to find Lily slouched on the sofa leafing through a magazine. One look at her face and Maisie knew this wasn't going to be easy. And, really, it was perfectly understandable, but Lily needed to get out and about.

"Please come, Lily. They're all your friends, and they'll be so pleased to see you."

Lily barely looked up as she said, "I'll maybe come a bit later. You go on."

"No, pet. We'll not go without you."

Lily threw the magazine down and threw a hard look at Maisie. "That's blackmail. If I don't go then you'll all miss out."

Maisie nodded. "Exactly! So go brush your hair, put on a bit of lipstick and get your shoes on. And I promise, pet, I will personally bring you home if you can't cope with it."

Lily looked down at herself, and said, "I have to get changed."

Maisie was sad to see she was still wearing Scott's tracksuit, wondering if she'd ever washed it. "So go and do it, pet, we'll wait."

As Lily left the room, Maisie grinned and gave the thumbs up to Adele and Jack. She was looking forward to the party, always lively and fun – she might even be asked to sing - and she genuinely believed it would do Lily good to get out of Scott's clothes, out of her house, and talking to people.

She'd find it hard, of course she would, but the more she did it, the easier it would become.

"We must all keep an eye on her," she said quietly, so Lily wouldn't hear. "She'll be remembering how it was last year, when she had Scott by her side. There'll be tears, but if she can stay even an hour, it'll be a good thing."

Adele agreed and told Maisie not to worry if Lily needed to leave. "Getting her there at all will be a major achievement," she said. "If she can't handle it I'll bring her back myself so you and Jack can stay and enjoy the day."

Chapter 38

After a spate of unsettled weather, Alex was delighted that it was going to be a fine day for George and Helen's barbecue. Since his week away in Scotland with his mother and Frank, then getting his hands dirty working on Lily's kingfisher at the workshop, he was feeling better than he had in ages. The only blot was the knowledge that Maisie had told Jack, Lily, Adele and goodness knew who else in the neighbourhood about his work as a medium, and he was worried how they might react. It wasn't that he minded people knowing, that would be ridiculous, but he did like to tell people in his own way.

He put on jeans and a pale-blue polo shirt, grabbed the bottle of white wine and six cans of lager that had been chilling in the fridge, and left his house.

The clamour of music and voices from the party was already loud; the Jameson's driveway and the street were full of parked cars. Lily and Scott had told him the day he'd moved here how good the Jameson's parties were, and he was looking forward to it. Would Lily be there, he wondered? Would she challenge him the way Maisie had?

Letting himself in through the side gate, Alex weaved his way through the crowd to the kitchen, and found Helen there preparing salads. She kissed him on both cheeks and directed him and his bottle and cans outside. A long trestle table was bent in the middle under the weight of an assortment of drinks, glasses and large metal buckets filled with crushed ice. Alex kept back a can of lager for himself, and pushed the others and the wine into one of the buckets, firmly twisting them so they all slid well down into the ice.

The smell of burgers and onions filled the air, and though Alex could not see the barbecue through the crowd of guests, he could tell where it was from the plume of smoke rising into the air.

He knew a couple of the party guests who lived in the street, and said his hellos and stopped for a quick chat. Then he spotted Jack in an armchair on the hexagonal area of decking at the bottom of the Jameson's long garden, beneath a green and white striped awning.

Alex strolled over and shook Jack's weakly proffered hand, holding it firmly, wishing as he always did when he saw Jack, that he was a healer, like Linda.

"Nice armchair, Jack. I notice you're the only one to have such luxury." He indicated the assortment of garden and kitchen chairs dotted about.

"I know," said Jack. "Privilege of my condition. George and Ray carried it out here just for me, wasn't that kind?"

"So where's Maisie?"

"She's about somewhere. Difficult to miss her, she's wearing the most monstrous dress you've ever seen. Oh-oh! She's behind you. I suggest you take a deep breath and turn round very slowly."

Alex laughed as he looked over his shoulder. "Hello, Maisie. My, you are dazzling today!"

"Has my husband been making horrible remarks about my dress?"

It was a bright green kaftan with knee-high slits up both sides. He couldn't make out the pattern at first, but Maisie opened her arms to let the wide sleeves fall free, and Alex found himself looking at a turquoise peacock in full display. Its beady black eyes seemed to stare straight at him. He was glad when Maisie dropped her arms again, and the peacock's body disappeared amongst copious folds of blue and green fabric.

She asked, "Have you seen Lily? Her sister is here, too – you've met Adele, haven't you? Lovely young woman; Jack's quite smitten with her. She's been no end of help at the shop. Her mother, too. I never thought I'd say it, but Irene's actually very nice when you get through the rather tough exterior. And the snobbery. And the bossiness. It's no wonder Lily's dad works such long hours and is always travelling somewhere. If you ask me-"

Jack stopped her with an exasperated "Maisie!"

"Sorry. Just saying. But really, Alex, Lily looks like the walking dead." Realising what she'd said, Maisie blushed a little and rushed in with, "I'll go and get some food."

Alex gestured to the beer on the table beside Jack. "Are you ready for another?"

Jack picked up his pint glass and drained the last drops before handing it to Alex. "They have a barrel of real ale, absolutely splendid. You'll find it on the end of the drinks table, right hand side."

"Sounds good. I'll try some myself."

Alex left Jack and joined the crowd again. Taller than most people who were standing about on the lawn, he looked over their heads trying to find Lily. Their infrequent meetings had always been a little awkward, but now she knew about his work as a medium, he thought he'd better be ready for whatever she had to say to him.

He finally spotted her, standing with Adele in front of the open French doors, talking to two women Alex didn't know. Maisie was right; she looked terrible. Drab in baggy dark clothes and utterly drained of vitality.

He located the beer barrel and filled Jack's glass and another for himself, mindful of not filling Jack's to the brim so Jack wouldn't spill it. He carried the beers back and sat down beside him, on a folding chair that thankfully turned out to be much more comfortable than it looked.

"Cheers, Alex, and thank you."

"Cheers."

They drank and Alex appreciatively studied the beer in his glass. "Not bad! Any idea what it is?"

Jack said he didn't. "But knowing George, it's something special and very, very strong, so I wouldn't drink too much of it if I were you."

Alex laughed, "I won't. I think a pint or two of this fine stuff will be more than enough."

"Alex, can we get something out of the way before Maisie comes back? She really is sorry that she blabbed to Lily, but I'm sure you've realised by now that she really is incapable of keeping anything to herself."

"It's okay, Jack. In one way it's better that it's out in the open, but it can make things awkward for me, as I'm sure you can imagine."

Jack gave a wry smile. "Yes, I can see that. And I need to tell you, Alex, that I like you, but I don't believe in what you do. Never have and never will. So now *that's* out in the open, let's just enjoy the day, eh?"

Maisie reappeared with two plates piled high with all kinds of food and cutlery wrapped in red paper napkins.

"Here you are. Burger, sausages, jacket potato, vegetable kebabs and a little salad on each. I couldn't carry three plates, so you have these and I'll just go back and get another plate. Alex, would you be a dear and find me a chair please?"

Alex stood. "Have this one, Maisie. Sit down and eat. I'll go and get something for myself. Oh, I can see Lily on her own, so I'll go and say hello to her first."

Alex turned to walk away from Maisie and Jack and almost collided with Adele, who just about managed not to spill any of her wine down Alex's shirt. Jack's face lit up when he saw her.

"Adele! I thought we'd lost you!"

Maisie smiled up at her. "Is Lily all right, pet?"

"She seems to be holding up. I left her chatting, and she said she'd follow me over here in a minute. How are you, Alex?"

Alex didn't miss the look of curiosity in Adele's eyes. Before he could reply, though, a commotion made them all look towards the house. People were running towards the terrace, and Maisie, Jack and Adele turned to each other and said with alarm the exact same word at the exact same time: "Lily!"

Chapter 39

It was late by the time Alex got home. He'd had a busy week since the eventful barbecue, and today he'd had to wrestle with a problematic job at the workshop that had a tight deadline. He'd only just had enough time to dash home to shower and change before driving into Salisbury to have dinner with friends. He was bone tired and knew he'd fall asleep the minute his head touched the pillow.

He didn't know she was there until she stepped out of the shadows and spoke his name.

"Lily! You... you gave me a bit of a fright there."

"I'm sorry. I thought you'd seen me. Can I talk to you, please?"

His tiredness swiftly dissipated at the sight of Lily's haunted face, a purple and yellow bruise still visible above her brow where she'd fallen at the Jameson's party. "Of course you can. Come on in."

He opened the door and switched on the hall light, standing back so she could enter the house ahead of him.

"What can I offer you? Would you like coffee, tea? I've got some herbal ones."

"Whatever you're making. Thank you."

"Go on into the living room and make yourself comfortable."

But she followed him and sat down at the rickety kitchen table. "This still reminds me of how my gran's kitchen looked when I was little," she said, as her eyes roved around the shabby room. "I often had a cup of tea with Mrs. Harrington in here. You've hardly changed anything, have you?"

"No, I haven't. The landlord is going to renovate it when I leave, but in the meantime I really don't mind the state it's in, and I have everything I need."

She put out her hand in an apologetic gesture. "Oh, heavens, please don't think I was criticising. Look, Alex... I know we haven't spoken all that much lately, and I have to admit that I've actually been avoiding you since Maisie told me what you do, but-"

"It's okay. I understand. But, Lily, how are you? You gave us all such a fright at the barbecue."

"I fainted, that's all. It was hot."

Her tone made it clear this was not open for discussion.

"Here you are. This is camomile tea; no caffeine and it'll help you to relax."

He asked where Adele was and Lily explained that she had had a day of meetings and was being taken out by some friends and would stay overnight in her own house. "She needs to go back fairly often for business reasons, and to check on her house. She'll be back here tomorrow."

"And you're okay on your own?"

"Um, yes, I'm okay. It's hard, of course, because I miss Scott so much, but I don't want Adele feeling guilty when she has to be away. I don't sleep well. I hardly sleep at all, to be honest, and her being there or not makes no difference to that. Look, Alex, I've been thinking about you a lot. I looked at your website, and a lot of others, and now I'm struggling with what to believe. I heard your car and I... Well, I just had to talk to you. I'm sorry it's so late."

"It's not a problem, Lily. Really. I don't sleep well either, so we can keep each other company." It was a white lie to make her feel more at ease, because he actually slept like the proverbial log, although he didn't know why. Sometimes he wished he didn't, because his dreams were

231

often quite disturbing. The setting differed in each of them, but the one constant was Grace, standing incredibly tall, her beautiful face impassive as she mouthed words at him that he could not hear.

"Now, let's go to the other room, where it's more comfortable, and I'll try and answer your questions."

For a moment, Lily simply wrapped her hands around the mug, and stared down at the table. He heard her take a shaky breath, as if she was coming to a decision, and she stood up, ready to follow him.

Once they were settled, he prepared himself to concentrate so he could at least try to give her the information she needed, because he must not be tempted into opening up his psychic senses. It was hard to keep on resisting, but he would not, *would not* compromise his promise to Beth.

"Alex, I hardly know where to begin. I've read about it, like I said, but I don't really know or understand what it is you do. All I know is what I've seen in films. People holding hands in darkened rooms and dotty old ladies with huge hoop earrings and crystal balls going into trances and speaking in strange voices." She gave a wan smile, "Oh, and the one with that little boy who sees dead people. Is that what it's like for you?"

Alex took a moment to work out how best to answer her, because he really didn't want her thinking he was some kind of crackpot. He had a chance here to help her, and he wanted to gently guide her towards what he knew to be the truth.

"In many ways, that is exactly what it's like for me. I can see and hear people who have passed over – which is, by the way, how I generally describe them. A euphemism, I know, but it's a more gentle way of saying it. Sounds more respectful, somehow." He gave a wry grin. "Obviously, I am not a dotty old lady, nor do I need to go into a trance in a darkened room. I do not have a crystal ball. And as far as I am aware, I have never spoken in a voice other than my own."

"But you say that you actually *see* them? The way I see you?"

"I do, yes, but… how can I describe it? They appear as if surrounded by a very pale mist. I usually see the mist first, and I know someone is coming through to communicate with me. I can see their features, clothes, colour of hair and eyes, but all ever so slightly… washed out, if you can picture what I mean by that. But it's not the same for all mediums, Lily, I'm only describing how it is for me. But I told Maisie, and I hope she told you, that I'm not able to it at the moment."

He watched her face as Lily mulled this over. He was pretty sure that she liked him. She surely knew that he was a genuine person, the sort you could trust and confide in. But maybe she was feeling that this conversation was already surreal, and it had only just begun.

"She did tell me. But you don't mind talking about it, do you?"

Alex replied he didn't mind at all, and she could ask whatever she wanted.

"So… hell, Alex. I thought I had it all worked out in my mind, but now I'm here, I have absolutely no idea how to talk to you about this."

She looked so confused, but Alex wanted her to find her way through it in her own time.

"Sorry. I should have written all my questions down. Okay. First, were you always able to do this?"

"Oh yes. Although I didn't realise exactly *what* it was I was doing until I was older. When I was very little it seemed absolutely normal to me and I thought everyone did it. I merrily told everyone that granddad or Auntie Norma, or whoever, was in the room, and was puzzled that no-one else could see them. My mum knew it was for real because I was able to tell her things I couldn't possibly have known, but I can't tell you how many times she passed it off as an overactive imagination."

"So your mother didn't like it?"

He sighed. "Yes, exactly. It made her uneasy – it still does a little, though she's much more accepting about it these days – but back then she chose to ignore it, hoping it would go away. When it became apparent to me that all of the grown-ups in my life and the other kids at school either didn't understand it or approve of it, or were downright afraid of it, I stopped saying anything. It was only when my father died when I was nine that I fully understood what it was all about."

Lily commented that nine was a young age to lose a father. She told Alex with a small smile that hers was quite a remote figure in her life because of his work, but she adored him, and knew he was always there for her.

"But I didn't lose my father! Look, would you like to know the story? I've been scribbling things for an autobiography that may or not come off, and I'd be happy to give you a copy of this particular chapter. It might help you to understand better." He looked at her drawn face. "I'll pop it through your door tomorrow, and when you've read it we can talk again. How about that?"

"You're being very kind." Lily glanced at her watch and apologised for keeping Alex up so long.

"Don't worry about that," said Alex. "You can stay and talk as long as you like."

"No, it's okay. I've kept you up far too long already, and I'm working in the shop tomorrow so I ought to try and get some rest. You've helped a lot tonight, Alex, and I'm so grateful."

Tears sparkled on her lashes as he said goodbye to her and watched her walk up his path and through the gate. He didn't shut his door until he heard Lily's door open and close, then he leant against it and wondered if he really had helped her. What she wanted, what anyone wanted, was evidence, incontrovertible proof, and he was unable to give her that. Not yet, anyway. Maybe he could talk her into seeing someone else though; Linda, maybe, she'd be more than glad to help.

Upstairs, he fired up his laptop and opened the document that contained the rough draft of his autobiography. Having found the chapter he wanted, he set it to print, and stared at the pages coming out without seeing them.

Should he have described to Lily how he had witnessed Scott's gentle passing? Tell her about the garden and the bridge and the flight of the kingfisher, seen in glorious iridescent blue and copper as it darted into the water and rose in a shower of crystal drops? About Grace? Would it help her to know these details?

Should he tell her how he had begged to be allowed to stay and for Scott to be sent back?

Should he, oh God, should he allow his psychic senses to open up so he could maybe, just maybe, see Scott? Oh, how he longed to talk to his father and to see Amber playing at his feet.

He thought again of the strange dreams that were occurring nearly every night now, always with the same theme: Grace, or his dad, on their own, together, or with crowds of others around them, all talking at him, but he couldn't hear or make out what they were saying. Grace's expression was always impassive; his dad's sorrowful.

But what was he supposed to do? He had made a commitment to Beth, yet all this time had passed and Beth had not once asked to see him. So would she ever? And thinking of her in that expensive clinic still rankled with him a bit. Paul had arranged it and insisted he would pay for it. "I know you want to take responsibility for her treatment, and I understand that," Paul had said to him, "But – and please don't be offended, Alex, but the bottom line is I can easily afford it whereas you have to admit that you'd be hard pressed to pay the bills. She's my sister, you're my best friend, so let me do this for both of you."

At the time Alex had still been suffering from his injuries and had been too weary to argue, even though he didn't like his brother-in-law funding Beth's treatment. But no way could he afford to pay for such a place, so he had to accept and be glad that she was getting the best possible care.

Forcing these thoughts away, he picked up the still warm pages from the printer and tapped them on the desk to make a neat pile, hoping he had an envelope to put them in.

Chapter 40

Lily walked quickly to The Lilac Tree. Maisie had needed the day off, Adele had to meet a client and her mother had a dental appointment, so she had either to bite the bullet and go in, or risk losing a day's business. This would be the first time in weeks that she had been there alone, and she was both looking forward to it and anxious in case she had a panic attack.

But her long talk with Alex into the early hours, drinking his herbal tea and learning first hand about mediumship, had definitely helped. She hadn't managed to ask whether she could learn to do it, but that would keep for now and, hopefully, the promised chapter would be there for her to read when she got home.

The sky was darkening by the minute and she worried that a cloudburst was imminent, would maybe catch her before she reached the shop. But she still wanted to walk. For weeks after the accident well-wishers had laid flowers at the accident site, and she had liked to look at them, to see who had been kind enough to leave them there in memory of Scott. They were gone now, but she never passed the spot without pausing awhile in silent contemplation.

Today, though, she had something to say.

When she reached the place, she took a deep breath and stood facing the hedge that still showed evidence of where the van had crashed through it before coming to rest in the garden on the other side. Alex had said he wasn't doing psychic stuff any more, but she felt sure that if Scott wanted to communicate, he'd find a way to make Alex hear him.

All she had to do was make Scott hear her.

Glancing around to make sure no-one was approaching, she licked her lips and said, "Scott. If you can hear me, please go to Alex. Please, Scott. Go to him and we could talk through him. I need you to do this. *Please*. Give me a sign that you can hear me."

She waited, half hoping for a thunderclap or a flash of lightning.

But there was nothing so dramatic, just the first large drops beginning to fall, dotting the pavement round her feet with circles like fast spreading grey freckles.

She hurried on to the shop, and by the time she'd switched the alarm off and the lights on, it was pouring and the road and pavements were soon slick with rain. It pounded against the windows, and car tyres made shushing sounds as they drove past. In the back room, she hung up her wet coat and switched on the kettle for a mug of tea. Holding it in her hands to bring warmth back into her fingers, she went slowly round her beloved shop, inhaling the gorgeous scents, ensuring that everything was as it should be.

But of course it was. Maisie would always make sure of it, keeping everything dusted and neatly aligned, that all the stock was clearly and correctly priced. And Maisie had assured Lily that her mother was a terrific help, with a good eye for display. She had made the window display her own personal project, and Lily had immediately noticed how stylish it looked when she'd arrived.

At some point, she knew, she would have to go around the other shops to see and thank those who were helping to keep things running. Thelma, Samantha, Max and Ellie were all sending someone over to cover lunch periods if Maisie, Adele or her mother were alone, so they could have a break. Maisie especially needed to be able to get home to see to Jack for at least an hour. Today, she saw from the rota pinned above the kettle, Samantha's assistant was due to come over at 1 o'clock. She'd use the hour to go through some paperwork.

She stowed her handbag under the counter and switched on the till, the card machine, and the laptop computer.

There were no people out on the High Street, and she accepted that it was unlikely she'd see any customers unless the rain stopped.

Maisie had made a note in the pad they kept for the purpose that they needed to order more of the luxury stationery they stocked. Lily decided she might as well do that, and quickly sent an order off by email. She wrote beneath Maisie's note that she had done so, so she wouldn't double order when she came in.

Next she chose a birthday card for her aunt, wrote a simple message inside, addressed the envelope and put a stamp on it. The post box was almost opposite the Lilac Tree, in between the bakery and the hairdressing salon; she'd pop over and send the card on its way when she left to go home.

There wasn't anything else Lily could usefully do, so she sat at the counter, allowing herself a little time to think.

Her long conversation with Alex last night had made something shift inside her mind. She'd already felt her beliefs change since reading the internet sites, and when she'd returned home in the early hours of the morning, she'd dared to *really* believe that Scott was out there, somewhere. Out of sight and sound for her, sure, but there. She went over a particular thing that Alex had said about his dad and Amber. Again and again his words rang in her mind: 'When my time comes, she and my dad will be there, waiting to greet me'.

And he'd said that Scott would be waiting for her, and she found that wonderful.

So wonderful, in fact, she couldn't let it go and return to her old way of thinking. Her old way had meant that there was nothing at all of Scott now but his scattered ashes and people's memories of him, and the material things he'd owned, like his clothes and tools.

Not long after Scott's death, Lily had contemplated suicide – had even started stockpiling pills in a shoebox - just to end the pain, believing that death was the end, the absolute end. Time and again during the sleepless nights, even as recently as last week, she'd retrieved the box from its hiding place beneath the folds of her only long evening dress and rifled through the contents: packets of paracetamol and aspirin, cold and flu remedies, and sleeping pills that had been prescribed by the doctor in the early days of her bereavement. He'd told her to use them sparingly and only if she really needed them. Take care, he'd said. Remember the baby, he'd said. And it was always the thought of the baby that had made her put the lid back on the box and return it to the wardrobe.

Now, thanks to Alex, she was imagining happy scenarios as she lay awake at night, where Scott came through to Alex, or, better still, where Alex taught her how to communicate directly with Scott. She may never have done it before, but she felt sure that, if nothing else could, desire and sheer determination would enable her to learn. Then it would feel as if they were a family again.

But she would keep this to herself, and not even tell Adele or Maisie about her conversation with Alex. Nor did she plan to ask Maisie to take her to the Spiritualist church. This plan of hers was to be strictly between herself and Alex. And, of course, Scott.

Thinking all this out made her feel so much better, and she felt inclined to start cooking again (which would please Adele, who hated it), to smile more, talk more, to enjoy watching television with Adele and discussing what they watched. Maybe she'd even manage to laugh at Adele's favourite sitcoms.

This chance of working in The Lilac Tree had come at just the right time, too, because it proved to her just how ready she was to pick up the pieces of her life.

And soon, yes soon, there would be the baby. She stroked her stomach and whispered to her baby to hurry up and be born.

When she got back home at 6 o'clock she was delighted to see an envelope on the doormat from Alex. Keen to read it straightaway, she nevertheless took it upstairs and laid it, unopened, on her bed for later. She did not want Adele to see it and start asking questions.

As she came downstairs, Adele was just coming in.

"Hi. How did the meeting go?"

"Great," Adele answered. "I've secured the business of a woman who's starting up a rather glam new jewellery company. How did it go for you at the shop?"

Lily answered that it had been a quiet day, but she had enjoyed herself.

"I'm going to change out of this suit and high-heels," said Adele. "Then I'll get dinner started and you can tell me how it went at the shop."

Lily said that she'd make the meal and it pleased her to see how delighted – and relieved - Adele looked. Her sister had done her best, but there was no doubt in either of their minds that Lily was the better cook. By far!

All through dinner she made a real effort to chat, and later, after watching television through to the end of the evening news and drinking a last cup of tea, she was at last alone in her room, with Alex's pages in her hands.

She settled back against the pillows to read, one hand supporting the comforting weight of the baby.

Chapter 41

Extract from A Different Kind of Life, by Alex Kelburn

My father passed away when I was nine years old. He was only thirty-seven and had been seriously ill for quite a while, so it was expected. It still came as a dreadful shock, of course, but in a way it's easier to deal with someone's passing when we know it's coming. It's still devastating, don't get me wrong, but sudden passings, like accidents or fatal heart attacks, are utterly devastating because we've had no time to prepare and say our goodbyes.

I can hardly remember when my father had been able to play rough and tumble games with me, but we did spend many happy hours playing cards and board games like draughts or monopoly until he was too weak to be able to sit up. I loved keeping him company in his room, and if he were too tired to play games, I'd cuddle up to him and we'd make up silly stories until he drifted into sleep. When he was too ill even for a cuddle, I sat on a chair next to the bed and chattered away, telling him about school, how much I hated homework, things like that.

The day he died was a day of blizzards in Scotland. I woke up in my freezing bedroom just as it was beginning to get light. My breath actually made little vapour clouds in front of my face, and I dreaded leaving the warmth of my cosy, heavy blankets when it was time to get up.

I was about to snuggle down again, when I became aware of a faint glow forming at the bottom of my bed. Then my dad was there, surrounded by a sparkly mist. I remember wondering how he'd managed to get up from his own bed and come to my room.

Then he spoke, and I remember the exact words he said, and the joy on his face as he told me: *I'm free, Alex. It's wonderful.*

I sat up, immediately forgetting about the intense cold, and asked questions in the typical curious way of a nine-year-old, and my father patiently explained what dying had been like for him. *There's no pain, Alex. I didn't suffer at all. Remember that in the days ahead, because they will be very hard on your mother and she will need you to be strong.*

I asked if we'd still be able to play draughts and snakes and ladders, and dad laughed and said he didn't think so, but we'd certainly be able to chat from time to time. We talked for ages, and then he stopped in mid-sentence and I felt the atmosphere in the room suddenly change. The air became sticky and charged, as if everything had become static. The temperature increased dramatically causing sweat to break out on my skin and the ice on the windows melted, running in thin, drizzly strands down the glass to pool on the sill.

Dad looked over his shoulder, and I could see that the misty cloud was getting bigger. From that mist emerged five or six people, a little hazy, but clear enough that I could see their features clearly. One of them was my granddad and he smiled at me.

When dad turned his face back to me, he was smiling the most glorious smile and his eyes were luminous with joy. He touched his fingers to his lips in a kiss, and he was gone in an instant, but I could still hear his voice, faint and fading to nothing, promising to return as soon as he could.

After he disappeared, the temperature of my room rapidly returned to freezing and I quickly snuggled back down into my bed. I wasn't at all sad or afraid; to me, as I'd seen people who had passed over all my life, this seemed perfectly normal, and I was happy that my dad was happy.

For me, he wasn't entirely gone. His physical body no longer had his life force within it, but I would still see him in spirit, I would still talk to him and I knew he would be watching over me as I grew up. I knew he would be there when my time came to cross over into that other place; he would be there to guide me, just as those people had come to show him the way.

The door opened a few minutes later and my mother looked in. Seeing that I was awake, she came in, and she was crying. Great gulping sobs and hiccups that utterly bewildered me. Her whole body shook, and she made me shake too as she gathered me up, still wrapped in the blankets, and rocked

244

me in her arms. That was the first time I cried myself, not for my dad so much, but because I was totally overwhelmed and confused by her grief.

She held me so tightly I could barely breathe. I wondered how and when I would be able to make her understand that dad hadn't really left us. She'd never wanted to accept that I could see and communicate with people in the afterlife, so I couldn't believe it would be any different now.

Chapter 42

Maisie was working the morning shift, and seeing the delivery van pull up, held open the door so the driver could carry in whatever he had for The Lilac Tree. Most likely it was the order Lily had placed, she'd seen the note in the book. It was just wonderful that Lily had managed a whole day in the shop, and Maisie felt sure she'd be happy to do more if she weren't so close to her time.

The driver opened the rear doors of his van and called out a cheery hello when he saw Maisie waiting. "Got lots of boxes for you, love. Where do you want them?"

"Lots, did you say? Are you sure they're for this shop? We're only expecting a small order."

He handed her the delivery sheet. "Says right here, love."

She scanned it and said, "I'm afraid there's been a mistake. We never order in this quantity. Is it possible for you to take them back while I sort it out?"

"Sorry, love. We're just a delivery service." He glanced at his watch. "And I've got a lot to do today, so…"

"Yes, of course. Sorry." She thought quickly. There was no point in putting them in the storeroom, as they'd only have to be carried back out again to be taken away. "Could you put them in front of the counter please?"

When she'd signed for the delivery and the driver, whistling some unidentifiable tune, had left the shop, she frowned at the order details. They had been sent ten times the amount they usually ordered; it had to be a mistake on the supplier's part.

She looked up the number and dialled, but as she listened to the ringing tone, a thought came into her mind.

The few times Lily had worked in the shop a couple of months ago, before the panic attacks had kept her at home, she had been vague and forgetful, so could it be that she had made a mistake?

Maisie thought back over what had been a fraught time one way or another. It wasn't long after Scott's funeral, and she and everyone else had advised Lily not to work. But she had insisted, and very soon had given a customer the wrong change, and lost her temper when the customer had said, very politely, that he'd given her a twenty pound note, not a ten. Maisie had had to intervene and sort it out. She'd known there were only three twenty-pound notes when she'd last served someone, and now there were four. The man had quickly been given the correct change, and Lily had mumbled an embarrassed apology. When another customer had come in just minutes before closing time and been unable to make up her mind about which of the large selection of scented candles she wanted to buy, Lily had been very impatient with her and lost the sale.

The following day, Lily had dropped a large ceramic plate worth £125 and had sworn so loudly and so crudely, that an elderly woman who had come in for gift-wrap and ribbon had left in an affronted hurry.

Maybe Lily coming in had been too stressful for her after all, even though she'd said she had enjoyed it.

She checked the book. Yes, there was her note, and Lily had ticked it as done. She searched for and found the order Lily had emailed, and saw that she had added an extra zero to the usual quantity.

Maisie picked up the phone and dialled the supplier again, sure they would be sympathetic and allow her to rectify the order.

The number was busy; she'd have to try again.

She wondered whether she should tell Lily about her mistake, or just sort it out and pretend it never happened.

Only one customer came in during the morning, and Maisie realised it had been a mistake to pile the boxes in front of the counter as it made things awkward. Maybe she'd better carry them out the back, because it could be a couple of days before someone collected them.

But the shop door opened again before she could decide what to do and in walked Lily's mother, come to relieve Maisie and do the afternoon hours.

Maisie smiled at her. "Hello, Irene. How are you?"

"I'm very well, Maisie. And you?"

Maisie answered she was fine too, and that the morning had been rather quiet and might stay that way.

"I see we have stock to put out. If you tell me the prices, I can do that this afternoon."

"Um, no. It's a mistake, actually. I have to send it back."

Before she could react, Irene had spotted the delivery sheet and picked it up. "100 sets of boxed stationery? That's rather excessive isn't it? Surely the supplier would have known a small shop like this wouldn't want such a quantity. Look, Maisie, you get off home to your husband, and I'll deal with this."

Maisie speedily ran the scenario through her mind. Irene calling the supplier and haranguing them in her inimitable way for making a mistake. The supplier insisting, quite rightly, that they were fulfilling the order that the owner of The Lilac Tree had sent.

She was forced to tell Irene what had happened.

She had expected any reaction other than the one she got: Irene started to cry.

"Oh, my goodness!" Maisie bustled her out of the shop and into the back room. "Here's a tissue. It's clean."

For once, words failed Maisie. She'd come to quite like Lily's mother because she had put aside her prejudices about Lily's business and stepped in to help, proving herself very capable and useful. But the woman was opinionated and hard as nails. Or so Maisie had thought.

The crying lessened and stopped. Irene blew her nose and apologised.

"No need to apologise. Would you like a cup of tea? I don't have to rush off, Jack's not alone at home."

Irene regarded her through teary eyes, as if weighing up her response. Then her shoulders slumped and she agreed tea would go down a treat.

Having wished for more customers all morning, Maisie now fervently hoped that no-one would come in. It was obvious to her that Irene needed to talk, and maybe their enforced intimacy would encourage it.

"Maisie, do you think Lily is coping? I mean, I know the poor girl is grieving and will do so for a long time yet, but there's something so... so fragile and brittle about her. I can't get through to her at all."

"Well, have you ever?" Maisie ignored the shocked and indignant expression on the other woman's face. "I've known Lily a long time, so I know that you and she have never really gotten along. You didn't approve of her lifestyle when she was a teenager, or of her choice of husband, or of her having this shop. You wanted her to be like Adele, university educated and high-flying in the business world. But Lily has done well for herself on her own terms, and Scott was a wonderful husband."

"You don't pull your punches, do you?"

"Never saw the point in holding back. If you've got something to say, you should say it. But am I wrong?"

Irene's jaw worked, and Maisie braced herself for a furious outburst. Maybe she had overstepped the mark, but someone had to tell the woman how it was.

But when Irene spoke, it was measured and quiet. "You are right. Yes, you are. From the day Lily was born it seemed we were at loggerheads. She was not an easy child and seemed to resist all my attempts to..." She shook her head and drew in a shaky breath. "Her sister was so different. Sunshine to Lily's storms. The gap between Lily and me grew and grew until we could barely be in the same room together, and when she left home so young and then she married Scott... well, I thought she was throwing herself away. It took Scott's death to make me see how wrong I was, and I deeply regret how I treated him. I never thought he was good enough for our family, and I've been trying to find ways to make up for it. But I can't, of course. I don't know if my daughter will ever forgive me."

The bell jangled and Maisie almost swore out loud. "I'll go," she said. "You finish your tea and I'll be right back."

Chapter 43

The kingfisher sculpture was finished. Alex stood back to have a good look at it and decided it was the best thing he had ever made. He wiped his hands on a rag, wondering how he was going to present it to Lily. He supposed he could simply tell her about it, and then let her see it and ask her if she wanted him to install it in her garden. Or maybe it would be better to arrange with Adele to install it while Lily was out, so it was in place when she got back. Either way, she would wonder why he had made it, so it could present the chance for him to tell her about Scott's passing.

All the time he'd been working on it, from the first tentative design to the intricate placing of the last pieces of copper on the breast of the bird and its outspread wings, Alex had not been able to stop thinking about Scott, wondering what he was doing, how he was adapting to his changed existence. It had been so tempting to open his mind and see if Scott would come through, so bloody tempting to open his mind so he could see his dad and little Amber.

If only Beth would ask to see him, talk to him, so he could see if there was any hope of reconciliation.

It was 6.30. The staff had said their goodbyes and left the workshop, and now it was time for him to be on his way too, as he'd arranged to see Lily that evening. He tidied up the workbench and then made a quick tour to see what other work was in progress. His order books were full, thanks in no small part to his dynamic manager, and he had a small but excellent team who loved working at Kelburn Engineering.

A spiral staircase of gleaming steel leant against the far wall. A garden gate, quite small and plain and only half finished lay on the workbench opposite. On the floor next to that was some kind of tank, with welding gear piled around it. Every surface was covered with work in progress. Taller items were propped against the walls. Finished items waited in the small warehouse for shipment.

He went back and studied every inch of the kingfisher once more, thinking it would be quite hard to let such an exquisite thing go, then he locked up and drove the short distance home to change and get ready for when Lily came round.

The phone rang as he was drying himself after a shower, and he had to dash to answer it.

"Hey, Paul. How are you?"

"Okay, okay." He sounded out of breath. "Look, mate, I just wanted you to know that Beth is out of the clinic. She's home with mum and dad."

Alex sat down on his bed, taking a while to process this news.

"How is she, Paul?"

"Better than she was, but not by much. I had a long talk with her last night, and there's something... I don't know how to describe it, but... it's as if there's a part of her missing. Amber, of course, is part of it, but I think it's you, Alex; she's not complete without you." There was a long pause. "Do you want a piece of advice?"

Alex didn't reply. Paul would say his piece whether invited to or not.

"Go and see her. Make her talk to you. Use those bloody psychic senses of yours to get right inside her mind, like I know you can. Can you go tomorrow? Damn it, whatever your plans cancel them. I'll prime mum that you're coming."

"Paul, I-"

"If you don't do this, I will personally come round there and thump the living daylights out of you."

Alex had to laugh. Paul was just not the type for fisticuffs. He had time to agree that he'd be at the house at 11.30 in the morning, and had to ring off because Lily had arrived.

She had his typewritten pages in her hand.

"It's so beautiful, what you say," whispered Lily. "I... Alex, is it really true?"

He nodded. "Every word, Lily. When people die, their spirit, their soul, their life force – whatever you want to call it – simply leaves the physical body, and they go on in a different form of existence. Some of us can communicate with them, we *do* communicate with them, and so we play a role in helping people who come to us by easing their grief a little."

"And did you make your mother understand about your father? You said she accepts it all now, but how did she feel about it back then?

Alex laughed. "Oh, believe me, it took a long while to convince her. That's why we try and give evidence by providing information about the person who has passed over, information that we couldn't possibly know."

"And do you still see your dad?"

Alex paused, formulating the answer in his head before speaking aloud. "He came to me off and on over the years, and then, when I was about seventeen, mum met Frank. Dad was delighted that she had another chance of happiness and he told me that it was time I started to use my abilities as a medium to help others and he'd chosen to be my guide. I joined what's called a development circle to really hone my abilities, and ever since, he's helped me when I'm working."

"So… your little girl… Do you see her too?"

Alex nodded slowly. Lily was forcing him to where he didn't want to go, and he'd expected that, but it was proving more difficult than he'd thought it would be. She didn't need to know the whys and wherefores of his current situation, especially as it might all change once he'd seen Beth tomorrow morning, but he had to be honest with her, because he could see where this conversation would eventually lead. "I *could* see her, yes. She's with my dad, and I saw her often until… well, until I had to stop. I don't want to go into the details, but it's all tied up with my wife's breakdown and… well, that's all I can say about it, for now."

Lily acknowledged this, but declared that if she had his gift she would never stop, no matter what the reason. She would have Scott with her every minute of every day. Then she commented on something he'd written that had really caught her attention.

"You say that you know your father will be there when you die, and I've read about this, but what does it mean? Will Scott wait for me?"

"Lily, we never die alone, no matter what the circumstance. Someone will always come to guide us to the other place. In all your research I'm sure you've come across near death experiences?" He hesitated, thinking for the first time that what he had experienced with Scott was surely such an experience? He hadn't been pronounced dead, not even for a minute, but what else could it have been, and why hadn't he considered this before?

Lily was looking at him expectantly, so he dragged his thoughts back to her question and said, "In a near death experience, many people who are medically considered dead but go on to recover report seeing a tunnel with a bright light at the end that they feel compelled to go towards. And then there's a moment, some barrier they come to. This is the point where they must decide or are told that they can go forward or they must go back. And if they are to go forward, there will be someone there to show them the way. In my case, it'll be my dad, and he'll have little Amber too."

"So Scott *is* going to be there for me?" She choked on the words and tears fell unchecked down her cheeks.

"Sorry, sorry." She fumbled in the pocket of her jeans and pulled out a wad of tissues. "God, I didn't know it was possible to produce so many tears. They just don't stop."

"I do understand, believe me. Even being able to see her with my dad, I still grieved deeply because I couldn't hold her. And when I cried, it was as if tears were actually leaking through all the pores of my skin. Grief makes you feel as if you are being turned inside out, but it's a process we have to go through. Tears are normal and it's healthy, so please don't apologise."

Alex waited while she dabbed at her eyes and composed herself. Gently, he asked, "Lily, have you ever considered bereavement counselling?"

Alex watched her face as she chewed her lower lip and looked down at her hands, where she was slowly tearing a tissue into strips. "My family wanted me to see someone, but I just... couldn't. Adele is being amazing, though. And my parents are doing their best. My dad travels a lot for work and I'm afraid mum and I don't always get on. Scott's family are struggling with their own grief, but they help out as much as they can. Friends are rallying round." Her voice dropped to a whisper. "But I'd give anything to have Scott back."

He touched her hand. "Of course you would."

For a moment he was so tempted to tell her about Scott's passing, and about the kingfisher. Then he'd tell her about the kingfisher he had made for her. But as he looked at her with compassion in his heart, waiting for her to ask the question she had really come to ask, he knew he could not tell her. Not yet.

The question came; she leaned forward and blurted it out. "Have you seen him, Alex? Can you bring him here?" Her eyes roamed the room, as if expecting to see Scott coming towards her.

"If I-" He stopped, the muscles of his jaw working while he tried to sort out what to say. Right now there was no way he could communicate with Scott, but tomorrow? Tomorrow could be so different. He couldn't tell her this, though; couldn't get her hopes up in case he had to dash them after his visit with Beth.

He started again. "It takes a while for a person who has passed over to come through, especially after a sudden death where there has been no time for preparation. The transition period can be short, but sometimes it's very long, years even. There are no hard and fast rules, I'm afraid, only that communication is initiated by them, not by us."

Her face crumpled and she suddenly bent forward as if she had been punched in the stomach. "Oh God, I c-can't stand this! It was easier when I thought he was completely gone from me! And then you gave me hope, only to dash my dreams by telling me I might have to wait *years*?" She shook her head in disbelief. "I thought you'd be able to help me!"

"Lily, Lily, I've told you I'm not working as a medium now, but I will try to help you. I know some very good mediums I could put you in touch with, and Scott *will* come through, I know he will. I realise it's hard, but have just a little more patience, Lily. Give Scott time to adapt and gain strength. It takes a great deal of energy to communicate."

He held her while she cried, a storm of weeping that soaked through his shirt.

When it was over, and she was limp in his arms, finally spent and exhausted, he dabbed at her tears with one of her tissues.

"Do you want me to call Adele, Lily? Is she home?"

"Yes, she's there, but no need to call her." She managed a wobbly smile. "I can manage the few steps to my own front door."

Alex hugged her. "Okay."

"You've given me a lot to think about, Alex. I never believed in any of it before, the life after death stuff. I suppose I didn't think about it because I didn't have to, but now... Now I can't accept that Scott has just...just *gone*. That there's nothing of him anywhere any more. I want so much to believe what you've told me."

"I wish I could give you more evidence. I know it's not enough, but I do assure you that Scott continues to exist and he will always be there for you. You two will meet again, Lily."

Lily stood up. "It's a lovely thought; something to hold on to. Thank you, Alex. I really will go now." Tears still shimmered on her eyelashes as he walked her to the door.

Chapter 44

As Alex parked his car outside the house of his parents-in-law, he felt his mouth go dry. A face appeared at the window, then the front door opened before he'd got out of his car, and Beth's mother came hurrying out to him.

"Alex, it's so good to see you."

He kissed her on both cheeks. "You, too, Anna." He glanced towards the house. "How is she? Does she know I'm coming?"

Anna shook her head. "I didn't tell her; I think it's best you just go in there and make her talk to you. She loves you, Alex, I know she does. I hear her crying at night, and it's not just for Amber; she cries out for you in her sleep."

Alex looked down at Anna's face, feeling a lump form in his throat as he saw the anguish in her drawn features. She had aged, and no wonder.

"Go on in, Alex. Beth is reading in the conservatory. I've got some shopping to do, so I'll keep out of the way for an hour or so." She smiled, then, and reached up to pat his cheek. "I know you can reach her."

He walked through the house and into the conservatory. Beth was curled up on the cushions of a wicker settee, a magazine open on her lap. She hadn't heard him come in, and for a few seconds he just stared at her, drinking her in. She was unbearably thin and fragile, but so lovely, he wanted to take her in his arms and never let her go.

She stiffened, at last sensing she wasn't alone. Her head came up and she gasped when she saw him. The magazine fluttered to the floor as she rose up, her hands out as if warding him off.

"What are you doing here?" she whispered.

But it was said more in wonder than anger, which gave him hope that she would not immediately send him away.

"It's time we talked, Beth, don't you think?"

"Did mum set this up? Where is she?"

"I asked Paul to arrange it. Your mum has gone out so we can have some privacy. Shall we sit down?"

By now she had composed herself a little, but Alex had seen the glimmer of something in her eyes that told him she had to work very hard to keep her distance. The conversation began in a stilted manner, with Alex doing most of the talking. Several times she'd seemed on the verge of saying something, something important, but she was prevented from spilling her heart to him, and without his psychic senses he couldn't fathom why.

Then she said she needed a glass of water.

"I'll get it," he said. "Promise you won't run away?"

She'd smiled at that, a fleeting thing but a smile nonetheless, and shaken her head.

In the kitchen, Alex ran the cold tap and got two glasses from the cupboard. He was at the sink filling them, when the back of his neck prickled and he knew he wasn't alone. Beth had followed him. He turned, intending to put the glasses down on the table before opening his arms in the hope she would run to him.

But it wasn't Beth.

The glasses slipped from his hands and shattered on the floor, spattering his legs with cold water.

Turning your back on your gift is helping no-one, Alex Kelburn.

Heart racing, Alex felt as if his very soul was being stripped bare by the coal-black eyes of the tall, beautiful woman who filled his vision and made him tremble.

She did not speak again, but before she faded back into the world she'd come from, she had made herself understood.

Alex had made the wrong decisions, even though he'd thought he was acting for the right reasons. He had shut down because he'd believed the woman he loved needed him to do so. He had been mistaken.

This time, though, there would be no mistakes, no misjudgements.

This time, he would allow his senses to open up so that he could read Beth's deepest feelings. He would find a way to heal her, to heal both of them, and then he would go back to using his psychic gifts to help others.

By now, Beth was in the kitchen and sweeping up the broken glass. Had she been here at the same time as Grace? How long had Alex been in communication with her? It felt like hours, but Beth would have come running the minute she'd heard the glasses hit the floor, and she didn't seem to think Alex was behaving oddly.

Mentally giving himself a shake, he helped to clean up the mess and they went back to the conservatory.

He went straight to it. "Beth, I feel you need to get something out into the open, something that is hurting you so deeply. Please, let me use my psychic senses, then you won't have to say anything, but I will know and I'll be able to help you. Please, Beth."

For a second or two she looked blankly at him, then frowned and asked in a hesitant voice, "I... I don't know, Alex. But... why do you ask me? Are you... are you not using them?"

Stunned in his turn, Alex had to struggle to find his voice.

"Beth! I thought you knew! It's what we argued about, what upset you so much! I closed it all down because you

260

were heartbroken that I could see Amber and you couldn't. I did it for you!"

Now Beth could only gape at him, her huge eyes filling with tears that soon spilled down her cheeks. Then, in a voice so soft he had to lean forward to hear her, she said, "No, Alex. No! Surely you... What about the TV series? Your demonstrations?"

He shook his head. "I put everything on hold so I could get you back. I thought it was what you wanted?"

"I would never ask that of you! Your work is too important. Surely... surely I didn't. Did I? Oh God, I was so confused. Alex, I... I'm so sorry! I can't believe this. Why didn't Paul tell me?"

Suddenly she was out of her chair and on her knees in front of him. She grabbed his hands, squeezing his fingers hard. "I thought you knew my reasons for leaving and that you stayed away because you agreed with them. But you don't know, do you? Oh, Alex, you shouldn't have done it, shouldn't have closed down. What about your career? And there are so many people who need you. What on earth have I done?"

Almost sobbing with relief, Alex allowed himself to open up, and the truth hit him like a sledgehammer. He felt the truth in Beth, and at the same time he remembered something Paul had told him when Beth had suffered the breakdown. She had said that she wasn't worthy of him because she could never give him the children he wanted.

Now, with his senses fully open, he *knew* this was the demon. They had misunderstood each other so badly, and it had almost cost them their marriage.

Almost.

Because he could put it right now.

He tipped her face up so she had to look at him. "I love you, Beth. With all my heart and soul, I love you. I know

261

now that you've been thinking I should walk away from you because you can't have more children; I know this is why you have kept your distance. But it doesn't *matter*. We were blessed with Amber, even though she was with us in this world for such a short time."

Willing her with every atom of his body to hear and believe him, he pulled her up from her knees and onto his lap, all the while gazing deep into her eyes as he said, "There are other ways we can have a family, but whatever happens, I need you to know that I could not, simply could not, be happy without you."

She kissed him then, a deep and loving kiss that took his breath away.

"I want so much to take you home with me," he said when the kiss ended. "Will you come?"

She laughed, a sound that made his heart skip a beat.

"I'm so exhausted all I want to do right now is crawl into my bed upstairs and sleep. Will you come back tomorrow? Come early, and I'll be packed and ready."

He stopped her with another kiss. "Would one minute past midnight be too early?"

He found it so hard to leave her, and made her promise over and over that she would be waiting for him in the morning. Now, standing beside his car, Alex let out a whoop of joy, startling Anna who was coming into the driveway carrying a bag of shopping. When she saw the huge grin on Alex's face, the bag dropped to the ground and she ran into his arms. He swept her up and spun her in a circle until they both felt giddy.

"I think I've just broken a dozen eggs, Alex," she laughed. "So when will you be taking her home? Although, from what Paul tells me, it's far from luxurious."

"I'll come for her tomorrow, Anna. I admit the house isn't much, but I'm going straight there to clean up, wash the sheets and towels, and put flowers in every room. When Beth feels ready, we'll start house hunting."

At home again, having stopped on the way to buy armfuls of flowers, Alex called his mother. She cried so much at the wonderful news that Frank had to take over the conversation.

Next up was Linda. Delighted to hear what Alex had to say, she promised to come and see them both soon, and reminded Alex to call Charles Hendry. "He's desperate to get you, Alex; you will do it, won't you?"

He then called Paul, who immediately started raving about getting Alex's TV career back on track.

"I'll pick you up at 7.30, take you out for dinner, so we can discuss everything."

Finally, before starting on the preparations for Beth's arrival tomorrow, he sat in the leather armchair and called out to his father.

Are you here, dad?

I'm here. I've never been away from you, Alex. It's so good to be talking again.

Why didn't I see you when I came over with Scott? I looked for you. I wanted so much to stay and be with you and Amber.

I know, I was there, but we were not allowed to meet because it would have made returning so much harder for you. It was not your time, Alex. It was all for Scott. Look who I have here. Happy to see her daddy.

His beloved baby girl sat happily at her grandfather's feet, playing with a rattle.

Tears of joy and relief flowed down his face and he didn't bother to wipe them away until his vision became too blurred to see her clearly.

His father reminded him then that he had work to do, so he put on some loud music and got down to the housework, hoping he'd get it all done before Paul came.

Chapter 45

Adele had enjoyed an impromptu meal out with a close friend, but on checking her phone before leaving the restaurant found a message from the client she was due to see in the morning. He was cancelling, and she was annoyed that he had left it so late, and then only done so by sending a text. She'd come home so she could get the train into London more easily in the morning for this meeting, and now it turned out she hadn't needed to. Still, it had been great to have an evening of carefree gossip and laughter.

She'd been worried about leaving Lily for the night, though. She couldn't put her finger on exactly why, but, despite all outward signs like the cooking, the conversation, something wasn't right with her sister. For days now she'd seemed nervous, edgy. Distracted. It was almost as if Lily was trying too hard and it was costing her.

Adele tried to convince herself that it was because Lily was so near her due date, but there was something else that niggled. When she had suggested cancelling everything and staying with her, Lily had been ridiculously over the top in insisting she do no such thing.

Practically shoving her out of the door, she'd said, "I won't hear of you not going to that meeting, Adele. You've a business to run. You can't be my nursemaid every minute of every day. If anything happens, I'll simply call an ambulance."

Sitting in her car in the restaurant car park, she checked the time, undecided whether to go to her house or make the hour long journey back to Lily's. She scrolled through her address list on her phone and clicked on Lily's number.

She would make her decision which way to turn the car when she'd spoken to Lily and gauged how she was feeling.

She tapped her fingernails on the steering wheel, listening to the ring ring ring. It went to Lily's answering machine.

And again.

Damn. Where was she?

She tried again, and again let it ring until the answering machine picked up.

Really worried now, she scrolled through her list and dialled Maisie.

"Maisie? It's Adele. Sorry to call so late, but-"

"Is everything all right, pet?"

"Well, I hope so. I just called Lily a couple of times and she doesn't answer. Do you know if she's there?"

"I'm pretty sure she is. I saw her earlier, and she was very cheerful and said she was going to have an early night. Just a minute, pet, let me look out of the window."

Adele waited.

"Her bedroom lights are on. Oh! Adele, I can see her drawing her curtains. Do you want me to go over there?"

"No, Maisie. She was probably taking a bath and didn't hear the phone. I'll be back in the morning, and I just wanted to check that she was okay."

"Yes, she's very near her time, isn't she? Don't worry, Adele, I'm keeping an eye on her."

Reassured, Adele started the car and turned on the radio, glad she only had to make the short journey to her own little house and not make the trip to Lily's when she was so tired.

Chapter 46

Reading through Alex's story about his father's passing for what could have been the tenth time, Lily thought again about how Alex had said it could take years for loved ones to communicate. Could she wait so long?

Grabbing her laptop she searched for sites about near death experiences, and marvelled at how many people described such similar scenes. In nearly every case they had experienced the tunnel, the light, some peaceful presence that gently sent them back into their physical bodies.

Another site detailed witness accounts of people who had watched someone pass away, telling how they had spoken to a dead loved one that no-one else could see, talking as if that loved one had come for them. Just like Alex had said it happened. Just like Maisie had said it happened for her mother.

Dying might be drawn out and painful or it might be instant, but the moment of death could be peaceful. You walked through that tunnel towards the light, straight into the arms of someone you loved, someone who had gone there before you and had come to show you the way.

Alex had told her when she'd asked that training her in mediumship would be a long process, not guaranteed to be successful. Not everyone can do it, he'd said, and he'd asked if she'd ever had any psychic experiences. She hadn't.

So that left her waiting for Scott to come through to someone like Alex, if he came through, and communicating with him third-hand. She wouldn't be able to see him or hear him; how could that possibly be enough?

She knew now what she had to do.

Imagining how Scott would receive her at the other end of that tunnel, she tipped out the contents of her precious box onto the bed and removed all the pills from their packets and bottles, piling them into one colourful heap.

Perspiration beaded her upper lip. Deep down she was really scared, but she needed to do this now. The baby could come at any time, and it was vital she accomplished this thing before that happened, so she, Scott and the baby would be a family in that other place.

The added bonus was that Adele was away tonight, staying at her own place.

The plan was to take a bath, put on something pretty, and… Her mind closed on what came next, but she was determined to see this through.

Lily padded over to the chest of drawers. From the top drawer she withdrew two envelopes from beneath her underwear, one addressed to Adele, the other to her mum and dad. A third envelope, a large brown one about the shop, she left in the drawer. She had mentioned this in Adele's letter; she would find it. She'd written these in the early days of her bereavement, when she'd started stockpiling the tablets, and was glad now that she had not destroyed them.

A dull ache started to throb in her lower back, and she had to hold tight to the banister to get downstairs. At the bottom, she paused and rubbed her back. It felt like something was clawing at her insides, making her gasp with pain.

"Not now, baby! Please, not now."

With the letters laid dead centre on the kitchen table, one below the other, she grabbed the bottle of brandy she'd hidden at the back of the dresser, and a crystal tumbler.

She took a last glance around her kitchen, a last walk through the other rooms of her house. Everything neat as a pin.

Upstairs again having bathed and dried herself, she plumped up her pillows and lit the vanilla scented candle she'd placed on her bedside table. She was wearing a beautiful maternity dress, pale blue and lacy. She'd had to order it online, because if she'd gone to Ellie's boutique, Ellie would have asked too many questions. Where was she going, to need such a fine dress? Did she have shoes to go with it? How was she going to do her hair? Friendly, social, *normal* chit-chat that Lily couldn't have tolerated.

The phone rang, and rang again, but Lily had no intention of talking to anyone tonight but Scott.

Awkwardly, she swept all the empty packets and bottles off the bed and heaved herself onto it, supporting the weight of the baby with one hand as she shuffled up until her back was against the headboard. She gathered the pills so they were well within reach, and filled the glass to the brim with brandy.

***

Vincent watched with dawning horror. Now he knew what she had been squirreling away in that box and her intentions now were perfectly clear.

Whatever it took he just had to get to Alex.

As he'd done before, he decided to go through the wall that divided the two houses. He tried to think himself through it, but this time he couldn't do it. He left Lily's room and placed himself right in front of the wall, tried again. Nothing.

With a howl of rage and frustration he ran at the wall again and again until suddenly there was the sensation of resistance that gave way so it felt he was moving through a thick, viscous liquid. He was in Alex's room.

It was immediately obvious to him from the silence that only occurs in unoccupied spaces that Alex was not there. Even if he had been home, though, Vincent had so far failed to make Alex aware of his presence, so why would tonight be any different? It was if the man was... Vincent searched for the word. Closed? Yes, closed.

So what kind of medium was he?

He paced up and down beside Alex's empty bed. What to do, what to do.

Well, what could he do?

Alex was not here. Neither Lily nor Adele could see Vincent. The older lady who visited often, Maisie, she couldn't see him either.

He slipped back to see what Lily was up to, wishing he had the ability to move things so he could make her take notice. But even if he could make her aware of his presence, could he make himself heard? Could he stop her?

There was nothing for it but to wait until Alex Kelburn came back.

Oh, Rose, Rose, I wish you were here to guide me! What on earth can I do for poor Lily?

Chapter 47

After an exhausting evening over a delicious meal, Alex was relieved when Paul refused his offer of coffee and dropped him off instead of coming in to talk yet more about his grand plans to get Alex's career back on track.

Falling back into the well-worn upholstery with a sigh of happy relief, he laughed out loud as the familiar ache began to pulse at the base of his skull.

Hi dad.

Alex. It's so good to see you looking so well and happy. And to think that Beth will be here tomorrow...

Yes. I can hardly believe it. But I feel so stupid, dad! How could I have got it so wrong? If I hadn't shut down, I would have understood Beth's fears so much earlier. I wouldn't have had to miss you and Amber for so long.

See it as a lesson you had to learn and put it behind you, Alex.

There was a sudden change in the atmosphere.

Alex?

Yes, I sense it too.

There was another presence in the room with them.

Startled, he concentrated hard, allowing his psychic senses to open fully, like a sunflower turning itself to the sun, revelling in the sensation after so long without it. He was half-expecting Grace again, but a man appeared in front of him, a man he'd never seen before.

Can you see me? Oh, thank God! You don't know me. I don't have time to explain, but you must help Lily. Call an ambulance, I beg you.

Is the baby coming?

The man hesitated. He was literally wringing his hands and hopping from foot to foot.

She's taking pills. So many pills.

Without another word, Alex bolted from the chair, the room, the house, and ran up to Lily's door. He pounded on it, shouting her name.

No time. Ambulance.

The man was behind him. Could he trust him? If he called an ambulance and there was nothing wrong with Lily he'd look such a fool.

But better to look a fool than take the risk that Lily really did need help.

Thankful that his mobile was still in his pocket, Alex fumbled trying to press in the three vital numbers, but finally he managed it and made the call.

Satisfied an ambulance was just minutes away, Alex ran over to Maisie's and rattled loudly on the knocker, all the while shouting up at her darkened window at the top of his lungs.

At last, a light came on above him, and Maisie was leaning out of the window.

"Alex?"

"Do you have a key for Lily's?"

"A key? Why, yes. What's wrong?"

"It's urgent, Maisie. Could you bring me the key? An ambulance will be here any minute and we need to get the door open."

"An ambulance?" He could see a grin spread on Maisie's face. "Oh, Alex! Is she in labour? I'll be right down."

Alex paced with impatience, coming to a sudden halt as he heard the siren. At the exact moment Maisie appeared, holding out the key, the medics were already jumping out of the ambulance.

Chapter 48

Her hands were trembling, the palms and fingertips sweat-slicked. Fear sat like lead in her stomach and the baby felt even heavier on her thighs as she leaned over, grabbing handfuls of tablets and shovelling them into her mouth.

Random thoughts chased around her head. What if Alex had lied to her about an afterlife? What if she was making a terrible mistake? What if it didn't work, and she damaged herself and her baby, or even killed her baby? No. Alex had said that Amber would be waiting for him when he passed over, so that meant, *surely* it meant, that Scott would come for her and their baby.

Another cramp gripped her insides, stealing her breath clean away. She felt the baby kick. Was it right to take the baby with her?

Yes, of course it was, a baby needed to be with its parents, both of its parents. This was the only way. Better to take her baby into the afterlife while he or she was still inside her. The baby would be born and live a full life, just not here.

But, oh God, was she right about that?

The questions went on chasing themselves round and round Lily's exhausted brain. Reasons why and reasons why not gnawed away inside her head, none of them making any sense now she was actually doing this. Would her parents understand? Would Adele?

She had a thought that almost brought a smile to her sweating face: perhaps she could speak to them from the other side - explain everything - through Alex! She and Scott would go to Alex, the baby in their arms, and he would know what to do, how to tell them.

She scooped up another fistful of pills - white and pink tablets, chalky and bitter, red and yellow capsules - and swallowed them in twos and threes, gulping them down with brandy, but mercifully tasting nothing now.

She needed lots of brandy as the tablets foamed in her mouth.

Pins and needles began to tingle in her hands and feet; the pain in her back was like a knife. Her eyes would not focus.

Her throat constricted as she tried to gulp down more of the dry tablets. She was gagging, and her stomach heaved in protest.

She felt herself getting heavier and heavier, falling, falling. For a moment she was aware of the soft support of the mattress and duvet and pillows, but then, like a lead weight, she kept on falling.

Suddenly, she was wracked with terrible spasms of pain. She convulsed, feeling as though her insides were being clawed out from between her legs.

She cried out. Or thought she cried out.

There was a loud buzzing in her ears that seemed to morph into a siren, like that of a police car or an ambulance.

Pain again, waves and waves of it. She felt wetness flood from her, burning her inner thighs, then, mercifully, she passed out.

Lily had no idea how long she'd been out before she opened her eyes again and blinked into blackness so thick it terrified her. Her thoughts were jumbled and confused as she tried to remember where she was and why. With a sickening jolt it all came back to her. A vile taste was in her mouth, her throat burned as if she had swallowed acid.

I haven't taken enough, she thought. *I need to keep going.* She put out her hands, wishing the candle hadn't gone out, trying to orient herself. But as she moved, there was a jolting, tugging sensation, and she sensed she was being lifted away from the bed.

Now she was standing, though she could not feel the carpet beneath her bare feet.

Fear prickled her skin and she had to fight the rising panic. She had no concept of time, of how long it had been since she had swallowed the first fistful of tablets. The darkness was so utterly thick it pressed into her body and felt icy cold on her wide-staring eyes.

There was a whimpering sound, which she did not at first realise was coming from her own mouth. She tried to turn, to move, and it felt like wading through tar.

Another noise started, a humming sound that vibrated deep within her head. She felt heat on the crown of her head and forced herself to look up. Suspended above her was a small, pale red globe, slowly spinning. It mesmerised Lily, seeming to lock her gaze onto it so she couldn't blink or look away. It grew in size at it started to lift upwards, and her eyes were forced to follow it.

The ceiling seemed to melt around the orb, which was glowing now, the pale red turned to a sparking scarlet, and Lily could see the night sky. It was pale in comparison to the darkness of the room, and she could see stars and a sliver of moon in the periphery of her vision. The sphere moved higher, straight up, spinning very fast now.

Unbidden, her arms reached above her head, fingers stretched out, wanting to touch the sky, feel the air. Now she was aware of soft carpet beneath her feet, but only momentarily, before she was being drawn away, pulled painfully towards the scarlet thing.

Terrified, screaming and shrieking, Lily struggled against the force that held her fast and pulled her inexorably upwards.

What had she done? What had gone wrong?

With a jerk, her body suddenly stopped, then she tilted and spun upside down, so she was looking down through the roof of her house and into her bedroom. Although it was far away, she could see the body on the bed – her body. But it was distorted, like looking at herself in a fairground mirror.

The lips were blue, and mustard-coloured vomit had leaked from the corners of her slack mouth and dried in crusty rivulets on her chin and neck. Blood had run from between her legs, soaking and staining the sheet beneath her. She was appalled and disgusted at the sight and a primal scream rose up within her. But this time no sound came. Instead, her intake of breath spun her body upright again and snapped her head back up until her eyes were once more locked onto the red sphere.

Where was the white light? And the tunnel? Where was Scott?

Caught between the earth and this terrifying, pulsing globe, she was two people, the pitiful woman on the bed below, and this one, experiencing the worst terror she had ever known. Frantically she tried to break free, but the pain was all consuming as the opposing gravity of the Earth and that terrible red moon fought for possession of her.

"This can't be happening, this can't be happening," she moaned, her voice sounding like a stranger's in her ears.

Then her fingertips touched the spinning globe and it felt like they'd been burned instantly to the bone. Her breath was sucked from her lungs and she thought she must surely suffocate. But the whirling scarlet thing suddenly winked out and Lily was left suspended in a fog so thick and sticky she could not move.

**

Sobbing, Vincent tried to tear away the sticky fog that was beginning to envelop Lily as she lay on the bed, shouting at her to hold on.

Hold on, Lily, help is coming! Don't go into the mist! Stay, Lily! Stay!

But she was fast being swallowed up and he could barely see her any more.

He could feel her terror, and wondered what she was experiencing. The same as he had, or something different? He didn't know if dying was the same for everyone, but he had not felt as fearful as Lily appeared to be.

Fight it, Lily! Come on, girl, come back!

Realising that there was nothing he could do to bring her back and anchor her here until help arrived, he stepped forward and allowed the mist to take him, too.

He could not let her face this alone.

Chapter 49

After a long, agonising silence, she could hear voices around her, but no matter how hard she strained, she could not make out the words. Then one voice seemed to reach her out of the hubbub and she heard her name being spoken.

"Lily?" The voice was soft, appealing, but she turned towards it with a heavy heart.

Whoever he was, he was not Scott.

They were standing in a dark space edged with pearly grey, yet she could see him clearly. Quite short and stocky. Dark, thinning hair. A stranger.

"My name is Vincent. I went to Alex, he knows what you've done and will get help for you. Meanwhile I'll stay with you, Lily. You're not alone."

"I don't know you!"

"No, but I know you. We used to live in your house, me and my wife, Rose."

Even in her frantic state, Lily remembered the fireplace. "You carved the initials in the fireplace?"

Vincent nodded. "Not long after we moved in. We were there all our married lives, until Rose got sick. We knew she was going to die. She asked me to end it quickly for her when she was too ill to want to go on, make sure she didn't suffer. I promised her that I would. But I couldn't bear to live without her so I..."

Lily waited for the man to compose himself and listened patiently as he described what he had done to Rose and to himself in the kitchen of her home so many years ago. He looked so sorrowful as he spoke, Lily reached out and touched his arm. "So where is she?"

277

"I don't know. We had a pact that whoever went over first, the other would wait. I made sure she'd gone ahead of me, but when I died, I couldn't find her. Something happened, and I found myself back in the kitchen, looking down at our bodies. I've been anchored to the house ever since. Lily, that was a long time ago, and I've never seen my Rose, not even once."

Feeling cold trickle down her spine at the implication of what Vincent was saying, Lily whispered, "So what happened?"

"I've thought long and hard about that, and I think this is some sort of punishment. The hard truth is, Lily, that I killed my wife and I committed suicide. I can only conclude that I am being punished."

"No! I've read loads of stuff, and I remember seeing that there is no judgement in the afterlife, that everyone is welcomed and cared for no matter how they die."

"Yet I am proof that it is not so. When I knew what you planned to do, I tried so hard to stop you."

Lily mulled this over. Could it really be that she had made some terrible, irreparable mistake? "Do you mean," she said, "That I won't see Scott? That because I committed suicide, I will be punished like you?"

"I honestly don't know. But I'll stay with you, Lily, whether we remain here or are sent back to Saxon Road."

Lily listened as Vincent told the rest of his sad story. He had truly loved his Rose, and had thought he was doing the right thing for both of them.

"She was suffering, see, and you can't bear to see someone you love in so much pain, can you. She wanted to die with dignity, and I wanted it too, so she could be free of it. But I knew I wouldn't be able to go on without her. Me without my Rose?" He shook his head. "Impossible."

"So you believed in life after death?"

"Oh yes. Rose taught me that. It's what gave me the strength to do what I did, knowing that Rose would be better. There's no suffering over there, see. We're whole again. Even young again, if we want to be. But it didn't work out for me." He shrugged. "As I say, I can only think it is a form of punishment."

"I didn't believe in it. Not until very recently. And everything I read told me that Scott would be here when my time came. I wanted that time to be now, to bring the baby with me, so we could be a family."

She stopped speaking and her hands flew to her stomach. It was flat.

"My baby! Oh my God, where's my baby?"

Lily tried to run, but the swirling grey fog held her fast, getting denser the more she tried to escape it.

Vincent grabbed her hand.

"Don't try to run, Lily. Wait. Be still. I'm with you and we'll work this out together."

Chapter 50

Barely able to stop the tears, Maisie put down the phone in Lily's hallway and said to Alex, "Adele's on her way, and she'll call her parents. I do hope she drives sensibly, she's in terrible shock."

Alex raked his fingers through his hair, making it stand up in spikes. "I wonder what's going on up there. Look, why don't we go into the kitchen and I'll make some tea. It could be a long night."

She followed Alex, shuffling in the baby-blue fluffy slippers she'd pushed her feet into, aware for the first time how she must look. To give him the key she had pulled her dressing-gown on over her nightdress and gone to the door, thinking for those few happy seconds that Lily's baby was on the way and she would have time to get dressed. But when Alex had told her the real reason for his calling an ambulance, she had all but staggered with stupefaction.

She'd dashed back upstairs and thrown on whatever came to hand, trying to explain to Jack as she dressed what was going on. He'd tried to get up, but she had insisted he stay in bed.

She looked down at herself, at Jack's striped shirt, incorrectly buttoned, so the collar was skewed; her white nightdress that was half in and half out of a voluminous skirt that she hadn't zipped up all the way. She knew that her gingery hair sprang out in all directions, and without makeup she looked old and pale. But she couldn't worry about her appearance at a time like this.

Alex handed her a mug of tea and she got the sugar bowl from the cupboard, feeling she needed at least three spoonfuls.

Spotting the two envelopes on the table, Maisie read who they were addressed to in Lily's neat handwriting, and had to gulp back the tears.

"She must have planned this, Alex. But why? She seemed to be getting on all right. Adele told me she was cooking again and she was smiling more, talking more. I saw her earlier and she seemed in such good spirits. Did we miss something?"

"I certainly did, Maisie. If I hadn't made some bad decisions and been so wrapped up in my own problems I would have known what she was thinking of doing."

Maisie covered his hand with her own. "How could you have known, pet? I see her every day and I had no idea she was feeling so bad. She seemed to be coping, she really did."

Seeing her reflection in the darkened window, she tried to smooth her hair down to stop it standing up around her head like gingery cotton candy. "But the baby, Alex! She's so near her time! How could she do that to her baby? Oh, she must have been desperate, absolutely desperate!"

Alex sat with his hands hanging loose between his knees, a picture of dejection. "She wants to take the baby over with her. She came to see me, Maisie. I can't help wondering if I said something that set her on this path."

Maisie sat down beside him with a heavy sigh. "We'll all go mad if we try to find ways to blame ourselves."

"I have to take some of the blame, Maisie. All my life I've been able to read people's inner emotions, but I deliberately shut it down. If I hadn't done that I would have *known* what she planned to do and I could have done something to help her."

Maisie took a shaky breath. "I don't pretend to understand quite what you mean, pet, but whatever you've done and why ever you chose to do it, you must have had your reasons."

"I did it to try and win my wife back."

"So you did it for love. And it didn't work? Or have I got it wrong? Sorry, Alex, I have no idea about your private life and-"

"It's okay, Maisie." Alex stared down at his clasped hands. "As I found out just this afternoon, it was all a dreadful misunderstanding. My wife has been recovering from an emotional breakdown, and all this time I thought I was doing the right thing by shutting my senses down." He gave a bitter laugh. "Turns out I'd got that completely wrong, and because of that I've made Beth's suffering go on far longer than it need have. And now I've failed Lily too."

"Oh, Alex, I'm so sorry. But no matter what any of us said or did, Lily might have gone ahead and done this anyway. But... how on earth did you know Lily was in trouble, and that she was taking pills?"

"She has a guardian angel, Maisie. His name is Vincent and he came to me and *ordered* me to call an ambulance for her. It's just lucky that I was open to communication again, or goodness knows how this would have turned out."

Maisie stared at him, shaking her head in wonder.

Having nothing more to say, they sat in silence on the sofa, hands clasped, wondering what on earth was happening upstairs in Lily's bedroom.

Chapter 51

The grey fog was so thick she could no longer see Vincent, and at some time he had let go of her hand. She couldn't move at all. What had happened to her baby?

She waited there, helplessly suspended, for what felt like an eternity. Just when she had begun to think that this was all she would ever know until the end of time, the fog slowly cleared and she could see Vincent again. He had his back to her, staring into – at last! – a dazzling white light. She was about to call out to him when she suddenly felt someone, *knew* someone was standing behind her.

She felt him with every fibre of her being.

She slowly, oh so slowly, turned around.

Scott was there, smiling down at her, such love in his eyes that she could hardly bear to look at him, she was so ashamed of losing their child.

To Lily's left a tall woman, taller even than Scott, strode into view, but she did not look Lily's way.

"Vincent," the woman said.

So much power was in the one word.

Vincent fell to his knees and started to sob.

Lily wanted to run to him as he started pleading for mercy, but Scott gently held her back. The tall woman's expression remained impassive as she went to Vincent and leaned over him, putting her hand under his elbow to make him stand up.

"I'm sorry, I'm so sorry," he sobbed. "What I did was wrong, I know it, but don't send me back. It's so lonely without my Rose."

"Vincent, listen to me. You were not sent back, as you believe. You were too impatient. We had Rose and were caring for her. By the time we came for you, your panic when you couldn't see Rose had sent you back and you were anchored to the earthly plane by your feelings of guilt. You may not have thought you felt that way, but in your heart you did. And not for what you did for Rose; you did that for love. But taking your own life and leaving Rose's sister to deal with the aftermath... that has played on your conscience, and we could not help you."

Vincent struggled to understand. "I thought I was being punished."

"We do not judge your actions, Vincent, nor do we impose punishment. You do that yourselves." She raised her arm and motioned with an open hand to the shimmering horizon. "Look."

Lily could see a crowd of people coming quickly towards them, chattering and laughing loudly. Two women suddenly broke away and one of them started to run, followed more slowly by the other.

Lily fixed her eyes on Vincent.

He was crying, tears streaming down his face, as he fell to his knees again. When the running figure reached him, he held out his arms and cried, "Rose! Oh, my Rose!"

The woman who was Rose laughed and pulled him up by the hand. They hugged and kissed, and then she led him back to the other woman. Vincent stopped in front of her and said, "I'm so sorry, Mavis, that you had to deal with that. So very sorry."

Mavis shook her head and smiled, then enveloped Vincent in a fierce hug. Rose and Mavis then stood either side of Vincent and led him into the crowd of waiting of people.

Even as Lily watched, they were enveloped by a light so bright, so pure, she could hardly bare to look.

The woman now fixed her unblinking gaze on Lily, and shame engulfed her again. She reached for Scott, wanting to be wrapped in his arms, held safe, but Scott's attention was on the other woman, and Lily sensed they were communicating without words.

"Thank you, Grace," Scott said at last, and he took Lily's hand and led her away.

She couldn't take her eyes off him, but he walked on steadily, facing ahead, saying nothing.

She tugged at his hand. "Scott?"

He stopped and drew her into his arms.

"Oh, Scott." She leaned against him, allowing the tears to flow unchecked. It was like coming home, but so much more than that. To touch him, see him, hold him. She really was in heaven.

Then a terrible thought struck her, so awful and so sharp it almost made her double over.

"Our baby! Scott, I lost our baby!"

Scott smiled and stroked her cheek. "She's fine, Lily. She's being taken care off. Trust me."

"She? We have a little girl? Oh, where is she? Let me see her, please! Where *is* she?"

"Lily, my love, not yet. She is safe, believe me. We need time alone, just you and me, and you will see her very soon. I promise."

"But-"

He placed his fingers on her lips. "Trust me."

Desperate to see her newborn daughter, she wanted to object, *demand* to see her, but something flowed from Scott's fingertips that seemed to act on her like a sedative. Of course she trusted him. Of course she would wait.

She tightened her arms around him, breathing in the scent of his skin.

"Come, Lily, walk with me. Let's talk awhile."

285

Hand in hand, they strolled together through green fields beneath clear gentian skies. There were flowers the like of which Lily had never see before, colours so bright and beautiful they dazzled her eyes. Scott was speaking, but she was so awe-struck by everything, she only heard the cadences of his speech and not what he said. Somewhere in the back of her mind she was aware that his voice was different, it had a different quality. And his *presence* was altered too. Before, he'd been always on the move, always busy with hands and brain. Now, he was... She searched for the right word and could only come up with 'serene'.

Scott stopped talking and smiled down at Lily's radiant face. He brushed her face with his lips, then just stood and gazed at her like someone blind seeing for the first time. "It's so good to be with you again. I'm sorry for all you've been through. I didn't want to leave you. I felt no pain, sweet Lily, I wasn't aware of what was happening until I woke up here and Grace came."

"Is Grace that woman who...?"

"Brought Vincent and Rose back together? Yes. She'll care for him now; it's what she does. Come on, Lily, come with me."

He laughed and started to run, pulling Lily by the hand, until they came to a river. They sat beneath a weeping willow with leaves of emerald green and gold, its long elegant branches swaying in the breeze and dangling in the pure water.

Lily gazed around her and then at Scott. There was a luminescence, a hazy glow around him, so pure she wanted to weep. She leaned into him and kissed his mouth, melting into the kiss as he parted his lips and brushed his tongue against hers. The contact sent shivers through her body and she felt the heat rise to the surface of her skin. "Oh, Scott, I've missed you so much."

They tumbled back onto the soft, fragrant grass. His hands were warm on her flesh and seemed to melt her clothes away. She wanted him naked too, and he was. Vaguely, Lily tried to remember what he had been wearing, but his caresses and kisses wiped all thoughts from her mind as she surrendered to the ecstasy of their lovemaking.

They cried out together at its climax, clasped tight in each other's arms, and then lay quiet and still, neither wishing to break the spell.

After a time, Lily didn't know how long, Scott stroked her hair and sat up. "Look around you, Lily, look at my home. I want you to see it all."

She raised herself up and rested her chin on her knees. Her fingers idly plucked at the grass around her bare feet. The river was so clear she could see pebbles like gemstones sparkling on the riverbed.

"Do you have a house somewhere?"

His sweet smile melted her heart as he thought about his answer.

"Yes, I have a house, and a beautiful garden, just like the one we always dreamed of," he replied. "But then I found this place and mostly I spend my time here. I love these meadows and this river, but if I wanted them I could have a stormy sea, a mountain, or even a moonscape."

As he spoke, Lily could see somewhere on the edge of her vision the scenes as he described them. The river transformed into a deep aquamarine sea, moody and wild with high, white-topped waves crashing against a stony shore. Then the waves seemed to stop at their crest and grow until they filled the sky as glorious snow-capped mountains, glowing pink in the setting sun. The mountains crumbled to rocks and dust, the sky to shades of inky blue and black and she was on the moon's scarred and cratered surface. But if she tried to focus on any one image, everything shifted again like desert sand and all she could see was the calm, cool river and the swaying willow trees.

"I have a gift for you, Lily. Something you'll always remember."

He stretched out his arm and gave a soft, low whistle. There was a blur of iridescent blue and copper in the corner of Lily's eye, and then she gasped as a kingfisher landed on the palm of Scott's open hand. The bird seemed to fix her with the black beads of its eyes, and then it spread its wings as if showing off to her its full glory.

"Oh, Scott," she whispered. "It's so beautiful."

She reached out to touch it, hoping the bird would tamely hop onto her own hand, but it flew up and away, and in a flash it was gone.

Scott's voice was wistful as he spoke again. "It's so hard to explain, Lily. I do not understand it myself, but I feel as if I belong here, as if I have been and shall be here forever. I'll still be here when your time comes, if that is right for us."

"It's wonderful, Scott, truly wonderful, and I'll love it just as much as you do. Let's fetch our baby now and be a family here, together."

Her eyes appealed to his, but his expression was unreadable as he calmly returned her gaze.

"No. You weren't listening, my love. I said I'd be here when your time came." He held up his hand as she started to protest, commanding her into silence. "You must listen to me. This is not your time, Lily. You have to go back."

"Go back?" Her voice was barely a whisper.

"Yes, sweet Lily, I have to send you back." He wiped the tears from her cheeks with his thumbs then drew her into his arms.

"I know this is hard for you, it's hard for me too to be apart from you again, but had you succeeded-"

"But I have succeeded! Scott, I'm here! We can be together, please-"

He shook his head. Lily was crying uncontrollably now, her heart breaking all over again because she had to let him go a second time. But she understood. Somewhere deep inside, she understood.

She recognised now that she had been driven to the edge of madness by grief.

She noticed that Scott was looking over her shoulder and, fearfully, slowly, she turned her head. The tall woman, Grace, was standing a few feet away from them.

Even at that distance, Lily was held fast by the black eyes that held a universe within their depths.

"It's time," Grace said.

"I love you, Lily. I thank you from the bottom of my heart for your love and the happiness you gave me. Please believe me when I tell you that you will be happy again."

Lily sensed their time together was running out fast and it would be futile to try to hold on, but, oh, she wanted so badly to hold on. Scott wiped away her tears again so she could look fully and clearly at his face once more. "You have to go back, Lily," he whispered.

He seemed lighter in substance, somehow, and as she gazed at him, his body seemed to fade a little and she could see the faint outline of the willow trees through his body. He took her hand and it was no more than a tingle in her palm.

They walked back to the place they had met, saying nothing because there was no more to be said. How long had she been there? A minute? An hour? A hundred years? She didn't know the answer to that question, but she did know it was over.

Scott spoke, his voice the merest murmur on the breeze.

"I love you, sweet Lily. Take care of our little girl. Be happy."

He slipped his hand from hers and she began to fall away from him and his world, back through the darkness.

She cried out his name, but it was lost in the void and she was suddenly enveloped in a damp, sticky mist. The whispering voices were back, but she didn't feel threatened by them this time.

Then there was pain, a stretching, tearing sensation.

She didn't think she could bear it.

Then, blessed numbness.

Silence.

A dream flashed somewhere in her mind. A dream of a river that was a raging sea that was a mountain that was a moonscape.

A dream of Scott, standing proud and beautiful in his world, with a kingfisher on the open palm of his hand.

The echo of a whisper on the furthest edge of hearing, "I love you, sweet Lily. Be happy."

Chapter 52

Amongst the thumps and muffled voices they could hear filtering down through the ceiling, there was a sudden, sharp cry and Alex almost laughed as Maisie jumped up and punched the air.

When she sat down again, they looked at each other and grinned.

"The baby! Oh, Alex, they've delivered the baby! That surely means everything's all right?"

A few minutes later, Adele staggered into the room. She'd arrived just fifteen minutes ago, wild eyed and desperate to see her sister. All colour was gone from her face, and she seemed close to collapse. "They wanted me out of the way so they could clean up."

"Adele, the baby?"

Adele dragged her tired eyes to Maisie. "A girl. A tiny, beautiful little girl."

For a second, Alex's stomach lurched and he thought he might cry out. His little girl taken, a little girl delivered.

Maisie ran forward and took Adele's hand, guided her to a chair. "And Lily?"

"She's alive. They're taking her and the baby to hospital."

"Would you like a brandy, pet? You look as if you could do with one."

Adele shook her head. "I'll have to follow the ambulance to the hospital. But you two go ahead."

Maisie went to the dresser, saying, "Alex and I will toast the arrival of Lily and Scott's little girl, we'll drink to Lily getting better, and we'll settle our nerves. Oh, no brandy. Never mind, it'll have to be whisky."

"My God," whispered Adele. "I keep going over and over it. How did we miss it? How did she manage to fool us? Alex, thank God she called you. It meant she didn't really mean to die, right? It was a call for help."

Alex didn't know what to say, how he could explain it to Adele, but Maisie caught his eye and gave a conspiratorial wink. Maybe it would be better to let Adele believe that's how it happened; it would be up to Lily whether or not to set her straight.

Adele was still speaking, almost muttering. "I had no idea. No idea at all that she was this desperate. I thought she was showing signs of recovery, and that the birth of her baby would be such a help. How could she do that to her baby?"

"We all thought the same, pet. The grief must have been too much for her to bear."

They all looked towards the sounds of a heavy weight being carefully manoeuvred down the stairs. A medic stepped into the living room and beckoned to Adele.

"We're taking your sister and your niece to the hospital now. I'm sure you'd like to come? There's room in the ambulance, or you can follow in your car."

"Thank you. I'd like to be with my sister please. My parents are on their way; I'll call them to meet us there." Before leaving the room she grabbed Maisie's glass and took a large gulp. "Oh, I needed that!"

Alex trailed after Adele and Maisie as they followed the medics out into the driveway. Lily was wheeled out on a stretcher, her face alabaster white tinged with grey, her lips a horrid shade of blue. A drip snaked from a bag filled with a clear liquid into her arm.

He'd not said a great deal to Maisie, but he was going over and over in his mind what he might have said to Lily when they'd talked through the night that might have triggered this. Had he said anything, *anything*, that had led her to think this was the answer to her grief?

Maisie held his arm as they watched the ambulance pull away, sirens blaring, lights flashing.

"She was trying to get to Scott, wasn't she?"

"Yes, Maisie, she was. I think she must have decided that by taking the baby with her, before she was born, they'd be a family over there."

Maisie blew out a shaky breath. "I'd better get back to Jack, he'll be wondering what's happening. Alex, when you said you needed a key, I simply thought Lily had gone into labour. I came over to see if I could help, feeling all happy and... Oh, I simply can't believe it."

"Nor me, Maisie. Nor me."

"Look, pet, I know it's late, but we're none of us going to get any sleep. Come back to the house with me and I'll make some cocoa, maybe something to eat?"

He considered the offer. Part of him wanted to be alone to think things through, the other part didn't want to think at all.

Should he have told Lily about Scott's passing, how he, Alex, had been sent back? Would that have made any difference?"

Alex.

Dad?

You could not have prevented this. I came to tell you that she was granted some time with Scott before being sent back. She understands now, Alex. She will be okay.

"Alex? Alex, you've gone deathly white, are you all right? Come on, let's go over to my place."

THREE MONTHS ON

Chapter 53

"Alex is moving out; he's piling boxes into his van. It reminds me of seeing him the day he arrived over there. You know, that seems like years ago now, so much has happened, and watching him pack up is like watching a film in reverse. I'm going to miss him very much."

"He's not moving all that far, Maisie, and he's promised to come and see us often."

"You like him, don't you." It was a statement rather than a question.

"Well, I can't be doing with all that psychic stuff, but yes, I like him. Now come away from the window, for heaven's sake."

"Oh, Alex knows I'm here. He just waved at me. I must say Beth is looking really well. She was so pale when he brought her here."

"It's been quite a roller coaster, one way or the other, hasn't it?"

"You're not kidding! What with Alex and Beth, and our Lily… well. Mind you, Lily told me she's been so glad to be back in her own home this past two weeks and away from her mother; I'm sure they must have driven each other mad." Maisie moved from the window, kicked off her slippers and curled up on the cushions.

Jack put his newspaper down and peered at Maisie over his glasses. "You're very good at the unfortunate turn of phrase. For a time there, Lily really *was* mad, you know. She could have had the baby taken away from her."

Maisie sighed and nodded. "It's thanks to her mother that she didn't. Irene was magnificent in the way she dealt with the doctors, social workers and all the busybodies that came wading in."

Jack nodded. "Yes, so maybe it's time you stopped being so critical of her. Now, have we got time for a cup of tea before we go over there?"

Maisie started to rise, but Jack waved her down.

"I'll make it, you can carry it."

She watched him carefully as pulled himself up out of the chair and used his walking stick for balance. Worrying about him pouring boiling water from the kettle but knowing she must not interfere, she forced herself not to get up and follow until he called her.

Why oh why, she asked herself for the millionth time, would he not accept some spiritual healing? Or, if not that, then some complementary therapy? She'd read that acupuncture and aromatherapy could help, but Jack would not even consider anything she suggested.

She gave a wry smile as the words Stubborn and Mule came into her mind.

Chapter 54

The baby was fast asleep in her sister's arms. Adele often said she hadn't thought it possible to love something so much, but her little niece had absolutely stolen her heart.

Lily was folding freshly laundered sleep suits and bibs into a soft pile to take upstairs to the nursery.

"Are you sure you want to do this, Adele?"

"Lily, how many times are we going to go over this? You know I genuinely, really and truly want to move in here with you. I've practically been here full time for months, so we may as well make it official. I think the question is really whether you want me here?"

Lily's eyes rested on her daughter and her face softened to such an extent that Adele had to laugh and say, "We're both absolutely besotted, aren't we!"

This was the best plan, best for Lily and her daughter, and surely best for Adele, too, for why should she live alone in her house when she could be here? Lily's house was large enough that they could live side by side and yet still give each other space. Adele worked from home a lot, so could help look after Hope when Lily started back at the Lilac Tree. She would get tenants for her cottage, and pay a generous rent to Lily to help her with expenses. Scott's younger brother had bought his share in the garage, so there would be nothing further coming from that source.

Lily had so much to be grateful for. She still had weepy days, but then all she had to do was hold Hope in her arms and tell her all about her short but blissful time with Scott in the afterlife. She had finished the nursery herself, and one day she would take great pleasure in explaining to

Hope why there was a missing tile on the fireplace, and who V and R were.

"I'm going to miss Alex and Beth being next door."

"Yes, me too," said Adele. "I think Beth is amazing."

"Isn't she? God, when Alex told me she was going to move in with him while they looked for a new home, I really panicked. She'd lost her baby girl and here she'd be, living next door to a baby girl."

"But she coped admirably. Alex told me that holding Hope had actually helped her." She nuzzled Hope's cheek. "But who could resist this little darling, hmm? Even a smelly little darling. She needs changing."

"I'll do it."

"Oh no, let me!"

Lily laughed. "If you actually want to change her, then you are beyond besotted. But please do get her cleaned up. The others will be here in a minute. Oh, maybe that's them now."

It was Maisie and Jack. She ushered them in quickly, so Jack could sit down, and Adele hurried to the nursery to get Hope changed.

Chapter 55

When Alex walked into the kitchen, he found Beth in rubber gloves, wiping the sink and draining board. She'd insisted on scrubbing the house from top to bottom, despite Alex telling her it was going to be gutted and refurbished by the owner.

"I hope I've left enough room in the van for the mattress and the last couple of things. We'll be ready for the off in the morning just as soon as we hear that we can get into the new house. Ready to go round and say our farewells?"

Alex watched Beth as she rinsed and squeezed out the cloth, a happy grin on his face. He still found it hard to believe that she was real and not a figment of his imagination.

Now she pulled off the gloves, moved across the kitchen and stepped into his embrace. "You know, I've grown rather fond of this funny house and I'm actually sad to be leaving it."

"What? If your brother heard you say that, he'd scream with frustration. He hates the place."

Beth laughed. "I know. But our Paul is more the luxury penthouse or five star hotel type, isn't he. If it isn't scrupulously clean and the height of luxury, he thinks it's a hovel." She looked around the kitchen, "I think this is cute. I hope we can come back and see it when Gary has finished the renovations."

Alex rested his chin on her head. "I can guarantee it, as Gary has already told me he has work here to put my way."

"I'll miss being able to pop into Lily's whenever I feel like it. It was so hard at first, knowing there was a little girl right next door. But in the end I think it really helped me."

"I must admit I've been impressed. I never thought you'd be able to face it, but... well, you did. You're truly amazing, Beth."

"At first it was for Lily's sake, if you remember. She was so worried when she returned home and found out I was here, thinking that seeing little Hope would send me back into madness. None of us could have seen it would have quite the opposite effect."

"You'll be able to see them often; we're not going to be that far away. Let's go round now, I saw Maisie and Jack go over a few minutes ago."

As they headed out, Paul was just getting out of his car.

"Paul! We weren't expecting you."

He kissed Beth on the cheek. "I know, but I thought you might want some help packing up."

Looking at his immaculate suit and handmade shoes, Alex could only laugh. "Right, as if you're dressed for it! And if you'd really wanted to help you should have been here hours ago."

Paul grinned cheekily. "Okay, I admit it. I just wanted to make sure you actually are moving out of this horrible house. Are you going somewhere?"

Beth said, "Just next door. A little farewell gathering."

"Perfect! I've got just the thing." He opened the back door of his car and heaved out a clinking bag. "Champagne!"

"Ooh, lovely," said Beth. "Chilled, of course."

"I've only brought three glasses, though, as I know you will have packed up everything by now. But before we go in, I've got some news."

Alex and Beth both waited, and Paul looked from one to the other, a slow grin spreading over his face.

"Eselmont rang me today to tell me your series will start to air in six weeks time. In fact, they're so confident it'll be a success, they're keen to get you back in the studio for a second one."

Alex grinned back. "Fantastic, Paul. Thank you!"

"This makes your autobiography even more of a priority. How's it going?"

"I'm working on it."

Paul gave him a long look.

"Honestly, I am! But with so much going on in the past few months..." He reached out and pulled Beth into his arms. "And this beautiful lady here especially has been something of a distraction."

"Oh, put her down, will you? We'll talk business some other time. Let's go, I want a drink."

Adele let them into Lily's house and directed them to the living room where the others were waiting. Hope, wrapped in a soft white blanket, was in Maisie's arms, and she was hardly able to drag her eyes away from the tiny face to say hello to the arrivals.

Holding up the two bottles and his three glasses, Paul announced, "I'm crashing your party, but I hope I can bribe you with chilled champagne. We just need a few more glasses."

He smiled rather wickedly at Adele, and there was an exchange of glances by the others as Adele's eyes widened and she visibly blushed.

"Allow me to do the honours." Paul deftly whipped the cork out of one of the bottles and poured champagne out.

Alex inwardly smiled as he watched his brother-in-law in action. Adele was positively glowing as her eyes followed Paul as he handed the filled glasses round, and Alex wondered if he should be a tad worried. Adele was far too good for his fickle brother-in-law.

He moved over to the French doors so he could see the kingfisher in the back garden.

Beth came over and leaned against him. "It means a lot to you, doesn't it?"

The bird had become, for him, a symbol of everything he believed in. In earthly life, its beauty could so easily be missed, its movement and colours seen as nothing more than a brief flash, there and then hidden again. In the afterlife it could be seen in all its glory. Every feather, every crystal droplet falling from its outspread wings as it rose from the water, in perfect slow motion so every detail could be captured.

He and Lily had talked for hours about this, another discussion that had lasted into the early hours. They had shared their experiences of being with Scott in the other world, tentatively at first, and then with vigour and excitement when each realised the other understood perfectly.

The next day, Alex had brought the kingfisher sculpture from his workshop and installed it on the back lawn. They'd stood hand in hand, and just gazed at it for what seemed an age. No-one else would ever know just what it represented for them.

"Now," said Paul. "I hope you don't mind if I say a few words?"

No-one objected; they all smiled and gave him their full attention.

"Well then." He moved so he was standing in front of the fireplace and planted his feet firmly on the hearthrug, giving himself complete command of the room. "I didn't understand why Alex moved into that ghastly house next door, but I can at least say that he has been surrounded by true, good friends. Let's drink a toast to a happy future for all of us."

There was a chorus of "Cheers!" as they all raised their glasses and drank.

Alex squeezed Beth's hand, feeling just about the luckiest man alive at that moment. His psychic senses had completely come back to him. Were, indeed, even stronger than before. His TV career was on track. The autobiography was taking shape, in his mind if not actually on paper. Amber was happy on the other side, being well cared for by his father. But most of all, Beth was beside him, looking healthy and happy. Oh, he saw the haunted look steal into her eyes all too often, but he knew she could cope now. She was even considering starting up some kind of charity for bereaved parents.

And Lily, sitting opposite him, had by now prised Hope from a reluctant Maisie and was kissing her and murmuring to her. She would be okay. She had had a rough ride since the suicide attempt, but her family had closed ranks to stop any attempt by the authorities to take Hope from her, and arranged for the counselling she needed to prove she was a capable mother.

It was excellent that Adele was going to live with her, though the way she was looking at Paul right now…

Maisie was, well, she was Maisie. Funny, direct, interfering, warm-hearted. And she had told him that she would try and get Jack to agree to see Linda for some healing.

There was so much to be grateful for, he felt a lump form in his throat and had to swallow hard. He was about to propose another toast in answer to Paul's, but out of the corner of his eye a grey, pearly mist was forming, sparking and glinting with tiny silver lights.

Dad?

Yes. And someone else.

Alex tensed, every nerve on alert, aware that the others had stopped talking and were looking at him.

Beth smiled and said, "I know that look. Who is it, Alex?"

Alex looked at the figure emerging from the mist and then at Lily. Her eyes were fixed on him over Hope's downy head.

Alex opened his mind and welcomed Scott to the party.

THE END

OTHER PUBLICATIONS BY THIS AUTHOR

ORDERS FROM ABOVE (J M Forrest)
A humorous fantasy novel

NATURAL ALCHEMY (J M Forrest)
A collection of poetry with black & white illustrations

ABOUT THE AUTHOR

J M Forrest writes novels, short stories and poetry.
For more information please visit her website:

www.jmforrest.com

Printed in Great Britain
by Amazon.co.uk, Ltd.,
Marston Gate.